Under Vanishing Skies

G.S. Fields

Under Vanishing Skies

G.S. Fields

Copyright © 2013 by G.S. Fields

First Edition

December 2013
ISBN 978-0-615-89849-0

ACKNOWLEDGMENTS

I would like to express my deep appreciation to those who supported me with my endeavor to write this book. Support came from many people in many forms. I hope that those whose names I failed to mention know that I truly appreciate their help and encouragement.

First and foremost I would like to thank my wife, Cherie, who allowed me the freedom to disappear into our room and write for hours without any questions or complaints. I love you. And I'd like to thank my daughters, Rachel and Stephanie, for their encouragement along the way. I love you both as well. I hope that you will take away one lesson from this…and that is to follow through on your dreams. And to my mom, I'd like to thank you for sharing your twisted sense of humor and wild imagination with me. I hope I put it to good use in this book.

I would also like to thank my friend, Javier "Jarv" Ramos, for his willingness to read through very early and very rough drafts. Your plot and characters suggestions helped make this story come to life. And thanks to my good friends and beta readers, Steve Eby and Jeremy Thompson. Your insights as readers were invaluable. Finally, thanks to my copy editors, Judy b. and Elizabeth Stock and my line editor, Dylan Garity. All of you did a great job of polishing a rough piece of coal until it sparkled.

Table of Contents

CHAPTER 1

Some say Fate is fickle. She isn't. She's a twisted psychotic bitch. It was the only way to explain why nearly everyone on the planet was dead…everyone including my family…and I was out here fishing.

I should have been with them when the storm hit, but I screwed up. Now this endless loop of a meaningless existence was my punishment. Every day was the same. Wake up, drink, eat, drink, fish, drink, and go to sleep. Death should be quick, not drawn out like this.

I tried to push the familiar dark thoughts from my mind and cast my line out. It landed fifty feet from my kayak. I set the reel and leaned back to wait.

Out of the corner of my eye, I saw Rick cast his line. It plopped a yard from where mine had just landed. I turned my kayak to face him.

"Come on! I said. "The Indian Ocean is a big place."

Rick laughed. "Lighten up, Aron. You really need to learn how to let go of all that negative energy."

"You sound like that yoga instructor that my wife dragged me to see," I said.

"I didn't know you took yoga."

"I didn't," I said. "I pulled my goddammed hamstring kneeling down on the mat. That was my first and last yoga class."

Rick laughed. "That's too bad. Yoga really helps clear the mind."

"That hippie shit doesn't work for me."

"How do you know unless you give it a chance." Holding on to his fishing pole with one hand, he held out his other hand and formed an O with his thumb and middle finger.

"Empty your thoughts and look around you," he said. You're fishing in the one of the most beautiful places on the planet. Think of this as your happy place."

"This may be your happy place," I said. "But it's not mine. My happy place is back in California. If I was back there, I'd let go of this negative energy in a millisecond."

His smile dimmed. "If you were there, you'd be dead." He paddled his kayak over by mine and said, "Come on buddy, it's been twelve years. You've got to let it go."

"Let it go? I'll let it go when I'm laid out on a funeral pyre and the flames are—"

A gust of wind whipped across the ocean and peppered my face with salt water.

"Goddammit," I said under my breath.

I squeezed my eyes shut against the burn of salt and blinked until I could make out the unmistakable silhouette of Lohifushi. A half dozen palm trees poked haphazardly up through its jungle canopy like a bad haircut. Lohifushi wasn't the smallest island in the Maldives, but at just over a quarter mile around, it was far from being the largest.

"You okay?" Rick asked.

"Yeah, perfect."

I wiped the water from my unshaven face and looked out beyond the island. A line of dark purple clouds bridged the gap between the grayish-blue morning sky in the east and the black, star-filled arcs that scarred the northern and southern horizons. The arcs appeared the day after the storm hit. Each arc was edged with an electric, greenish-blue hue that twisted around like the Aurora Borealis. I leaned forward, rested my arms on the paddle, and watched a steady stream of fire streak across the black zones.

The kids who were born after the storm probably didn't think twice about the arcs, but I did. I paid close attention to how much larger they grew each year. They didn't grow by a lot, but they grew enough to reassure me that in a few more years the atmosphere above the islands would be gone. I just wished it would hurry up.

"What are you looking at?"

"Nothing. Just watching the solar particle show."

"I told you a million times, those are meteors."

"And I told you that meteors burn up in the atmosphere. You know damned well there isn't enough atmosphere in the black zones to burn up anything."

He bumped his kayak into the side of mine and said, "Those meteors are burning up in the sky above your thick head." He shook his head. "Solar particles...you're such a moron."

"And you're a know-it-all asshole."

I knew that he was probably right, but I'd never give him the satisfaction of telling him. And besides, he had no way to prove it. Nobody outside of the Mars colony knew how bad it was.

About a year ago, they'd sent a reconnaissance ship down to search for survivors. They told us that we were all that was left...or at least all that was left worth saving. They didn't say much about the solar storm or the atmosphere. Their silence on the subject told me all that I needed to know. We were screwed.

Instead, they talked about the rescue mission. I remembered how proud they were when they announced that a cargo ship would arrive in a year to take a thousand lucky passengers back to the colony. Lucky my ass. They'd been terraforming that planet for fifty years and they still weren't finished.

Rick rammed my kayak again, knocking my paddle into the water. I managed to grab it before it floated away.

"Asshole," I said beneath a smile.

At thirty eight, Rick still had one foot firmly planted in his childhood. I supposed that was another reason why I liked him. He could make me forget about this hell hole for a while. But I never forgot about it for long.

"Come on," he said. "We should head in before Helen sends out a search party." He counted the fish in the empty front passenger compartment of his kayak. "I got over four dozen. What about you?"

"About the same," I said.

"She's not going to be happy."

I shrugged and grabbed my paddle. The size of the catch had decreased steadily every year since the storm. In another few years, there'd be nothing left to catch.

I dug my paddle into the water, turning the boat towards the dock. I could hear Rick sloshing behind me. After all these years, that clumsy son of a bitch still paddled like a drunken tourist.

It didn't take long before I slipped into the easy, relaxed rhythm of plunge, pull, lift, rotate, plunge, pull, lift, rotate. Each breath I took was in perfect sync with the stroke of the paddle. Within seconds, my conscious thoughts were replaced with the hypnotic lull of paddling. Forget all that yoga bullshit, this was my happy place.

A light in the east caught my eye. I looked over and saw the sun's rays shoot up behind the cloud bank on the horizon. The scene looked like the cover of a Watchtower pamphlet, the kind I used to find wedged in my screen door back home.

"Hey Rick," I said looking over my shoulder.

"Yeah?"

"Do you think any Jehovah's Witnesses survived the storm?"

"What?"

"You know, Jehovah's Witnesses, the guys in white shirts and black ties. They always seemed to show up around dinner time trying to save souls."

"What about them?"

"I'd bet a bottle of Mohamed's moonshine that if any of them had survived, then they're still out there somewhere knocking on doors and pissing people off."

I heard him laugh and I kept paddling.

***

Twenty minutes later we reached the dock. William was waiting for us, his bony legs dangling over the edge. Rick coasted in beside me, and I saw the concern in his eyes when he saw his son.

I had arrived at the resort on the same day as Rick and Sarah. I came here to do some serious fishing.

They had come here on their honeymoon to do some serious fucking. I guess we both succeeded. Nine months after we arrived, William was born into this dying world and I was still fishing.

Despite my best efforts, the kid ended up calling me Uncle Aron. Don't get me wrong, I liked William. He was smart, a lot smarter than any ten-year-old I had ever known. But the kid was like a tick. He kept showing up uninvited in unexpected places.

"You can't keep doing this," Rick said as he climbed onto the dock. "You've been here all night again...haven't you?"

William lowered his head, hiding his bright hazel eyes behind his long, blond bangs.

"I told you last night to go back home and get some sleep."

"But I wasn't tired."

"Don't give me any of that crap. Your mom's probably been up all night worrying about you." Rick glowered at him. "Come on William, you know how sick she is. What if she needed help in the middle of the night and you weren't there for her?"

William looked up and glared back.

"Take it easy on the kid," I said. "He's here now, so put him to work."

Rick's face softened and he said, "It's just that hanging out on the dock all night by yourself is dangerous and...look at you." He pointed at William's legs. "You're covered in mosquito bites."

William shrugged and studied his dirty bare feet.

I'll be goddammed if William didn't look just like his old man. They both had that stupid cowlick that stuck straight up and bounced around like a spring. Even the scowls on their faces were identical. I chuckled.

Rick looked at me and asked, "What's so funny?"

"The two of you. You're like different versions of the same software."

Rick smiled and then looked over at William. "Alright, you heard your uncle." He pointed to a stack of plastic buckets next to the old bait shack at the foot of the pier. "Go bring a couple of those buckets over so we can unload the fish."

William ran over and returned a few seconds later with the buckets.

We worked as a team. Rick and I tossed him the fish and he dropped them in the buckets. His face lit up when he spotted the stingray in the bottom of my kayak.

"Wow!" he said. "Everyone said they were gone, everyone except Mr. Thompkins. He said the stingrays and some of the other fish would return once the weather got better. Do you think he's right? Are they coming back?"

"I'm sure they are," Rick said, giving me a cautionary glance.

He must have sensed that I wanted to tell William that Mr. Thompkins was a dumbass. And like the other dumbasses who thought things would get better, he handed out false hope with a stupid smile. Instead, I tossed William a fish. He caught it, but he paused to study my face before dropping it into the bucket.

"What the hell do I know?" I said. "I'm just a dumb computer geek. You should listen to your dad. He's the college professor."

When we finished unloading the fish, I picked the stingray up by the tail and said, "Let's get these fish to Helen before she comes out here after us."

We walked in single file up the hard-packed sand through the dense jungle foliage. Rick led the way, followed by William. They each carried a bucket of fish. I brought up the rear holding the stingray.

I watched William stagger up the trail, bending from side to side as he tried to counter-balance the weight of the bucket. He looked like an omnidirectional antenna: tall, lanky, and wobbly. Despite his wiry build, he managed to lug the heavy bucket without stopping.

"Doing okay?" I asked.

"Uh huh," he grunted.

I smiled.

The path soon opened up and the dining hut came into view. Six thick wooden poles held up the thatched roof like some kind of Tiki circus tent. The sides were open, allowing the breeze to pass through. A dozen years ago, this place had fed up to three hundred hungry tourists who'd wander in from the beach to graze on the gourmet buffet. Now there were under two hundred people left on the island and no one ate in the main dining room anymore. People only came here to pick up food from Helen and then take it back to their huts to eat.

We worked our way through the empty, large, round tables and headed for the door on the back wall. Light peeked through the cracks and I could hear the clanging of pots and pans, along with the unmistakable sound of Helen humming some Australian folk melody. Rick pushed the door open and the familiar sweet smell of fresh baked plantain bread filled my nostrils.

Helen turned from the sink and wiped her hands on her apron. She gave us a warm smile and said, "G'day boys. What have you got there? No wait...let me guess. Is it fish?"

A smile spread across William's face. Helen had a way with William. Hell, with all the kids. She was their surrogate grandmother and she took the role seriously. Most of them were born after the storm and she knew they would never meet their real grandparents.

William set his bucket down, ran over to me, and snatched the stingray out of my hand. "Guess what Helen?" Without giving her time to respond, he held it up. "Look!"

She put her hands on top of her overripe breasts, which sat on her barrel shaped belly. "That will make a marvelous brekkie! It should keep everyone's mind off of today's small catch." She glanced at me over her bent, wire-framed glasses.

After twelve years on the island, I still couldn't understand all of her Aussie lingo, but I sure as hell understood that look.

"Don't blame me," I said, pointing at Rick. "The honorable Council member over there wouldn't shut up and kept scaring away all the fish."

"You're not pinning this on me," Rick said, "You were the one who was splashing around."

Helen shook her head and said, "My old Bob used to say that fishermen were born honest, but somewhere out on the water they learned to get over it." Helen and her husband had come to the island to celebrate their fortieth wedding anniversary. After Bob died from a heart attack a year after the storm, Helen had busied herself by becoming the island cook.

She barked out some orders and we followed her directions. After setting the buckets down by the sink, Rick and William put on an apron. They each grabbed a knife and started filleting the fish on the stainless steel counter next to Helen. I dropped the stingray on the wooden butcher block that sat in the middle of the kitchen and I prepared to cut up the prize catch.

"So Rick, why were you out fishing this morning?" she asked. "Don't you have to head back to Male for the Council meeting?"

"Nope. It's postponed for a week while they find a replacement for Hans Garrettson," Rick replied.

"Oh my, another one quit?" she asked.

"That's what they told me," Rick said.

From the tone of his voice I knew that he didn't believe it. There was obviously something behind the recent string of Council members quitting. Rick had tried to talk about it a couple times, but I had managed to change the subject. I didn't give a rat's ass about the Council of Thirteen.

I mean, what was the point? Even if the ship managed to make it to Earth, pick up the people who were selected by the Council to go to the colony, and then somehow make it back to Mars, their chance of survival was no better than if they stayed here. I didn't care how much the Mars colony had expanded over the last decade or how much the terraforming had progressed. I knew deep down in my soul that, like all dominant species before us, it was mankind's turn to disappear. That's why I told Rick to scratch my name from the list. I planned to die right here, drinking and fishing.

Helen looked over at Rick and said, "Well, I guess you can spend some quality time with your family then."

"Unfortunately, I agreed to go out to Makunudhoo and make some repairs on the communications tower. I have to leave right after breakfast."

"What?" William threw his knife on the counter and it hit with a loud metallic clang

"I'm sorry," Rick said. "I was going to tell you after we brought breakfast to mom."

"Why can't Uncle Aron go?"

"Because it wouldn't be fair," Rick said. "Your uncle has been doing most of the repair jobs since I've been on the Council."

I made the mistake of looking over at William. Tears fell down his freckled face.

"I don't care!" William cried out.

Helen draped her flabby arm around his shoulder, but he shirked it off.

"Mom's sick and can't do nothing and you're always at that stupid Council thing. It's not fair." He ran out of the kitchen.

Rick took off his apron and said, "I'm sorry Helen." She nodded, and he took off after William.

I looked over at Helen and was momentarily trapped by her gaze, but I managed to break free. I focused my attention on the stingray that I had butchered. Now she had two reasons to be pissed off at me.

I felt the guilt rising up within me, but I shoved it back down into its place. Just because I didn't have a family, everyone seemed to think that it was okay for me to travel around from island to island and fix the goddammed communications equipment. Well, they were wrong. I'd done my share of work and I deserved some rest and relaxation. Rick was the only one who understood. I'm sure that's why he took the job before it came my way.

I put the knife down, closed my eyes, and took a few deep breaths. When I opened them, I found my thumb absently tracing the thick scar across my wrist.

If Rick had really wanted to do me a favor, he should've walked away and let me finish what I had started twelve years ago on the end of that pier.

***

I skipped breakfast and lunch, partly to avoid a lecture from Helen, but mostly because I didn't want to run into Rick. I knew that if I saw him, I'd probably change my mind and take his place. But he left a couple hours ago, so I decided to go on a run. Running, like kayaking, helped me shake off funky moods like this.

I searched for my shorts and then remembered that they were still in my backpack. I'd taken them along with me on the last repair trip, but never got a chance to run.

Kneeling on the floor, I blindly hunted for the bag under the bed. My hand brushed against the thread-worn shoulder strap and I yanked it out. I stood up and gave it a good shake before throwing it on the bed to dislodge any insects that had made my bag their home. The musty smell brought back a flood of memories.

The pack had been my constant companion after the storm. Rick, Jin and I had hopped across the islands in search of electronic parts that hadn't been completely fried by the electromagnetic pulse that preceded the solar storm.

When we showed up on the island, everyone used to say the same thing. They said we looked like the start of a bad joke, "A Harvard professor, a Chinese officer, and a drunken computer geek walked into a bar."

Despite the odd composition of our team, we had managed to cobble together a crude VHF radio network thanks to Rick's electrical engineering background, Jin's military experience with radio systems, and my lackluster programming skills. It took four years before we finally set up the first of over two hundred relay towers across the islands. Finally, a year ago, we completed the Intra Island Communications Network, or IICN as everyone called it.

I couldn't understand why people felt compelled to create acronyms with the end of humanity looming in front of them, but they did. I had tried to discourage it with my own acronym. I wanted to call it the Communications Unified Network Trunk, but I got overruled.

The IICN wasn't much of a network, but it provided everyone who had a data mat with the ability to send and receive text messages. There was also just enough bandwidth to provide a rudimentary voice and video communications channel. However, because of that limitation, the Maldivian Defense Force controlled all video and voice communications. Only MDF personnel and a few others were authorized to use it.

Even though the IICN only provided text message service, people went nuts when it was completed. But I didn't help build it to make people happy. I built it to keep my mind off Kelly and the girls.

I had become obsessed with finding out what had happened to my family after the storm, but with no communication to the outside world, I didn't know whether they were dead or alive. I never did find out, but I didn't need to.

Six months after the storm, refugees began to trickle in and the stories they told crushed any hope I had of my family's survival. The stories painted a picture of hell.

The atmosphere somewhere north of Spain and south of Bolivia was gone. This was the area we called the black zone. In my opinion, the people who were in the black zone when the storm hit had been the lucky ones. They had suffocated to death when the air bled off into space. Not a great way to die, but at least it was quick. Those between the black zones and here had it worse. We called that area the middle zone. Not very creative, but I guess there were only so many ways to describe hell.

The middle zone extended from about the tip of Mexico up to the northern black zone and from the top of Australia down to the southern black zone. There was just enough atmosphere in the middle zone to breathe, but not enough to block the x-ray radiation emitted from the sun. Most of the people in that zone either died from radiation burns or from the extreme change in weather caused by a sudden decrease in atmospheric pressure.

The refugees who made it to the Maldives described brutal massacres, rapes, and cannibalism as civilization crumbled. I tried my best to avoid listening to their stories. Kelly and the girls had been in that zone. If I let my mind go there, I'd probably go completely insane.

I shook my head to knock out the depressing thoughts. Grabbing my bag, I reached inside and found my running shorts wadded together with some t-shirts that had seen better days. I got dressed, walked outside, and took off.

Lohifushi wasn't a runner's paradise. One lap around the island equaled a mile. It was like running around a big parking lot, but as long as I kept moving I didn't care. Running enabled me to mentally escape from this tropical island prison. And soon I lost myself in the run.

As I turned the corner by the old bait shack at the base of the pier for the tenth time, I could feel my mind preparing to make a break for it. Another few laps and I'd be off this Godforsaken rock, if only mentally.

I followed the lush green canopy that covered most of the white sand trail that circled the island, connecting the different groups of huts. I loved this part of the trail. The trees provided protection from the sun's strong rays and the breeze, cooled by the shade, felt good against my sweat-soaked skin.

Each hut that I passed looked exactly like the next, with white stucco walls and thatched roofs. At the end of one of those groups, I ran past little Emily. She was still on the front deck of her hut playing with her dolls. She looked up, smiled at me, and made one of her doll's hands wave at me again. Emily was a sweet girl, but every time I looked at her it brought back too many memories of my own daughters, Katelyn and Theresa. They used to play with their dolls like that and would stay out all day long if I had let them. The memories squeezed my heart like a vise, making it hard for me to breathe. I looked the other way, pretending not to see her, but she yelled out, "Hello Mr. Aron!"

I forced a smiled, waved, and then looked ahead just in time to avoid getting whacked by a massive palm frond that hung low over the path. I ducked under it and when I looked up, the old surf bar came into view. It sat on the northern tip of the island where some of the world's best left breaking waves gently rolled along the coastline that was now void of surfers.

Farther on, the path opened up onto a long, weathered boardwalk that hung out over the shallow water in a big, sweeping half circle. I ran through the gauntlet of huts that lined it on either side, each one suspended over the water by stilts. Once highly desired honeymoon suites, they now served as warehouses and workshops.

Up ahead, I saw a small group of people milling around in front of the hut where coral was crushed into the powder we used to filter our drinking water. They were talking amongst themselves and didn't pay any attention to me. I ran through their cloud of thick coconut fiber cigarette smoke. The acrid haze stung my eyes.

I reached the end of the boardwalk and continued down the eastern shore. The wind pushed my back as if telling me to pick up the pace. Sweat dripped into my eyes as I sprinted around the corner. I wiped them clear and saw the ruins of the old observation deck. It was just visible through an opening in the foliage. All that remained of the deck now was a broken pile of salt-bleached wood.

When I had first arrived on the island, I spent a lot of time on that deck drinking beer and trading fishing stories with other tourists. Fishing had been one of my greatest pleasures, but now it was just a way to survive…and an excuse to get away from everyone.

Those bastards at SatComm Control Services had known that and they used it as bait. They knew that I wanted to cancel their contract. So to keep me from making any hasty decisions, they flew me out to India for a couple of meetings and then had generously offered me a three-day, all-expense-paid fishing trip to the Maldives. I'd been offered bribes before, but I'd never taken one. But they had offered me a trip to the Maldives. It was number three on my list of places to fish before I died. I could have sent for Kelly and the girls to join me, but I didn't. I lied to Kelly. I told her that I had to stay in India for more meetings. Now I lived with that lie every day of my life.

I stumbled over a tree root, but managed to stay on my feet. The jungle closed in around me as I approached the end of the lap. When I reached the entrance of the pier, I saw Mohamed running toward me. He waved his arms and I slowed down.

"Aron! Aron!"

Fighting to catch my breath, I stopped a few yards in front of him and put my hands on my hips while looking at my feet.

Mohamed was the island doctor, only he wasn't really a doctor. He had been the sports trainer at the resort. The fact that he was a sports trainer had always struck me as funny. He looked like one of those Buddha statues that sat next to the cash register in a second rate Chinese restaurant. The only difference was that Mohamed was from Bangladesh, not China, and unlike Buddha, Mohamed wore bright flowered shirts, a sarong, and flip-flops.

"Hey Mohamed, what's up?"

"The pirates have attacked Makunudhoo."

I looked up. My stomach suddenly twisted like the vines of a Banyan tree. Rick was on Makunudhoo!

"When?" I finally managed to say.

"I just received a message from one of the survivors. He's requesting medical assistance. Kamish is readying the boat over there," he said, pointing toward the pier. "He will be ready to leave in a few minutes."

"What about Rick? Did you hear from him?"

"I sent him several text messages, but..." The look on his face made the vines in my stomach twist tighter.

These pirates weren't like the ones in the bedtime stories my father had read to me. They were like locusts. They plundered and consumed every resource in their path. Their leader was Jamal, a self-proclaimed prophet.

Most of the pirates were from Somalia, but some were from other parts of Africa and the Middle East. The pirates saw themselves as religious soldiers who were finishing what Allah had started. They called it the final Jihad against infidels. I called it mass murder.

Three years ago, they had turned their attention on the Maldives. At first, there had only been a few attacks and they were limited to couple of long-range supply ships. Recently, they started raiding the outlying islands. I'd gone to some of those islands to help. The image of the carnage they left behind was seared into my brain like the brands they burned onto their victims.

"Aron, you must have faith that Rick—"

I ran toward the boat and yelled, "Let's go!"

CHAPTER 2

I watched as the flames of Rick's funeral pyre whipped in the winds of the approaching storm. There had to be at least four hundred people around the fire, most of them from other islands. All of them cradled a coconut shell candle in their hands. They sang a religious hymn that I'd heard too many times in the recent months. I didn't want to be here, but Helen had insisted. She had come to my hut and refused to leave until I agreed to go with her.

Standing to the rear of the crowd, I looked around. A little ways in front of me I spotted Little Emily. Her back was to me, but I knew that it was her. She held a doll in one hand and clung to her mother's sarong with the other. The sight of her brought back memories of when Kelly's mom had passed away. My girls had clung to Kelly's skirt the same way. I looked away.

Kamish and his two brothers, Lanka and Senil, stood together with their wives on the other side of the fire. They were barely teenagers when I had arrived on the island twelve years ago. Originally from Bombay, they had worked as cabana boys, raking the sand and keeping it clean for the tourists. They were grown men now in their late twenties. All them dark skinned and muscular. Kamish was the oldest and tallest of the three. He was built like a prize fighter and his brothers followed him like a general. Lanka stood to his right. He was the middle child. Short and shy, Lanka always seemed to be studying everyone and everything around him. Senil stood to the left, his arm draped around his very pregnant wife. He was the youngest of the three and the first of the brothers that I had met. He was a skinny little kid then, with a mischievous smile. I recalled the day that I had met him.

I had just settled into my beach chair for a nap when I heard a weird bird call. I looked up and saw Senil. He held a finger to his lips as if he were about to commit a major crime. Then he shimmied up a nearby palm tree and brought me a coconut. He had hacked it open with a machete that was nearly half his size. We weren't supposed to tip the resort employees, but I tucked a few bucks into the shell after I had finished drinking from it. I tossed it to him. When he saw the money, his smiled doubled in size.

I studied his face now. I searched for some hint of that mischievous boy. All I saw was the somber face of a grieving young man.

Off to the left I spotted Mohamed and Helen. Mohamed held her in his arms as she sobbed inconsolably into his chest. The image tore at my heart. I looked away, but my eyes fell upon a sight that nearly brought me to my knees.

Sarah stood there holding William's hand. Neither one sang. Her stoic face belied the grief that I knew she had to be feeling. Given her illness, I was amazed that she could stand. A glimmer of light reflected off a single tear that rolled down her cheek, so I looked at William. That was a mistake.

Tears rolled freely down his angry face. I watched as he tried unsuccessfully to control his sobs. He looked up, fixing my eyes with his gaze. They screamed out to me, begging to know why his father had to die. I knew the answer, but I couldn't face it...not with him staring at me like that. So I looked up to safety of the early evening sky. But the sky just provided a backdrop for the the memory of how I had found him on Makunudhoo.

When I had arrived on the island, I saw a dozen other men tied up to palm trees. Rick was one of them. I ran to him. His pants were around his ankles. His legs covered in blood. And his head hung down to his chest where they had branded a circle inscribed with a crescent moon and a single star. It was the symbol for Jamal. I'd seen the it six months ago on the island of Embudu, burned on the corpses of men, women, and children.

I knew that Rick was dead, but I had to be sure. As I stood in front of him, the nauseating smell of burnt flesh filled my nostrils. I had to fight the urge to throw up. Gently, I lifted his head by the chin and looked into his open, dead eyes. They seemed to stare at a killer who was no longer there. Blood dripped from his half-open mouth onto my hand. I saw something wedged inside. I looked closer and then jumped back. The fucking bastards had choked him with his own balls!

I shut my eyes tight. Now my head was filled with the song that everyone was singing. The rage that I tried to push deep in the pit of my stomach suddenly broke free. I opened my eyes and threw my candle against a boulder. It shattered with a loud crash. The singing stopped and everyone stared at me. I suddenly felt like I was on trial.

Fuck them!

I turned and ran off.

As I ran through the jungle, I felt Rick's accusing dead eyes following me. I picked up the pace, but I knew that I couldn't outrun the truth. If I had gone to Makunudhoo yesterday, then Rick would be back there singing with his family at my funeral.

I couldn't breathe. Stopping outside the dining hut, I bent over. The taste of bile filled my mouth. I don't know how long I stayed like that, but it seemed like forever.

Then I felt a soft hand on my back. I didn't need to stand up to know who it was.

"I'm sorry, Sarah," I said. "I'm just no good with—"

"I know. It's okay."

I stood up and looked into Sarah's gaunt, tear-stained face and said, "Goddammit, it's not okay! I even fucked this up."

"What are you talking about?"

"This," I said motioning to her and me. "I'm supposed to be the one who consoles you."

She reached out, took my hand, and smiled. "You know what Rick would say about this?"

"That I'm a dumbass?"

Her sad smile grew. "Probably, but he'd also say that you shouldn't beat yourself up over this. It wasn't your fault, Aron. None of it."

I looked away. I didn't want her to see the tears welling up in my eyes. "Well...then he was the dumbass."

I heard her laugh, softly at first, but the laugh quickly grew louder. I looked at her and for a split second, the heaviness that had been crushing my chest vanished. But then the memory of Rick's dead face flashed in my brain. Suddenly the pressure on my chest returned with a vengeance.

Her laughter turned into a coughing fit. She let go of my hands to cover her mouth. When the coughs subsided she said, "You're right. For such a smart guy, Rick used to say a lot of stupid things." Then a gentle look spread across her face. "But he was right about one thing."

"What's that?"

"He was right about you."

I tilted my head, confused.

"I remember the day he came home and told me about..." she looked down at the scars on my wrists. "He told me how he had found you that day, sitting on the edge of the pier holding a piece of glass from a broken bottle."

Why was she doing this? I didn't want to hear this...not now.

"He said you felt guilty about not being at home with your family when the storm hit. And do you know what I told him?"

I turned and looked away again.

"I told him that maybe he should've left you alone and let you finish what you had started."

I turned back and looked into her eyes, unsure if I'd heard her right.

She smiled softly and said, "It's not that I wanted you to die. It's just that it was such a terrible time for everybody, so much pain and suffering. I simply didn't understand why he had stopped you from ending your pain."

The same thought had crossed my mind a million times over the last twelve years and I still didn't know the answer.

She continued, "Well...he just smiled at me and told me that if humanity had any chance to survive, then we couldn't stop helping one another. That's why he wanted to be on the Council of Thirteen, to help people."

"I don't want to get into that right now."

"Into what?"

"Into the Council bullshit."

Her eyes glistened with fresh tears.

"That was something he believed in, Sarah...not me." I said, "You know my thoughts on the Mars mission. It's just a shell game. The people up there have the same probability of dying as we do down here...maybe greater. So what's the point?"

"The point is hope," she said. The tears spilled out of her eyes. "Everyone needs hope. I need it, William needs it, and even a thick-headed jerk like you needs it. Rick believed that the Council gave us that hope."

"But you've heard him talk about the Council. You know all the politicking and backroom deals that go on. The only people with hope are the ones with connections to Ahmed and some of the other scumbags on the Council."

"Not everyone on the Council is corrupt and you know it. You know Shannon and you've met Michio. Rick trusted them because they're good people. It'll be hard for them to keep the Council in line without Rick there to help."

I knew where she was heading with this, but I wasn't going to follow her there. "I don't really know Michio that well, but I know Shannon. She's as tough as they come. I'm sure everything will work out."

I turned to leave, but she grabbed my arm. I stopped. I couldn't look at her.

"I'm not asking you to do anything that you don't want to do. I just...I don't know...I guess I'm just worried about William. Rick and I wanted to give him a chance at a future. You're a father. You understand, don't you?"

I understood, but I wasn't a father, not anymore. Besides, some fucking father I turned out to be. All I had cared about was cashing in on a fishing trip to the Maldives. It was all about me and what I had wanted. Well...I got what I wished for and it cost me the opportunity to be there with my family at the end. And yesterday I fucked up again. I needed some alone time.

"Aron?"

"Yeah?"

"Are you okay?"

I nodded, but took off down the path. I needed a drink.

***

I watched as wave after wave crashed relentlessly against the rocky shore, sending plumes of water high into the air. From the look of the storm clouds, I could tell that it wouldn't be long before the rain hit.

I took another swig from the bottle and winced as the moonshine burned its way down my throat. Holding the bottle up to the light I wondered where Mohamed had learned to distill alcohol. It just didn't seem like something that an Allah-fearing Muslim would or should know how to do. From the taste of this shit, I wasn't convinced that he did know.

A long weathered board off to my right sprang up a few inches and then slammed back down with a crack. I jumped to my feet, but fell back on my ass.

"Still can't hold your liquor, I see."

I turned and saw Shannon standing above me on the ruins of the old observation deck. Her short golden locks of hair danced

20

high above that sexy smirk of hers. The last time I saw her was over three years ago, but as the wind pressed her thin dress tight against her athletic body, I recognized every inch of her. Not that I'd ever seen her naked. Shannon and I were drinking buddies, that's all.

Even if I could get Kelly out of my mind long enough to consider having sex with someone, I'd never have a chance with Shannon. I mean, what could she possibly see in me? I was fifty-two years old. Sure, I still had a full head of thick brown hair, but despite years of kayaking, I had a small floatation ring of fat around my waist. She was eighteen years younger than me and had the body of a twenty year old.

Shannon was originally from Ireland, but a few years before the storm she had moved to the Maldives to be a full-time surf instructor. I had met her a year after the storm when she delivered supplies for us during construction of the IICN. She ended up ferrying us from island to island over the first five years. From the moment she had knocked me into the water by tossing a box of parts at me from the deck of her ship, we were friends. I was in awe of her sharp wit and unshakable nerve. She was like no one I had ever met...no woman anyway.

"I have not yet begun to drink," I said in a really bad impersonation of General MacArthur.

"Good. Then there might be enough left in that bottle to wet my lips."

She maneuvered her way down the pile of broken wood with the ease of a gymnast and plopped down next to me. I handed her the bottle.

Looking into my eyes, she said, "Here's to Rick who will live on in our hearts. For to live on in the hearts of those left behind is never to die." She took a drink and handed me the bottle.

I held it up and said, "To Rick!" Then I chugged.

"Easy there, hot shot," she said.

Wiping my mouth, I asked, "Where the hell did you come from, Shannon?"

She motioned with her thumb behind her. "Up there. Weren't you paying attention?"

"Don't be a smart ass. You know what I mean."

"I came in from Male for Rick's funeral, but the bloody batteries on our boat ran out. We had to wait an hour to recharge them. By the time we arrived, the service was over."

"Better late than never, I guess," I smiled. "It's good seeing you again. It's been a long time."

"Yes it has," she said matching my smile.

I knew she wouldn't broach the subject, but I had the courage that comes from drinking a half bottle of moonshine, so I did. "Where the hell did you disappear to for the past three years? I asked around, but nobody seemed to know. I heard that you sailed off one day and never returned. Everyone had you figured for dead." I know that I did.

Lifting an eyebrow she said, "You sound like my father." And then she laughed. "I've been on what the Aussies call a walkabout, only I've been using my boat instead of my legs."

"Walkabout?"

She grabbed the bottle, took a drink, and then said, "Three years ago I got a bad case of island fever. So one day I decided to go back to Ireland. I loaded up my boat with food and water and took off."

I shook my head. "You're nuts. We're in the middle of the fucking Indian Ocean. And from what the refugees said, there's nothing left that far north...not even air."

"I guess I just had to see for myself." Her face darkened and she took another drink. Handing me the bottle she said, "I made it as far north as the Persian Gulf."

I choked as I swallowed. "You're shitting me! How long did it take you to get there?"

"I don't know really. I didn't keep track of time. Maybe a couple of months. Anyway, I wasn't in a hurry which was a good thing. My batteries only held enough charge to power the boat five hours a day."

I took another drink and then asked, "Well...what was it like? Did you find anyone alive out there?" I knew the answer, but it was one thing to hear about it from some refugee and another to hear it from a friend.

"If there is anyone out there alive, I didn't see them." She took a sip. "The weather up there is fucked up. The farther north I went, the colder it got at night and the hotter it got during the day. I'll bet the temperature reached a hundred and forty degrees. Anyway, I spent about six months exploring the coast of India. By the time I reached the Persian Gulf, my common sense caught up with me and I decided to get the hell out of there. I didn't want to end up like all of those dried up corpses that littered the streets."

"And it took you three years to get back?"

"No. Just a little over a year."

Tilting my head, I asked, "If you got back a couple years ago, why didn't you drop by and say hi or at least answer my messages? When Rick told me that you were on the Council, I thought he was joking."

"I met a guy," she said, looking away.

"You picked up a guy in the middle of the ocean?"

"I didn't say I picked up a guy. Now who's being the smartass? I said I met a guy, Saravan. He was one of the Bangladesh refugees that resettled on Gan. Until a few months ago, I'd been living with him down there. I guess I just got caught up in the relationship, that's all. Anyway, when word got around about the Mars mission, everyone convinced me to run for the Council…so I did. Not sure why."

"I know."

"You do?"

"Yeah. Like I said before…" I grabbed the bottle out of her hand. "…you're nuts."

I took a long, deep drink and didn't stop until she said, "Easy now or I won't get any more."

I brought the bottle down and smiled. "Sorry. It's been a while since I had a drinking partner. I guess I forgot how to share."

"Well, we'll just have to fix that now, won't we?" She reached for the bottle. "So listen, before you say no…and you will say no…just hear me out. I want you to come to Male and be on the Council with me."

"No! Uh uh. The Council is—"

"Hey!" she said cutting me off. "I said hear me out."

I crossed my arms over my chest and let her continue.

"Most of the hard work is done. We've already compiled information about all the inhabitants, assessed their health, collected their bloody skill sets, blah, blah, blah. It's all done. And the candidate list is just about complete. We're just quibbling over a few names, mostly people that Ahmed and his buddies keep putting on the list, people who don't meet the criteria for going to Mars."

"Then why do you need me?"

"Two reasons," she said. "With Rick gone, Michio and I are the only two people on the Council who aren't in Ahmed's back pocket and it takes two votes to block passage of the list."

"I'm pretty drunk, but I can still count. You plus Michio equals two."

She smiled, "That's true. We can block their bullshit candidates now, but some members have been mysteriously dropping out of the Council."

I nodded. "I heard. Rick mentioned it."

"So you understand why I'm a little nervous about Michio and I being the only two left. If Ahmed manages to get Michio to quit, then Ahmed will get his people on the ship and a lot of people who deserve to go will get left behind."

"What makes you think that one more person on the Council would make a difference?"

"Because," she said. "We've only got a couple more weeks before the ship from Mars arrives. If it arrives before we finalize the list, the captain of the ship takes charge."

"Really? Why?" I asked.

"Because they only have a two-week window to return to Mars. Michio tried to explain it to me, but orbital mechanics and space trajectory math is beyond me. The point is that if the captain takes over the selection process, then Ahmed's candidates won't have a chance. Of course, that axe swings both ways. We may not get all of our candidates on the list either."

"Who cares? Let the fucking captain decide."

She slapped me on the side of my head, not a friendly slap either, a sharp crack to the noggin. "I care!" she said. "I've gotten to know the people around Gan and the other surrounding islands. There are some very good people down there who deserve a shot at going."

I shrugged and she continued. "So to answer your question of what difference one more person on the Council would make...a big difference. There's no way Ahmed could push two people out in such a short span of time without raising a lot of suspicion. Suspicious people get angry and angry people can overthrow an asshole like Ahmed."

I grabbed the bottle back from her and took a swig. "Okay, fine. You need another person on the Council who isn't on Ahmed's side. That's only one reason. You said there were two?"

"Very good," she said. "I thought maybe you were too far gone to remember back that far." She smiled and winked.

"Well?" I asked.

"The second reason is because I miss you."

My stomach flopped and I wasn't sure if it was the booze or what she'd just said. But if I was a betting man I'd take odds that it was what she'd said.

"We used to have so much fun back then, Aron," she said. "Remember? You guys were hilarious, always joking around as you put up those god-awful, ugly communication towers."

"They may be ugly, but they work," I said sticking my finger in her face. But she was right. Those years were pretty damned fun. We worked hard and partied harder, at least Shannon and I did. Rick and Jin had usually headed home to be with their families, but Shannon and I didn't have families. So we drank. Sometimes we fished and a few times she even got me out on a surf board, but mostly we drank.

She knocked my hand away from her face and said, "My point is that I don't have anyone to share a drink with and I don't have fun anymore...not like we did back then." Her smile magically transformed into that sexy smirk again. "And once we get the list finalized, we could start having some real fun."

"But when the list is done you'll be off to Mars and I lose my drinking partner again."

She shook her head and her expression changed. I saw sadness behind her smile. It seemed to reach out to me for help. "No. I'd prefer dying on this planet, the planet that God put me on."

"I don't know, Shannon. Don't get me wrong...I'd love to hang out with you again, but the Council..."

"I know, I know...but it'll be over before you know it. I swear."

I took another drink and said, "What makes you think I could get elected? I'm no politician."

Her smile brightened. "First of all, everyone with a data mat knows your name. For the love of God, Aron...you're a bloody hero. You're the erector of the almighty IICN."

"I'm no hero," I said.

"It doesn't matter. There's no need for an election. As chairman, Ahmed has the power to appoint a replacement as long as the Council votes to approve it."

I laughed so hard I almost pissed myself.

"What's so funny?" she asked.

"Ahmed hates me. You weren't on Male then, but he and I had a little run-in and...well...let's just say that it ended with me showing him how I felt."

She laughed. "I may not have been there, but everyone in the Maldives heard about how you mooned Ahmed from the communications tower during the dedication ceremony."

"So you know why there's not a chance in hell that he'd appoint me." I said

"He'll appoint you. Because if he doesn't, then Michio and I will block any other appointment he tries to make. Without thirteen members on the Council, the list can't be approved. If the list isn't approved when the ship arrives, then the captain takes over and if that happens—"

"If that happens then Ahmed doesn't get his people on the list. I get it." I tipped the bottle back, but it was empty.

I looked over at Shannon and found her smiling at me. Suddenly I wondered if her offer was more than an invitation to drink. Then I remembered her boyfriend. What was his name again? Oh yeah, *Saravan* . What kind of a stupid name was Saravan?

My head felt like it was bobbing around out on the ocean. I couldn't get my brain to slow down long enough to come up with an excuse to say no. Then I thought about Rick and how the next several weeks were going to be hard around here. There were too many memories. And then there was William. I couldn't face the kid...not yet. I knew the Council would suck, but the memories of Rick and facing William would be worse.

"Alright," I finally said.

"Really? You'll do it?"

I nodded. The thought of spending time with Shannon filled me with a warm feeling in my gut, but there was something else swimming around down there, something other than Mohamed's bathtub booze. And even as I nodded, I had already regretted my decision.

CHAPTER 3

A wave crashed against the kayak. I countered with a stroke of my paddle and kept myself upright.

Shit! It had only been two weeks since Ahmed appointed me to the Council and already I was getting rusty. I had hoped that Ahmed and his boys would see the light and we could put this whole Council bullshit behind us, but the chance of that happening was slimmer than the chance of the atmosphere spontaneously healing.

Getting up to speed on Council business was a lot tougher than I had thought. For eighteen hours a day, seven days a week, I had pored over the lists, familiarizing myself with the inhabitants and the pool of candidates. Then I studied the profiles of those who were on the proposed list. What was it that Shannon had told me? They were just quibbling over a few names? Maybe it was the Irish in her, but the word quibbling turned out to be an epic understatement.

The list was stuffed with hundreds of ineligible candidates. Vote after vote was held, but the same people kept showing up on the list. I felt like Don Quixote in some new level of hell. At least in this hell, they offered an occasional break. This break was only one day. But that's all I needed. One day of fishing could help me flush two weeks of the Council bullshit out of my system.

I looked down through the water at the razor-sharp coral that lay a few feet below the surface. The black, green, and gray colors blurred together under the lens of the choppy ocean. It reminded me of those French abstract paintings that Kelly had once dragged me to see at the San Francisco Museum of Modern Art. Like those paintings, the colors and shapes of the coral were beautiful. The only difference was that I'd never heard of anyone getting shredded by a painting before. Death-by-coral wasn't a good way to kill myself, but that fucking Council had me considering it.

"I hope you're getting a good laugh out of this," I said to Rick, as if he were floating out there next to me. "But goddammit...this isn't funny."

The rain suddenly began to fall and the patterns of the coral took on an almost mosaic look. A few minutes later the swells began to rise. I picked up my paddle and turned the kayak to face the waves head on.

I still couldn't believe that I had volunteered to take Rick's place on the Council. Mohamed's moonshine must have killed the brain cells that governed common sense.

A wave broke over the bow and water poured into my seat compartment. Perfect. What else could go wrong? As if to answer my question, it began to rain. Shit. I decided to head in.

Paddling against the wind was hard, but as I slugged my way back towards the beach I felt some of the stress begin to melt away. Despite the weather, I found myself enjoying the rush of speed as I slid down each swell. That's probably why I didn't see the rogue wave that knocked me over.

The world spun. A wall of water rushed over me. Instinctively, I jammed my paddle down and wedged it into the reef. One of my hands lost its grip. I fell sideways, my hand smashing into the coral. The wave pulled the boat sideways. I screamed as my hand grated across the coral like a hunk of cheese. Water rushed into my mouth. I began to choke. A swell lifted me up and I somehow managed to grab the paddle with my bloody hand. But it was too late. I felt myself rolling over. I paddled frantically in a futile attempt to keep the boat upright. In a second, the swell would fall and I would fall with it, head first into the bottom. So with all the strength I could muster, I pushed my paddle back in a long, sweeping stroke. Then, leaning back, I swung my body hard to the right. It worked. I was upright again.

Leaning over the side, I coughed up a lungful of water. At some point, my coughs turned into laughter and it took me a second to get the joke. God had just offered me a chance to get off of the Council and I didn't take it.

***

I walked slowly back to my hut through the pouring rain. It was coming down in sheets now, blowing almost horizontal with the wind. As I passed in front of the dining hut, Mohamed poked his head out and yelled, "Aron, my friend! You will catch a cold out there."

I just waved and kept walking, but Mohamed opened an umbrella and ran after me.

"What are you doing out in the rain?"

"Just coming back from kayaking."

He looked incredulous. "In this?"

"I get wet kayaking, so what difference does a little rain make?"

He must have seen the blood dripping from my cut hand. "You're injured."

"I'm fine. It's just a scratch."

"It is more than a scratch and you know it. Come on." He tugged on my arm. "Let's get this cleaned up."

"I'm fine," I repeated.

"I insist," he said tugging at my soaked shirt. I didn't have it in me to argue, so I went with him.

We walked past the old swimming pool that now served as a cistern for the island's water reserve. A couple of smart people had converted the three-tiered swimming pool into a water treatment plant. Rainwater was collected from across the island and hauled to the upper pool where it made its way through a series of two filtration waterfalls before ending up in the main reservoir at the bottom.

We continued along the path, walking past fruit trees and the vegetable garden that was planted in the old soccer field. It was the only place on the island with soil deep enough to sustain agriculture. On the other side of the field was Mohamed's infirmary. We walked onto the porch and Mohamed closed his umbrella, leaning it against the wall. I followed him inside.

"Mango juice?"

"No thanks." I said. "Water if you've got it."

"Mango juice is better for you. Here, try some." Mohamed grabbed a small plastic jug and filled it with a thick, orange liquid. He handed it to me. "Here...drink."

"Really," I said. "A glass of water is fine."

Pushing the glass into my hand he said, "Mango juice will help protect you against staph infection."

I had never heard that before. True or not, I knew better than to argue with Mohamed about the miraculous power of mango juice. So I took the glass and smiled politely before taking a sip. It was like drinking syrup. Not the kind of thing that hits the spot after paddling through a storm. "Mmm," I choked out. "Thanks."

Mohamed rummaged through some plastic containers and seemed to find what he was looking for. "Please, please...sit." I sat down on one of his wicker chairs. He sat down next to me. Then leaning over, he began to bandage my hand.

"So, how is it going?" he asked.

"I can't complain."

He smiled. "You know what I mean. The Council. How is the Council going?"

Stalling to think of a tactful way to answer, I took another sip of the syrup and immediately regretted it. After forcing myself to swallow, I said, "It sucks. Ahmed doesn't run a very tight ship."

I winced as he poured some of his moonshine over my hand. "This may sting a little."

"You're supposed to say that before you pour it over the cut," I said.

"I am sorry," He said. Then, as he began wrapping my hand with a cloth bandage, "So Ahmed is causing you problems?"

I shook my head. "He's causing everyone problems, but I can deal with him. I dealt with him and his cronies when we were building the communications hub on Male."

He finished bandaging my hand and then sat back. His expression changed. The smile was gone. "Just be careful. This time will be different. He was nice to you back then because he needed you to complete the IICN. He doesn't need you now."

"Nice my ass! He was a pushy, pig-headed, stubborn son of a bitch."

His smile returned. "He is that...and more. But he is also dangerous, so be careful."

The stress that I had lost out on the water had found its way back into my neck and shoulders. I rolled my head from side to side until my neck cracked. "Thanks, Mohamed. I'll keep that in mind." I looked at my hand and wiggled my fingers. It hurt, but not bad. "And thanks for patching me up."

"It is my honor." He smiled. "It is the Islamic way. We must always help the injured."

"Tell that to Jamal."

From the expression on his face, I knew I'd crossed the line.

Why the hell did I say that? "I'm sorry, Mohamed. That isn't what I meant."

"You said what is in your heart and the heart speaks only the truth. But I know your words were not aimed at me."

"No...of course not. I'm...after what they did on Embudu and Makunudhoo...I don't know. Look, I probably should go."

I started to stand, but he put his hand on my shoulder pushed me back down. "Please, my friend, sit. It is not healthy to keep this anger inside of you."

I sat back down, but looked away.

Mohamed broke the silence. "It is natural to feel anger when something like that happens. And it is understandable that you direct that anger at the source of those attacks. But you must try to separate how you feel about the pirates and the religion that they hide behind. Jamal and his followers are fanatics. That is true. But they are no different than the New Crusaders." I looked over at him and he continued. "The unthinkable atrocities that the New Crusaders carried out in the name of Christ did not make Christianity an evil religion."

Memories of the stories my grandmother had told me about the vigilante groups called the New Crusaders flooded into my head. She had told me that after the terrorists blew up over a hundred high schools in the states back in 2018, a bunch of holier-than-thou right-wing shitheads went around killing anyone who looked remotely Muslim. And the damned president and congress argued about what to do and in the end did nothing. Thousands of innocent people were slaughtered. I couldn't remember how many had died. Fifty thousand? One hundred thousand? It was enough to force the military to stage the first coup in American history, although the history books called it an intervention.

Mohamed was right. Religions didn't kill people. People killed people. People killed people. And sometimes people hide behind religion.

I said. "I'm sorry…really."

Mohamed stood up and smiled. "We must sit down and have a long discussion about this someday when you have more time."

I stood up. "Be sure to have a bottle or two of your moonshine ready. I'll need it for that discussion."

He laughed and said, "How many times must I tell you. It is medicine, not moonshine."

I looked at my watch and said, "It's almost time for me to head back to Male."

"How long will you be gone for this time?" he asked.

"Just a week. They're taking a three-day break for the Remembrance Day Weekend."

"They are taking a break so close to the arrival of the ship?"

I shrugged and walked to the door. He reached out his pudgy arm and pushed it open for me. I stepped outside and said, "Thanks again for fixing me up and for the advice. I'll see you when I get back."

"Stay safe, my friend."

I turned to leave, but stopped when he said, "Wait. I almost forgot." Turning around, I watched him disappear into his hut. A few seconds later he reappeared with an old water bottle that I knew wasn't filled with water.

"Here, take this. It will help with the stress of the Council."

I took the bottle and smiled. "You of all people should know that booze is prohibited in Male. What are you trying to do...get me arrested by the morality police?"

He smiled and said, "If anyone says anything, you have them call me. I am a doctor, remember? I am prescribing this medicine to help ease your hypertension."

***

Two hours later, my teeth rattled in my skull as the hull pounded against the waves. It was useless to try to read anymore, so I bunched up my data mat and tucked it into my back pocket. There would be time to finish reviewing the updated list when I got to my room on Male.

I stood up and grabbed the railing to keep from falling over. After getting my sea legs, I climbed two steps up to the bridge. Kamish sat behind the console, steering the twenty-four foot speed boat through the shallow channel that ran between a chain of islands. He kept one hand on the wheel and the other on the throttle, cutting back the engines every time we launched off the top of a big wave.

His younger brother, Lanka, was strapped into a fishing chair up ahead on the bow. I watched for a second as Lanka swept the horizon with his binoculars. If anyone could find something out there, it was Lanka.

Then I turned around and saw Kamish's youngest brother, Senil, on the aft chair doing the same thing. Both of them held fast to their rifles.

Above the high-pitched whine of the electric engines and the roar of the wind I yelled, "How much longer?"

Without taking his eyes off the waves, Kamish said, "Maybe ten minutes. I can just make out the light from the port." He nodded toward the horizon.

At first I didn't see anything, but when we crested the next big wave I saw the light for a brief moment before we slid down the backside.

Ten minutes was a long time out here, but it didn't used to be. For the first several years, the MDF Air Patrol had kept the pirates outside the atoll. But there were fewer functioning boats and helojumpers nowadays, and there were more pirates. So nobody took anything for granted.

I felt my shoulders tighten and I tried unsuccessfully to crack my neck. It wasn't that I was afraid of getting killed; it was what they did to their prisoners before they killed them that bothered me. That brought back the image of Rick tied to the tree.

I checked my watch. It was seven o'clock. The heavy storm clouds that blanketed the entire sky made it seem later. At least the rain had stopped, so visibility wasn't too bad.

"How are we doing on juice?" I asked.

Kamish glanced at the gauge and said, "Should be enough to get us into port, but I will have to swap out batteries before we head back. There wasn't enough sun today to get a full charge."

Like most vehicles manufactured after the gas crisis of 2021, the boat was solar powered. Its paint passively collected the sun's energy and eventually converted it into electricity. The technology used to work pretty well before the storm, but the weather patterns had changed and it was a lot cloudier than it had used to be. Most boats had to deploy a floating solar net to help them get a full charge.

I walked aft to add my eyes to the watch. Besides, it wasn't as bumpy back there. Senil greeted me with his mischievous smile. In this light, his teeth looked luminescent.

"Better hold on. It is a bit bumpy back here," he said.

"That's okay," I replied. "It's better than up front where Lanka is." I held fast to the boat rail and crouched down next to his chair. "See anything?" I yelled.

He must have picked up the concern in my voice because he winked and said, "Do not worry. The pirates won't bother us tonight. They do not like the rain. It makes their prayer rugs all wet," he laughed.

I forced a smile and said, "Kamish said you guys aren't staying in Male tonight? What's the rush to get back?"

His smile got wider. "Mohamed told me that Jemil will deliver soon and I want to be there when my son is born."

"What makes you think it's going to be a boy?" As far as I knew, there wasn't a working ultrasound in the atoll.

"I can tell. My grandmother used to say that if the baby rides low in the belly then it will be a boy. Jemil's belly is almost touching the—"

Blood poured out of his mouth as he tried to finish his sentence. I didn't hear the shot that killed him, but I saw who did it. The pirates were coming up fast behind us in a large, rigid-hull inflatable boat and they were shooting wildly at us. One of the bastards had gotten lucky.

Where the fuck did they come from? I looked around. They must have been hiding in one of the small coves of the island off to the right. I reached for Senil, but his lifeless body slumped to the deck before I could get a hold of him.

Crouching next to him, I yanked the rifle from his hand and yelled towards the front of the boat, "Pirates!"

Kamish looked back and I saw the horror in his eyes and he screamed, "Senil!" Then, looking out ahead, he blasted the horn to alert his other brother. Lanka unbuckled himself and sprinted to the back of the boat. Kamish was already on the radio calling the MDF for help.

Lanka took a quick look at Senil and then crouched down next to me. Putting his hand on my shoulder, he pulled me further down below the railing. Then, shouldering his rifle, he took aim and fired. I just knelt there and watched. It took the ricochet of a bullet near my head to remind me that I had a rifle of my own. I brought it up and fired.

Kamish must've had the throttles pegged because we were bouncing so hard that I couldn't aim. It didn't matter. I kept firing. At the rate they were closing, I could tell that we wouldn't reach the protection of the port in time. And the damned MDF Air Patrol wouldn't get here in time either. It took at least fifteen minutes for those assholes to get a helojumper off the pad.

I was about to fire another shot, but stopped when I saw something that looked like a snake flying through the air. It took me a few seconds to realize what I was looking at. It was a grappling hook on the end of a rope and it was heading straight for us.

Lanka shoved me hard out of the way. I rolled into the corner. When I looked up I saw Lanka pinned against the rail. The hook was in his back, and two of its metallic prongs protruded through his chest. I watched in horror as the rope tightened. I tried to get up, but before I could reach him the hook ripped his body in half. He collapsed onto the deck next to his brother. The hook was now solidly jammed into the back of the boat.

I heard Kamish scream above the rush of wind. "No!"

I looked toward the bridge. His face was filled with rage. He pushed the throttle as far as it would go. It didn't help. We were slowing down. Our engines were no match for their diesel hybrids.

I looked around for something to cut the rope. They usually kept an axe in one of the storage containers. I crawled over and looked inside the rusty metal box on the starboard side. All that I found was a solar net pack. I pulled it out and threw it overboard so I could look for the axe. The box was empty. Out of the corner of my eye I saw something behind us in the water. I turned to look. It was just the solar pack automatically deploying. Thousands of miniature water activated servos stretched the net to its full one hundred foot diameter.

I could hear rifle shots above the roar of the wind now. They were almost on us. I laid flat on the floor and crawled over to the box on the port side. The floor was covered in an inch of bloody water that sloshed around. I reached the box and opened the lid. I peered inside. It was filled with life preservers. I started pulling them out and throwing behind me. Then I spotted it. The axe was attached to a metal clasp on the inside of the box. I freed it and crawled back to the hook. Raising the axe above my head, I brought it down on the rope. The rail bent, but the rope held. Two more shots whizzed by me and I ducked. Peeking up over the rail I saw them. They were less than fifty feet behind us. We were out of time.

Suddenly I heard their engines strain and then cut out completely. I peeked up expecting to see the bastards boarding our ship. Instead, I watched as they ran to the back of their boat. I suddenly realized what had happened. The solar net had tangled in their propellers. Taking advantage of the diversion, I brought up the axe again and swung down hard. This time the axe cut clean through the rope. We lurched forward and I fell back. Lanka and Senil's lifeless bodies slid across the bloody swill and joined me.

After a few seconds, I peeked over the railing and watched as the pirate boat shrunk into the distance. We were finally out of range.

I got up and walked slowly toward the cabin. I looked down. My clothes were covered in blood. When I reached the bridge, I looked over at Kamish. Tears streamed down his cheeks, his face tight with hatred.

I turned away and stared at the light shining out from the lighthouse at the Port of Male. Tears streamed down my face and I pictured Senil as a boy, shimmying up the palm tree to get me a coconut.

CHAPTER 4

A fried fish stared up at me from my plate with an accusing eye. I looked away and filled my empty glass from the bottle that Mohamed had given me. Half of the bottle was already gone and I still felt like shit. No medicine was strong enough to help me forget what had happened out there on the boat.

I took a sip anyway, winced, and set the glass down. Then I pushed the plate away. There was no way I could eat tonight and tomorrow wasn't looking good either.

I looked around the hotel's grand dining room and saw about a dozen people finishing their meals. It was late and the dinner rush was over. Most of them were Europeans who, like me, were stranded here while on vacation. This hotel was their home now. A few looked like locals, Maldivians, although I guess technically we were all locals now.

I listened to the conversion of the couple at the table next to me. They spoke English, but based on the guy's accent I guessed that he was either German or Austrian. He was telling the middle-aged redhead about his day. He described a fight that took place at the loading docks in the morning.

Macho bullshit. Probably trying to get laid.

Then he complained about how few cargo loads there were lately. He had only unloaded five boats today. It was what he didn't mention that I found interesting. He didn't say a word about the attack on our boat. I wondered if the news hadn't gotten out yet or if he didn't want to scare the woman.

I drained my glass and refilled it. Some of it spilled on my data mat, which sat unfolded and untouched on the table. I'd been avoiding it all night.

"Fuck it," I said under my breath.

Using the side of my hand, I wiped the moonshine from the data mat and then tapped the screen to open the Council database. I navigated to the Evacuation Eligibility spreadsheet and opened it. I scrolled down until I found what I was looking for: Lanka and Senil's names. Their entire lives summed up on two rows of the spreadsheet. I highlighted their information and let my finger hover above the CHANGE STATUS button. I grabbed my glass with my other hand, drank a silent toast to them, and then selected one of the options from the drop down list. Their status changed from ELIGIBLE to DECEASED. I hit the CONFIRM button and polished off what was left in my glass. A second later, my data mat chirped as an automated message popped open.

SUBJECT: CHANGE NOTIFICATION

THIS AUTOMATED NOTIFICATION WAS SENT TO INFORM YOU OF A CHANGE TO THE LIST. THE FOLLOWING INFORMATION WAS CHANGED:

NAME ISLAND CHANGE
LANKA CHANDRA LOHIFUSHI STATUS-DECEASED
SENIL CHANDRA LOHIFUSHI STATUS-DECEASED

Every member of the Council should've gotten the same message. I sat back and sighed because I knew what they were all doing. They were scrambling to submit their next top two candidates to fill those empty slots. Sure enough, a few seconds later I began receiving candidate submission emails.

"Bastards!"

I must have said it louder than I had intended because the room went silent. There was no point looking up. I knew that everyone was staring at me. To hell with them!

After a minute, people started talking again. I heard someone say hello, and from the sound of the voice I knew who said it. I looked up and saw a short, bald Maldivian strolling through the room like he owned the place. He did.

Before the storm, Ahmed Walheed was a successful business man. After the storm, he became the Prime Minister of the Maldives. He still held the title, but it didn't mean much anymore. His new title, President of the Council of Thirteen, was what he preferred. The president wielded more power.

Shit! He saw me and was headed this way. An unconvincing sympathetic look was plastered on his face. His eyes were sad above his ever-present smile. It was the kind of smile that would look at home on an undertaker who sold used cars on the side.

Ahmed stopped in front of my table and pulled out a handkerchief. As he wiped the sweat off his forehead, I couldn't help but notice the massive sweat stains that stretched from his armpit to the hip pockets of his seersucker coat. Hell, I could be standing on the other side of the island and I'd be able to see those stains.

When he finished mopping his brow, he shoved the handkerchief into his pocket and said, "Aron, I am so sorry about the unfortunate incident today. It was disturbing to hear that pirates are operating so close to Male."

Getting a flat tire was an unfortunate incident. Losing your fucking wallet was an unfortunate incident. But the brutal slaying of two young men…two good young men, was a goddammed tragedy and it took all the will I could muster to keep from burying my fist in his face to convey that message.

"I'm not in the mood, Ahmed."

"I understand. I just wanted to make sure that you were okay. We all heard about the attack and everyone was asking about you."

I'm sure they did. They probably wanted to know if another slot on the list would open up. "Well, as you can see for yourself….I'm fine." I held my arms out. "No bullet holes. No giant gashes through my body. So just tell everyone that I'll see them tomorrow at the Council meeting." I grabbed my glass to take a drink and realized it was empty. I set it back down. "And if you don't mind, I'm tired and I'm going to bed."

Ahmed looked at the water bottle and then at me. I'm sure he knew that it wasn't water.

Come on, bastard. Say something. Give me an excuse to slug you.

But he was too smart for that. He let it go and said, "Yes, yes, of course. Go and get some rest. We have a long week ahead of us."

He patted my shoulder with his puffy hand, making the hairs on the back of my neck prickle. Before turning to leave, he said, "But there is one thing that we should discuss before tomorrow."

Here it comes.

"I know that you are new to the Council and that it must be difficult for you to understand the give-and-take that must occur to finalize the list of evacuees."

"I got no problem with give-and-take, Ahmed. What I got a problem with is the give-and-give that you guys expect from me."

He shook his head. "That is not what we expect. Anyway, it doesn't matter. I think we should look past our differences and rise above these petty issues. We have less than two weeks before the ship arrives and if we don't come to a consensus, then as you know, the ship's captain will make the decision for us."

I pushed my chair away from the table and said, "Petty issues? Are you trying to piss me off!"

Ahmed pulled out his stained handkerchief from his hip pocket and wiped the back of his neck. "Now Aron, please settle down. I am sure that it will come as no surprise to you that there are some members of the Council, not me mind you, but others, who think that you are responsible for the stalemate."

I stood up. My chair fell onto its back. "Responsible? They think *I'm* responsible for the bullshit that's going on?"

Ahmed held his hands up in front of him like a traffic cop and looked around. "Please, lower your voice." He smiled at the people next to us. Then he leaned close to me and whispered, "The Council just thinks that you are being a little…unreasonable."

I shook my head and laughed. "I'm being unreasonable. Are you shitting me? I'm not the one stacking the list with people who don't meet the basic selection criteria. And I'm not talking about a couple of people. Last week alone I identified over one hundred candidates who were over the age of sixty and another two hundred who have serious physical and mental health issues and I—"

"Aron, Aron…" he said nearly in a whisper. "I am on your side. I too want to do the right thing, but you must understand that sometimes rules must be bent. Surely there are a few people you would like to see on the list, but perhaps they don't meet all of the criteria?"

"Don't try that pulling that shit with me! I know how that games ends." He sounded just like those bastards at SatComm Control Services. They just wanted a one-year extension on the contract in return for a vacation in the Maldives…a little quid pro quo. They said nobody would know and they were right. A week later the storm hit. Nobody ever did find out. They couldn't…they were dead.

"What game?" he asked. "You're not making any sense."

The room began to spin and I held on to the edge of the table. A little voice in my head agreed with him. I wasn't making any sense and I should've probably shut up. But I hated that little voice, so I ignored it.

"Look," I said as calmly as I could. "You helped write the damned charter for the Council. The charter states that we're supposed to choose candidates who can contribute to the growth and welfare of the Mars colony. Most of the candidates you've submitted have nothing to offer the colony. Just the opposite, they'll require the welfare of the colony to stay alive."

"I think you are exaggerating a bit."

"Exaggerating?" I reached down and snatched my data mat off the table. My head was still spinning and that little voice kept talking. It begged me to walk away. That voice was such a pussy. I hadn't listened to that voice in years and I wasn't about to start now.

My fingers stumbled as I typed in a search string. Eventually I found what I was looking for.

Holding the data mat in front of Ahmed's face I said, "Here! Here is what I'm talking about. It's one of yours. Why the hell are you sending this guy? He's seventy-three years old with a chronic heart problem. What makes you think he'd survive the ten-month trip to Mars? Even if he did, he'd probably be dead within a month of arrival. Am I exaggerating about him?"

Ahmed's face turned a deep shade of red and he wagged his stubby index finger an inch from my nose. "Prasad Rannabandeyri Kilegefan is a very important man. Very important! He is the great grandson of Ibrahim Nasir Rannabandeyri Kilegefan, the first president of the Maldivian Republic. He is a symbol for all Maldivians. He must go to Mars."

"Do you hear yourself? This isn't about saving the Maldivian society. This is about saving mankind. The colony doesn't need symbols. The colony needs people with skills."

I was about to slap the bastard with my data mat when Melana, a young Maldivian girl who helped her mom work in the dining room, suddenly appeared between Ahmed and me. She picked up my uneaten plate of fish and quietly asked, "Are you finished with your food?"

I stared at her for a second, thrown off guard by her question. I nodded. She smiled and returned to the kitchen. I watched her walk through the kitchen doors and just stood there as the doors swung back and forth. Finally, I looked back over at Ahmed.

A strained smile filled his face as he dabbed beads of sweat on his forehead. "I can see that you are still upset from your trip," he said. "Let us save this discussion for chambers tomorrow. I am sure we can find some common ground."

Ahmed turned and walked out of the dining room, stopping by a few tables along the way to shake hands and pat backs. As I watched him go, my hand found the bottle. I raised it to my lips and took a gulp.

What the hell was I doing? The sooner this list was finalized, the sooner I could get back to fishing.

CHAPTER 5

"Mister Chairman, point of order," Michio said.

Almost everyone on the Council ignored Michio's call for order. Some people spoke quietly in small groups along the walls, while others talked loudly to one another from across the U-shaped, mahogany table that was set up in the center of the room. It was a huge table full of elaborately carved palm trees and tropical flowers on the legs and corner moldings. As big as the table was, it looked like a piece of children's furniture in the giant banquet hall.

The room had once hosted conferences and wedding receptions. Wedding receptions…what kind of people would have a wedding reception in this room?

The floor was covered in a loud, jungle print carpet that smelled moldy. On the far side of the room, a series of tall, multi-paned windows lined the wall. The windows looked out onto the ocean. Hung between each window were neon purple draperies. The color somehow amplified the pounding hangover in my head. The loud, gaudy decor just didn't seem like a good venue for a wedding event, but it seemed perfectly suited for the Council of Thirteen.

I rested my elbows on the table and cradled my head in my hands just in case it exploded. When I awoke this morning, I thought it already had.

I looked over at Ahmed, who reclined in the only high-backed chair in the room. He sat at the head of the table next to his cousin, Viyaja, and both were ignoring Michio's plea to restore order. Ahmed and Viyaja appeared preoccupied with their game of whisper tag. Viyaja laughed and I cringed when I saw his teeth. They looked like something out of a novelty catalog; long, square, and jumbled together. He was either afraid of dentists or he practiced some archaic religion that forbade braces.

"Point of order, mister chairman," Michio repeated for what seemed like the hundredth time.

Michio was nothing if not persistent. I bet he never had this problem back when he was a mid-level bureaucrat in the Japanese government. The Japanese were pretty well known for their devotion to rules and order. This must be an absolute hell for him.

Besides Shannon, Michio was the only other person on the Council that I trusted and genuinely liked. Rick had told me about him. He told me that there was a lot more to the guy than met the eye, but he never explained what he meant. It didn't matter. Michio helped me get up to speed on the Council and taught me about the parliamentary rules that governed it. It was during those lessons that I had discovered that we shared a few things in common.

Like me, he came to the Maldives on a vacation to fish. Unlike me, he was smart enough to have brought his family with him. And like me, he hated Ahmed. But unlike me, he was able to hide it.

I looked over by the door. Three members from the eastern islands congregated in a tight huddle. There was Bill Mathers, a sixty-year-old New Zealander with a brand new thirty-year-old wife. I'm sure his long, crooked nose and bushy eyebrows had won him that trophy and not his position on the Council.

To his right was Abdul-Wahid, a skinny, dark skinned Pakistani who, rumor had it, once had been on the national cricket team. He had a boyish face with an overcompensating mustache and he always seemed to be in a bad mood. Shannon said his bad mood was because he was a bit of a religious fanatic and resented working with infidels. I figured it had more to do with the Pakistan Cricket team's loss to India a few months before the storm. No chance for a rematch now.

On Abdul's left, Karl Kopperstag leaned against the wall. He was a mean-looking South African with a shaved head.

Further down the wall I saw Hari Singh and Raj Balamudi, or as I liked to call them, the bobble-head brothers. They never nodded or shook their heads. They bobbled them from side to side so I never knew if they were indicating yes and no. It drove me up the wall.

They were the youngest members of the Council, both in their early thirties. They represented the western island alliance, although in practice they represented the best interests of Ahmed. They referred to Ahmed as uncle. And while I knew that term was used in this part of the world as a sign of respect for elders, it wouldn't surprise me to find out that Ahmed was actually their uncle.

Ahmed laughed at something and I looked over at him. That stupid laugh of his, that machine gun blast of ha-ha-ha, ha-ha-ha just pushed me over the edge. I stood up and yelled, "Ahmed, for

Christ's sake! Take control of the Council." I reached up and grabbed my forehead to make sure it was still attached.

Ahmed looked at me and smiled. Then he picked up his gavel and struck it twice on the table to bring the room back to order.

"Gentlemen, gentlemen. Please, take your seats." He continued hammering until, one by one, all of the Council members were seated.

The last three in their seats were Chen Liu, Jun Wong, and Kim Pao, all originally from China, except Jun Wong, who still preferred to be called Korean despite the annexation of the Korean peninsula by China twenty years ago. They represented the central islands and while they had once been considered swing voters, like the rest, they'd been voting with Ahmed lately.

Michio remained standing. When everyone was seated, he said, "Mister President, point of order." He said it as if it were the first time he had uttered the phrase all day.

Ahmed looked amused and said, "The chair recognizes Mr. Shimitzu, the representative of the Hurra island chain."

"Thank you, Mr. President. A motion for a vote on the list was proposed and seconded. With the motion on the table, you must call for a vote."

"Yes, yes...of course. I apologize." Then Ahmed addressed the entire group. "A motion for a vote has been proposed and seconded, so will those in favor of the current list, as amended, please signify by a show of hands."

Ten hands shot up from the Ahmed caucus.

"Very good. And those opposed?"

Michio, Shannon, and I raised our hands.

"Will the secretary please note that there were ten in favor and three opposed. Having not met the required twelve votes, the motion fails."

Michio nodded and sat down, his face devoid of emotion. I made a mental note never to play poker with him.

Abdul-Wahid took off his sandal and began to beat it on the tabletop while glaring at Michio, Shannon and me...but mostly at Shannon. Shannon smiled and blew him a kiss. She was the only female on the Council and her action sent Adbul into a rage. He stood up and beat his sandal harder. I waited to see Shannon's next move, but a melodic Islamic chant worked its way into the room from the mosque down the street. Abdul froze, sandal still in hand.

"Allahu Akbar," someone said and then repeated, "Allahu Akbar." The words had a Pavlovian effect on almost everyone in the room. One by one, people got up and started to shuffle out.

"Gentlemen. It is call to prayers," Ahmed said for formality's sake. "Therefore, I propose a thirty minute recess. Is there a second?"

Abdul-Wahid, who was now putting his sandal back on, mumbled something unintelligible.

Lifting his gavel, Ahmed asked, "We have a second, so all in favor?"

Half the room was already gone, but it didn't matter. End of the world or not, the Maldives was still a Muslim state, so voting against daily prayers was not really an option. Those in the room raised their hands and Ahmed declared a recess with a thump of his gavel.

Shannon came over and plopped down in the chair next to me. Without a word, she lifted her long legs and rested them on my lap. I pretended like I couldn't see up her skirt, but I was never very good at pretending.

She represented the far southern islands, the Gan atoll. The islands were populated predominately with refugees, most from Sri Lanka. I still thought it was odd that she ended up as their representatives, but she was a very likable person. I mean, what's not to like?

"You know," she said. "I think I'll teach Abdul how we used to settle our differences in the back streets of Dublin. We didn't use sandals back there, we used our fists." She smiled and winked at me as she pushed a loose strand of blond hair behind her ear.

I smiled as an image of Shannon kicking the shit out of that little creep popped into my head.

Michio walked over and joined us. "This is pointless. We have just wasted four days of work because they refuse to follow the rules."

"You said this would be easy, Shannon."

"I don't recall using those exact words," she said.

"Well, whatever words you used, I'm getting really tired of this shit and I've only been on the Council for a couple of weeks. I don't know how you two have lasted so long. I still think it would be easier if we let the captain of that ship decide for us," I said.

Both of them stared at me.

Michio spoke first. "No. We must stand strong. The rest of the Council will eventually see that we all have too much to lose if we do not compromise. In the end, they will honor the charter."

"What the hell are you talking about?" Shannon said. "They have about as much honor as the fucking Irish Republican Army back in 2096 when they broke the hundred-year truce."

"The IRA uprising was over forty years ago," I said. "I think it's time you let it go."

"We let it go once and look what happened," she said. "You can never let your guard down with bastards like that. We need to watch our backs."

I chuckled and Shannon asked, "What's so damned funny, Yank?"

"Us. There are only three of us, for God's sake. The only way we can watch our backs is if you watch Michio's back, Michio watches my back, and I watch your back."

Her smile widened and her incredible green eyes twinkled. "Sounds like some kind of excuse for you to stare at my backside." She flipped another lock of hair off her forehead with a suggestive toss of her head.

"Come on," she said. "They'll be gone for a good hour. Let's go grab a cup of tea."

She swung her legs off my lap, placed a hand on my thigh, and pushed herself up. Michio stood up next to her.

"What are you waiting for?" she asked. "An invitation from the bloody queen?"

No. I was waiting for the blood to stop rushing to a particular part of my body.

***

Down the street from the hotel was a small café with three tables set out on the sidewalk. Like most businesses in the post-storm world, the owner operated the café under the barter system. When we ordered our tea, Shannon gave him a small jar of fish paste, a product of her island chain, and a kiss on the cheek. I'll bet he would have given us the tea just for the kiss. I would have.

I sat down and listened as Shannon launched into one of her many tall tales. It was a story I hadn't heard before. She was a great storyteller and I could listen to her for hours.

"And so there I was, out in the middle of the channel trying to teach these six Buddhist monks to surf. The boat had dropped us off and wouldn't be back for an hour. I had to admit that for pudgy fellas, they had pretty good balance. Anyway, after about ten minutes, I grabbed a beautiful curl and thought I'd show them a few tricks. The curl broke unexpectedly and I went down like a sack of potatoes. When I came up for air, I realized that my bikini, top and bottom, were gone...just gone."

Michio and I laughed.

He asked, "So what did you do?"

"Well, I figured these gentlemen paid for a full hour lesson and I wasn't about to welch on the deal. So I climbed onto my board and paddled right back to the where I left the pack of them floating. I sat up, legs straddled on either side of the board, and said, 'Alright gentlemen. Who wants to be the first to shoot the curl?' I'm not sure what they thought I was talking about, but all six hands shot up, and a few were raising other parts of their anatomy, if you know what I mean."

Tea spurted out of my nose. I grabbed the edge of the tablecloth to dry my face. When I looked up, Jin was standing there. I sprang out of my seat, nearly dropping my cup.

"Well I'll be goddammed...look who it is." We shook hands and I asked, "What are you doing here? Did something break in the radio tower again?"

"It is good to see you too, Aron." He nodded politely towards Shannon and Michio before saying, "No. There is nothing wrong with the tower as far as I know. I came to speak with you."

I gave him a puzzled look, but Jin's round baby face remained impassive. The only indication that something was amiss was his eyes. Jin was the third member of the IICN musketeers. Rick, Jin, and I worked our asses off building the IICN. I knew him almost as well as I had known Rick. So when I saw his eyes, I knew something was wrong.

"It is a private matter," he said. "Can we go for a walk?"

Looking at my watch, I said, "I don't have a lot of time. Can we meet later for dinner?"

He shook his head. "It is important that I speak with you now."

I looked over at Shannon and Michio. "I'll see you guys back in the Council. Send me a message if something important pops up." Not that I expected anything important to happen in that worthless meeting.

I looked at Jin and said, "Okay, let's go." Jin's expression worried me. The last time I saw him like this was when his son had almost fallen from the top of a hundred-foot communications tower.

We walked in silence on the cobblestone street in front of a string of small, pastel-colored hotels facing the ocean. Hell, most of buildings on Male faced the ocean. The island was only a mile long and a half mile wide. It was hard not to face the ocean.

We crossed the street and headed down toward the beach along the promenade. When we reached the base of the communication tower he stopped.

Sheathed in overlapping curved stainless steel panels, it looked more like a modern art sculpture than a communications tower. A hundred years ago it had housed equipment used to detect signals from tsunami buoys. Later, it became a memorial for the thousands killed during one of the largest tsunamis in recorded history. Now it was the main equipment hub and communications tower for the IICN.

Jin didn't say anything, so I did, "What's up, Jin? You look worried."

He looked around, and then finally said, "I have learned something disturbing."

"Okay." Now he had me looking from side to side and I didn't know why. "It's just you and me out here, what is it?"

"You know that I was once in the Chinese Army?"

I nodded.

"Did I tell you that I was in the Cyber Warfare Division?"

I nodded again. He had brought it up one night about six years ago. Rick, Jin, and I were celebrating the first operational test of the IICN with one too many bottles of moonshine. We all let a few skeletons out of the closet that night. The Chinese Army secret was his, although it wasn't a big deal. The United States and China hadn't been at war for over twenty years and either way, I didn't care. And it wasn't likely the war would start up again given that the United States and China didn't exist anymore.

"Yes." He nodded as if he had remembered that night too. "But what you don't know is that my specialty was hacking into satellites."

I wasn't surprised. During the war, both sides hacked into each other's communications systems. "So? There's nothing left up there to hack. What's this all about?"

He looked up and said, "You are wrong, Aron."

I stared at him, not sure what he meant.

He continued, "Three years ago, I built a device to transmit signals to satellites over a secret command-and-control frequency."

"You did what? Wait a minute. There is no way that any satellites survived a solar storm as big as the one that hit twelve years ago. And even if one did, you'd need a laser uplink station to communicate with it. Are you telling me that you built a laser uplink?"

"No. I did not build an LUS. I did not need to. You see, most satellites have back doors, communication paths that use radio frequencies."

"Jin, I worked in the satellite communications software business for twenty-three years and I never heard of any back door RF channels." From what I remembered, the last RF satellites were decommissioned around 2030.

He looked down at his feet. "These were not...official communication capabilities. My government had some of our manufacturers surreptitiously install this capability in the satellite components. It enabled our military to keep track of certain information."

"So wait...you're serious. You actually communicated with a satellite."

He nodded.

I walked a few feet away and stepped onto one of the massive concrete rocks that served as a breakwater for the harbor. Closing my eyes, I let the ocean breeze fill my lungs. I needed to let this sink in.

Jin stepped onto a rock next to me. I opened my eyes and looked at him. "What was the point of building the transmitter?"

He shook his head. "After we completed the IICN, I needed something to keep my mind occupied, so I built the transmitter. Each night I would point it at a different part of the sky and try to connect to a satellite. I never really expected to find one, but it helped me pass the time. Then, a few weeks ago, I received a signal from a satellite."

"So what kind of satellite? A communications satellite? A weather satellite?"

"No. It is a military reconnaissance satellite, an Indian reconnaissance satellite. It is in orbit over Pakistan. It sustained some damage from the storm, but I was able to hack in and assume control."

"So you're in control of a reconnaissance satellite? This is big, Jin. Really big. The MDF could use it to—"

"No! Nobody must know about this."

I flinched and took a step back.

"I am sorry," he said in his usual quiet tone. "Please…let me explain. The guidance system was broken, but I managed to fix it. Before trying to reposition the satellite, I needed to calibrate it. So I took a photograph of something that was within range of its current orbit. It had to be something that I was familiar with so I could calculate the distance between a series of geographical points."

"So what did you take a picture of? China? The Great Wall?"

He shook his head. "No, I pointed the camera at the Maldives. I knew that I could measure the distance between some of the communications towers we built."

Jesus Christ, he was smart. I never would have thought of that.

"It was when I studied the image that I saw it."

"Saw what?"

"I saw an MDF boat docked alongside a supertanker positioned about a hundred nautical miles south of the Maldives. When I zoomed in, I saw the symbol of Jamal painted on the hull of the tanker. It must be their mother ship. The MDF boat was docked alongside a pirate fast attack boat and they appeared to be transferring crates between the ships."

"Are you sure it was an MDF boat? Maybe they painted one of their boats to look like an MDF patrol boat."

Shaking his head, he said, "I am absolutely sure. The clarity of the image was very good; good enough for me read the numbers on the hull and identify some unique characteristics of the boat. Before I came to see you, I went to the harbor." He pointed over to where the MDF boats were usually docked. "I confirmed the identity of the boat in the photograph."

I turned, stepped off the rock, and walked back to the base of the tsunami tower. Jin followed.

"Why are you telling me all of this?"

"Because it is evidence that Ahmed is involved."

I shot him a look and said, "No it's not. It's circumstantial evidence at best. Look, I hate the bastard as much as the next guy, but you can't accuse him of cozying up to the pirates unless you have ironclad proof. He's a dangerous son of a bitch."

Jin walked next to me and said, "You are the only person I have told this to. You are my friend and a man of honor. I know that you will help me do the right thing."

"Whoa! What do you mean, 'do the right thing'?"

"If he is involved with the pirates, then we are all in danger."

"Yeah, well... unless you have a high-res glossy of him hugging a pirate you don't have anything that proves he is guilty. Do you have a picture of him on the boat?"

He shook his head.

"Then you have nothing."

"I have the messages that they sent to each other."

"How?'

"SIGINT," he said.

"SIGINT?"

"Signal Intelligence. I was able to use some of the signal collection sensors on the satellite to intercept messages that were transmitted across the VHF channel. I triangulated the signals and isolated the location of where the messages were sent from. They were sent to and from the location of the mother ship."

"Wait," I said. My brain felt like it was about to explode again. "How'd you crack the IICN encryption?"

There were only two ways he could have cracked the encryption that we put into place on the message server. Either he convinced Ahmed to give him his personal encryption key, and I don't think that Ahmed would hand over something like that to Jin or anyone else. Or else he built a quantum computer to crack the code for him...and not even Jin could do that.

Jin shook his head again. "I did not break the encryption. I simply stripped the user information from the header, which is not encrypted. I then mapped the ID to Ahmed's account by searching the server logs."

I grabbed his shoulders. "Then that's it! That's proof that he was communicating with the pirates."

He shook his head. "Unfortunately, there was an anomaly."

My hands dropped to my side.

Jin continued, "I discovered Ahmed's User ID was on messages that originated both from Male and from the location of the mother ship. Some of these messages were sent within minutes of each other, so—"

"So you don't have anything." I shook my head. "I'm sorry, but there's no way in hell that I'm going to expose Ahmed with this information. I'm no lawyer, but even I know that this wouldn't hold up in court. For all we know, Ahmed has been sending threats to the pirates. I doubt it, but it's possible. Hell, maybe he gave them his User ID so they could communicate a ceasefire or something."

Jin looked like I'd just kicked him in the gut.

"I'm sorry, but I can't do it... not without more proof," I said.

This wasn't like Jin. He never acted rashly. And he knew better than to accuse Ahmed without hard evidence. Eight years ago, someone else had tried that. He accused Ahmed of stealing supplies and trading them for his own profit. The guy that accused him ended up dead. They said it was an accident, but I had a hard time believing that someone could accidently fall out of a helojumper.

My data mat chirped in my back pocket. I pulled it out and read the message.

"Look, Jin...I've got to get back. They're starting the meeting. Let me know if you find anything more conclusive." I turned and started to walk away.

"Aron, wait!"

I stopped and turned around.

"There may be a way to decrypt the messages. Can we meet later, so that I can explain?"

Throwing my arms up in the air, I said, "Yeah, okay, sure. The Council should finish around five o'clock tonight. Meet me at the café, the one where you found me. But Jin, keep quiet about this. Okay?"

He bowed, and I took off for the hotel.

CHAPTER 6

I ran up the stairs, two at a time, and darted down the hallway. Out of breath, I pulled the oversized teak doors open and found Shannon standing in the middle of the room. Around the table, people rolled their eyes and ignored her. At the head of the table, Ahmed absently tapped his gavel in the palm of his hand while Shannon continued to talk.

"...and so that brings us to how you behave after you drop in on, snake, hog the wave from, or simply run over another surfer. It is not a good idea to pretend that nothing happened. That will likely lead to a brawl on the beach. So if you find yourself in this situation, paddle over to the person and apologize. Accidents happen out on the waves, but that doesn't excuse not having good manners." Shannon looked over at me and winked. Then she looked back at Ahmed and said, "And so Mr. Chairman, I think that's all I have to say about surfing etiquette. I hope that it is useful information that we can use to assess prospective candidates. I now relinquish the floor."

I almost laughed out loud. She had filibustered to buy me time to get here.

Ahmed turned to me and said, "I am so glad you were able to make it back in time. We were about to have another vote on the amended list."

Glad my ass.

Ahmed started the procedure to call for a vote. Shannon motioned for me to follow her to the back of the room where the refreshment table was setup.

"What took so long?" she asked when I got there. "I had about run out of things to talk about. Another few minutes and I would've had to stall for time by doing a lap dance for Ahmed." She cringed.

"I'm sorry. Jin had something important to tell me."

"What was so important that you're willing to risk a vote on the list without you?"

"You got to promise to keep this under your hat," I said.

"I never wear hats, but I promise not to tell," she said. "So come on, what is it?"

"Jin hacked into a satellite…a reconnaissance satellite."

"You're kidding, right?" She studied my face and then said, "You're not kidding! How?"

"It's complicated."

Putting her hands on her hips, she said, "Are you saying I'm stupid?"

"No, it's just that Jin isn't ready for this to be made public yet. To be honest, neither am I. There are some things he needs to figure out first."

She stared at me another few seconds and then said, "But can he control it? Take pictures and whatever else a reconnaissance satellite does?"

I nodded.

"That is pretty big news. I can see why he wants to keep it quiet," she said. "Don't worry. I won't say a word. Just promise me that once he figures things out, you'll tell me what's going on."

"I promise."

Ahmed's voice carried across the room. "So we have a second on the motion to vote, so let us begin."

Shannon and I returned to our seats. We spent the rest of the afternoon embroiled in the same old debate, whether we should allow exceptions for unqualified candidates…and there were still a lot of them. When it became clear that the debate would stretch beyond four o'clock, I sent Jin a message that I was running late. It wasn't until after five that Ahmed eventually called for the three-day recess in honor of the Remembrance Weekend.

***

Before heading down to the café, Michio, Shannon, and I made plans to meet up in the hotel dining room for dinner around seven thirty. I figured I'd have plenty of time to talk with Jin about his idea before dinner. I checked my watch for the third time and realized that I was wrong. Jin was late…over an hour late. I took a sip of tea and grimaced as I swallowed the lukewarm brew.

Where the hell was he? This morning he couldn't wait to tell me about this conspiracy theory and now he was a no-show. I checked my data mat to see if he'd replied to any of the messages I had sent him. My inbox was empty. The only thing new was a reminder from my calendar that I was late for dinner with Michio and Shannon.

It wasn't like Jin to be late, but it happened sometimes, usually when he was working on something particularly complex. Maybe he was still working out the details on his decryption plan. He hated presenting anything that wasn't thought completely through. I hoped that was the case. Either way, I had to go.

On the walk back to the hotel, I passed banners and decorations that had already been hung up along the street. One read, "We will never forget." Another one read, "Remember and They Will Never Die."

As far as I was concerned, Remembrance Weekend wasn't a holiday; it was a fucking waste of time. I mean, what kind of sadomasochistic son of a bitch wants to spend a weekend remembering the day the human race was nearly wiped out? Not me. I had better things to do, like stand watch out on North Point and look out for unidentified boats.

I didn't have to stand watch now that I was on the Council. In fact, since we got the automated maritime monitoring app installed a few years ago, nobody had to physically go out to North Point to stand watch. I just liked it out there.

As I continued walking to the hotel, I thought back to that weekend when Rick and I had developed the app. We had been on watch and were bored. Rick suggested that we have an old-fashioned hack-a-thon. By the end of the day, we had figured out how to pipe the video streams from four remotely controlled cameras mounted on an observation deck into a simple app that compared pixel patterns with known boat profiles. If a boat was detected, the app sent out alerts to the MDF and nearby islands. It took some tweaking to get the pattern recognition dialed in. When we first deployed it, a flock of birds triggered a false alarm. Luckily, there weren't enough birds anymore to cause that problem, not since the fish began to disappear. Lucky for us...not the birds.

App or no app, I volunteered to spend my three-day weekend out there away from everyone and everything. North Point was little more than a coral outcropping, but that didn't stop the Maldivians from counting it as one of the two thousand islands that made up their nation. If there was a way that I could've moved out there by myself, I would have done it years ago. Other than paddling around in my kayak, North Point was the one place where I truly felt alone.

I reached the hotel and climbed the stairs up to the third floor. When I entered the dining room, I scanned the tables for Michio and Shannon. It was eight o'clock so only a few tables were occupied. Even if every table was full, I wouldn't have had any problem spotting Shannon, not in that dress. She had apparently spotted me too. She pointed at her watch, shook her head, and motioned me over.

"I'm sorry," I said when I reached the table. "I was waiting for Jin, but he didn't show. That's not like him. I'm starting to get a little worried."

"Relax. I'm sure he's fine. Knowing him, he's geeking out on that special project you told me about." She flashed me a smile so intoxicating that it threw me off balance. "You're probably just upset because he stood you up. It's not nice getting stood up, is it?"

I fumbled for something to say. Why the hell did this feel like a date? It wasn't. I needed to pull it together. That damned dress of hers was making it difficult. It was tight enough to be a tattoo. I had to focus, but all I could focus on were her amazing tits.

"Well? Are you going to apologize or just stand there and gawk?"

"I'm sorry," I repeated and sat down. I suddenly realized that we were alone. "Where's Michio?"

"He sent his apologies. There was a helojumper leaving and it was going past his island, so he snagged a seat on it. He said that he wanted to squeeze in a little more time with his family."

"I don't blame him. What about you?" I asked. "Don't you want to get back to Gan and spend some time with what's-his-name?"

She picked up her water glass, took a sip, and then said, "It's Saravan and no...we're taking a break from each other." She set it down without breaking eye contact and began tracing the rim with her finger.

I took a drink to rinse away the taste of the foot in my mouth. When I finished, I said, "I'm sorry. I didn't know."

"Stop apologizing for everything. Besides, what are you sorry for? Saravan and I had a physical relationship, not an emotional one. Things were getting stale lately so we decided to sail in different waters, so to speak. That's all." She shrugged.

My mind searched for something to say, but I had no idea how to respond to that. Almost every relationship I ever had was a serious relationship. Take Marcy Davis for instance. Sure we were in the second grade, but I was in love and I had planned to marry her. I probably would have too if she hadn't dumped me by the jungle gym at recess. All of my relationships were like that, right up until college when I met Kelly.

I knew that I'd marry her the moment I spilled my beer on her at the student union. Only once did I ever have a physical-only relationship with someone. It was during a time when Kelly and I had broken up. I only remember the girl's first name, Jessica. She lived in the dorm room down the hall and rumor had it she had a morally casual attitude towards sex.

I'd been drinking way too much one night and crying about Kelly. Apparently my roommate had enough of my moaning because he sent for Jessica. She was all too happy to help. Had I not been so drunk I probably would have sent her away. But I was drunk, I was twenty three, and she was naked. Afterward, I felt cheap and guilty as hell. I guess I never understood how people could separate the physical and emotional components of sex. For me, they were like two sides of the same coin.

Shannon and I sat in an awkward silence for a little while. Thankfully, she broke it.

"I took the liberty of ordering for both of us," she said. "I hope that's alright."

"Sure. What were the choices?"

"Well, it was a choice between the fried fish plate with spicy mango relish or the fried fish plate with spicy mango relish."

I smiled and asked, "So what did you order?"

"I don't want to spoil the surprise."

Her foot brushed my leg. I looked at her, but she was looking at her finger as it completed another lap around the top of her glass. She gave me no sign of whether the foot contact was an accident or something else. Twelve years of celibacy had done funny things to my brain, so I waived it off as a figment of my sex-starved imagination.

This was nuts. I needed to get a hold of myself. We were having a dinner to discuss the evacuation list, nothing more. I took another sip of water.

Melana, the cute Maldivian girl that kept me from killing Ahmed a few nights ago, brought out our food. Like William, she was the by-product of a procreation epidemic that had spread across the islands during the first few years after the storm. It must have been some kind of instinctual human response to the imminent end of our species that made all of those people screw each other silly. Thankfully, when it became apparent that we were going to be stuck on these islands for a while, people slowed down. Overpopulation led to starvation, and starvation was a powerful libido inhibitor.

"Thank you, dear," Shannon said to Melana with smile. She reached out and softly stroked Melana's cheek.

Melena tilted her head from side to side and said, "You're welcome, Miss." Before returning to the kitchen, she did a half curtsy and then skipped away.

We ate our food over small talk, mostly about the Council; what moves and counter moves had played out over the last four days. And we talked about the upcoming holiday weekend. Shannon was looking forward to a good party and I was looking forward to avoiding it. As the conversation began to wind down, I felt pretty stupid for thinking there was something going on between us. I mean for Christ sake...someone like her coming on to someone like me?

We finished dinner and Melena returned. She brought us tea and some kind of pastry. When we finished desert, I looked at my watch and said, "I've got to go. I have to get up early to catch my ride. Guess I'll see you in a few days." I stood up, turned towards the door, but then turned back. "Oh yeah," I said. "Thanks for dinner."

She looked at me with a raised eyebrow and said, "You're not expecting me to pick up the bill are you?"

There was that playful smile again. It was a good thing that I didn't have any of Mohamed's moonshine tonight. "Oh yeah, the bill." The meals for Council members were free, but I played along. "I'll tell you what. I'll get the tip. How much should I give?"

"It all depends," she said, looking over her teacup. "Shall we discuss gratuities up in my room over a drink?" She took a sip of tea.

And just like that...bam, I realized that I was in way over my head. For twelve years I'd avoided getting mixed up in any kind of relationship. What was the point? Why get involved when people were dying of curable diseases like cancer? And besides, Kelly had been my soul mate, the one true love of my life. The thought of getting intimate with anyone else still felt like I'd be cheating.

I tried to play her comment off as a joke. "You have booze in your room? Aren't you afraid of the morality police?"

She set her cup down, "Diplomatic immunity, remember? One of the perks of being on the Council."

Council members did have some diplomatic immunity, but it was intended to make sure that nothing prevented us from missing Council meetings.

I said, "I'm not sure that immunity covers violations of Islamic law. If I had known that I could have brought some booze up to my—"

"Do you want to debate the law, or join me for a drink?"

Kelly used to cut to the chase like that, and the thought of her suddenly sent a flood of guilt coursing through my soul.

This was ridiculous. She'd been dead for more than a decade. So why the hell should I feel guilty?

"Some other time," I said. "I know how you Irish are. You'd end up drinking me under the table and I'd miss my boat."

Her smile turned into a disappointed frown. She leaned forward on her elbows, rested her chin on folded hands, and said, "Missing a boat is better than missing an opportunity." Then sighing, she added, "Well, if you change your mind, Aron, you know where I'm staying."

I left before I had a chance to reconsider.

***

The next morning, before the boat departed, I checked with the harbormaster to see if she'd heard of any new pirate activity. Nothing had been reported since my trip to Male four days ago. I hoped that it would stay that way, but I couldn't stop thinking about Lanka and Senil.

The uneasy feeling in the pit of my stomach was still there as I waited for the captain of the boat to finish preparations for departure. To keep my mind from dwelling on the last boat ride, I checked my messages. Jin still hadn't replied. I considered sticking around Male and searching for him, but where would I look? He didn't say where he was staying, and for all I knew, he might have already gone back to his island or still be plugging away at his decryption scheme. In the end, I decided to leave. I could try to contact him again before I left Lohifushi for North Point.

By the time we left the dock, the winds had shifted northward, pushing the clouds away and revealing a clear blue sky for the first time this week. As we got underway, I looked out on the ocean and remembered how awestruck I had been when I first arrived in the Maldives. The water was crystal clear and I remembered looking over the side and seeing the corral thirty feet below the surface. The water reflected the sky and sparkled like a brilliant turquoise gem.

An MDF patrol boat passed by and the drivers exchanged a wave. I looked at the hull number. Wracking my brain, I tried to remember if it was the same one that Jin had mentioned, but I couldn't remember. I looked away and tried to put the thought out of my mind.

Ten minutes later, we passed Noonu, a small island about halfway between Male and Lohifushi. Like Lohifushi, it had once been a popular resort. A flash from the top of the communications tower caught my eye. The red and white tower stood a hundred feet above the jungle canopy. I strained to make out what had caused the flash. There were two men up in the tower. One held binoculars to his eyes and he seemed to be looking at us. Few islands in the interior of the atoll posted guards in the towers. Something had to be up. A few minutes later, we passed another island and I spotted another manned tower. Clearly, I wasn't the only one who was worried.

The calm waters provided a smooth ride and yet I couldn't relax. Nearly every island we passed was the same. Those with towers had men on them. Those without a tower had people standing watch on the beach. An hour later, we finally entered the Lohifushi marina. The muscles in my neck and shoulders were strung tighter than a cocked spare gun. If I didn't get to North Point soon, I'd snap.

We docked next to the thatched roof boathouse at the end of the concrete pier. Grabbing my duffle bag, I patted the driver on the shoulder and thanked him for the lift. Then I hopped off the boat and headed over to my hut. As I followed the well-worn trail under the jungle portico, I passed a dozen or so people. Some smiled politely. Most avoided making eye contact. I'd noticed this change in everyone's behavior the minute I was appointed to the

Council. It was as if by not making eye contact, they thought they would somehow improve their chances of making the list. I didn't get it.

When I reached my hut, I found William sitting on the white plastic recliner outside the front door. I could tell by the expression on his face and the way his fingers flew across his data mat that he was playing a video game. I also could tell that he knew I was there, but he didn't look up.

"Morning, William."

"Uh huh," he said.

"What are you playing?"

"A game."

"Yeah, I kind of figured. Which game? I don't recognize the tune."

"I call it Pirate Hunt."

"Pirate Hunt, huh?" I set my bag on the ground next to the door and leaned over for a closer look. "Where'd you get it? Trade it with someone from another island?"

"Nope. Made it."

I looked at him, but he was focused like a laser on the data mat. "You made it? Let me see." I reached for it, but he swung his arm up and knocked my hand out of the way.

"Wait!" he yelled. "I'm just about to sink the mother ship." His fingers flew across the screen, tapping icons along the side and then touching what looked like a large, old-fashioned pirate ship. Orange and red flashes erupted on the deck of the ship. Within a few seconds, it exploded and sank. Without looking up, he said, "Here." He handed me the data mat.

The graphics were good, really good. And the user interface was pretty damned sophisticated. "So how do you play?"

Now more interested in a mosquito bite on his leg than the game, he said, "You start off with fifty people and two boats. The pirates attack the boats and raid the islands. That's it."

"Uh huh. And what's the objective?"

"Are you serious?" He looked up at me, and then talked slowly like I was an idiot. "You kill the pirates. If you sink the mother ship, you win."

I ignored the attitude and said, "When did you get to be such a good coder? Hell, I remember that tic-tac-toe game that you and your dad had developed and—" He got up and snatched the data mat out of my hands.

"I'm sorry, William. I didn't mean to...well, I'm sorry."

He shoved the data mat in his back pocket and started to walk off.

"How's your mom doing?" I asked.

He paused and without turning around said, "She wants to see you." Before I could ask why, he ran off.

"Shit." Why did I have to ask? I knew how she was doing. Helen had sent me a message. She was getting worse.

I picked up my bag, went inside, and unpacked. Stalling for time, I took my dirty clothes to the laundry hut and threw them in the washer. When the wash finished, I folded my clothes and tried not to think about what I'd find when I got to Sarah's hut.

There were a lot of reasons why I chose to study computer science instead of medicine. One reason was that I didn't mind being around dying computers. Dying people, on the other hand, were a different story. I didn't like being in the same room with them. I mean, what do you say to someone who's dying? Bon voyage? It was nice knowing you?

As I entered Sarah's hut, I suddenly wished that I had studied medicine. Maybe they taught doctors what to say. Right now, my mind was a blank.

Sarah was in bed covered with a single, dingy white sheet. The open window next to the bed let a soft breeze into the room. Helen sat in a chair next to her, trying to get Sarah to eat something.

"Come on, dear. Just eat one more spoonful for me, okay?" She held the spoon out in front of Sarah's face, but Sarah just looked at me and smiled.

After a few seconds, she said, "I'll eat more later, Helen. I promise."

I could tell that Helen didn't believe her, but she set the spoon in the bowl, got up, and wiped her hands on her ever-present apron.

"Okay, dear. I'll leave you alone so you can visit with Aron."

As she walked past me on her way out the door, she whispered, "Mohammad will be here in another hour to give her another treatment, so don't stay too long."

The word treatment was a stretch. Maybe Mohammad's potions and yoga therapies were better than nothing. Who knows? But as I looked at her withered body, I found myself wishing that they would leave her alone and let her die with some dignity.

"Come here." She patted the edge of her bed. "Sit next to me."

I passed Helen on her way out of the door. She gave me the "I'm serious" glare before leaving. I opted for the chair instead of her bed.

"You're looking better. That jungle juice Mohammad's been giving you must be doing some good."

Her laugh immediately turned into a coughing fit. When it subsided, she said, "It's doing something, alright. It's giving me diarrhea." She looked out the window as Helen walked past. "Poor Helen. She's been changing sheets twice a day. I told her that I didn't want any more medicine, but when I saw the look on her face I promised to keep taking it."

I tried to smile, but I must have failed because she said, "Aron, relax. I know that it's hard for you being here, so I won't keep you long. It's just that...it's just that I need to ask you something. Okay?"

"Sure. No...I mean...I'm fine. Really. It's just that with the Council meetings and all the other stuff going on—"

"Aron Atherton, you were always a lousy liar. That's why Rick loved playing poker with you. He said that he wished he had known you before the storm, so that he could have won your money instead of coconut chips."

I ran my hand through my tangled hair that was getting too long in the back. "He cheated, you know. I never figured out how, but he cheated. Nobody is that lucky."

She smiled and we sat in silence. Finally, she said, "Aron, I want to talk to you about William."

"He was waiting for me this morning outside my hut, you know." I was speaking too fast, but couldn't slow down. "I saw that video game he wrote. Pretty impressive. He's definitely got a knack for programming. A chip off the old block, I guess."

"Unfortunately," she said. "He got something else from Rick. A tendency to keep all of his feelings bottled up inside. That's part of what I wanted to talk to you about. I'm worried about him and what he'll do after I'm gone."

"Sarah, come on. You're not going anywhere. Helen wouldn't allow it."

"Aron, let's not do this. Don't make me play games like I have to with Helen and Mohammad. I'm dying." She reached out and took my hand. "It's okay. We don't need to talk about it, but don't pretend. Okay? Just sit there and listen to me. Can you do that for me?"

I cleared my throat. "Sure. Go ahead." I looked up and pretended to study the cheap painting that hung on the wall above her headboard, hoping the tears that I felt welling up in my eyes didn't roll out.

"Do you remember a few years ago after the raid on Embudu?"

How the hell could I forget something like that? Body parts scattered around the island, women raped, and children...children skewered on bamboo stakes, some roasted over open fires.

I nodded.

"Well, Rick and I talked about what if something like that happened here. I mean, who would take care of William if we both died and he survived? As we started to run through possible candidates, we both said your name at the exact same time and then laughed. That was all there was to it. We had decided."

Shocked, I looked at her and said, "Sarah, I'm honored...really I am. But I can't take care of a ten-year-old kid. I don't have the time. I'm running back and forth to Male all the time, and when I'm not there I'm out fishing and that's dangerous and..." My mind went blank. I just needed one good excuse, but nothing came to mind.

She smiled and seemed amused. Clearly, I hadn't made a good case, so I tried a different tactic. "It should be Helen," I said. "She's great with him and she knows how to raise a boy. Come on, you've heard all of those stories about her and Bob raising six boys in the outback. She's the one you want, not me."

Sarah shook her head. "Helen is great and she'll help you out when you're off island, but William loves *you* . He looks up to you, he always has and after Rick died—" She paused and her eyes began to tear up. "After Rick died...well...he never lets you out of his sight. Do you know why?"

I looked up at the painting again.

"Because he needs you, Aron, and I think you need him too. And right now, I need you to say yes so I don't have to worry about what will happen to him."

As a tear rolled down my cheek, I got up and walked to window and looked outside. Something moved up in the palm tree, and I realized it was William's feet, visible just below the roofline. Every kid had a favorite hiding spot and that tree was his. I wondered if he could hear us way up there.

"Okay, I'll make you a deal." I kept looking outside so she wouldn't have a chance to read my crappy poker face. "I promise to take care of him, but you've gotta promise me something too. You can't die...not yet. Okay?" I turned and looked into her eyes, "Just promise me that."

She wiped the tears from her eyes, smiled, and nodded. I knew that it was a promise she couldn't keep. I just hoped that when the time came, I could keep my end of the bargain.

CHAPTER 7

It was late afternoon by the time Kamish dropped me off on North Point. We hadn't spoken much on the trip over. What was there to say? His brothers died while getting me to Male. It was my fault. He'd never say it, but he had to be thinking it.

After the boat left, I walked up to the shack. Before stowing my gear, I checked to see if Jin had replied to any of my messages. Still nothing. That sense that something was wrong grew a little stronger. But there was nothing I could do about it now. Climbing the ladder to the observation deck, I spent the rest of the day scanning the ocean for unidentified vessels that I knew wouldn't be out there. It didn't matter. Searching an empty ocean helped keep my mind off Jin, the Council, Sarah…everything.

From the deck, I had an unobstructed, three-hundred-and-sixty degree view. There was nothing out there but water and a tiny sliver of an island called Bandos. It sat a mile and a half south of North Point and was barely visible even with my binoculars.

As the evening sky darkened, I let the binoculars hang from the strap and I sat back into the plastic beach chair. I watched the sun as it sank into the ocean. And when the last rays finally disappeared below the horizon, I took a deep breath, closed my eyes, and willed my body to relax. It was nighttime, which meant that I was safe. Nobody in their right mind would try to navigate the maze of reefs that fenced the northern entrance to the atoll. And they'd have to be completely insane to try it at night.

I took another deep breath and opened my eyes, drinking in the western sky. It was alight with hues of blue, orange, and pink. As I watched the colors slowly melt together, a pang of nostalgia coursed through me. Kelly and I had once watched a sunset like this from the top of Bishop's Peak in San Luis Obispo. The nostalgia quickly turned in to sadness as I tried to imagine what a sunset must look like there now. The colors in the sky dimmed along with my spirits, so I climbed down the rickety ladder and went into the shack.

Hastily constructed following the raid on Embudu, the one-room structure served as an early warning post. Barren except for a handful of scrub brush that had somehow found the will to live in the crevices of the dead coral and sand, the island itself was a perfect place for an observation post. It was positioned at the northernmost tip of the atoll and the view from the observation deck was totally unobstructed.

The only electricity on the island came from a small solar panel that powered the cameras on the observation deck. There was no plumbing, no air conditioning, no food, and no water. Everything I needed to survive I had to bring myself. Two five-gallon jugs of water and a plastic crate filled with food sat in the corner. I called that corner the kitchen. The other three corners were designated as the bedroom, the living room, and the office. The bathroom was outside. The toilet was a large flat rock that hung out over a small tide pool. It was the easiest place to maintain balance while squatting. And nature took care of flushing the toilet.

This shack was nothing like the huts on Lohifushi. With its earthen floor and palm frond walls, the shack took the word austere to a whole new level. The huts on Lohifushi were designed to look rustic for the tourists who wanted an authentic island experience without sacrificing any of the modern conveniences of home. The curtains, manufactured to look like hand woven fibers, were made from a fiber optic solar fabric that helped power each hut. There was even air conditioning, although I hadn't used mine in over eight years. The sweltering heat and humid nights were a thing of the past. The weather now was more like what I had grown up with back on the central coast of California, pleasant days and cool nights.

Smiling at the simplicity of the place, I unrolled my data mat and set it down on the office floor. With a few flicks of my finger, I opened the surveillance app. A four-paned window appeared on the screen, each pane displaying a view from each of the four cameras mounted on the deck. The cameras had already switched themselves to night vision mode. It wasn't like the modern, full-color, three-dimensional night vision system that was built into car windshields. No, these were basic infrared cameras that showed objects in ghostly black and white. It was all that Rick and I could manage given the parts we had to work with.

I made sure the app was fully operational and then stood up and stretched. The dim light of the data mat reflected off the snorkeling mask perched on top of the fishing gear. I had brought it along with a snorkel, fins, spear gun, and fishing pole. With any luck, I'd get a chance to do some fishing and maybe even snorkel off the reef. There was nothing like fresh fish cooked over an open fire in the middle of nowhere.

North Point sat off of a reef that extended out a hundred feet before dropping off a massive underwater cliff. What tropical fish were still around were usually swimming along the cliff's edge. The fishing was nothing like when I had first arrived here, but it was better than nothing.

The soothing cadence of the waves lapping the shore filled the room. The more I listened to it, the sleepier I got. It had been a long day and I decided to turn in for the night. But I had to run my radio checks first.

I sat down on my bed roll and flicked an icon on the sidebar of the data mat. A communications panel opened. I clicked the address icon and a long list appeared. As I scrolled through the list, I only found three addresses that were colored green. Green meant that the data mat was within range for voice and video communications. People on watches and patrols were the only ones besides the MDF who could use that communication channel.

I clicked on Dhonakulhi and waited as the word CONNECTING blinked on the screen. With a ping, the word changed to CONNECTED and a small window opened. Inside the window was a familiar brown face. I knew who it was, but for the life of me I couldn't remember his name.

"Dhonakulhi, this is North Point with a radio check. How do you read me?" I asked.

"I see you fine, Aron. How are you? It has been a long time."

I fumbled for his name. It started with an A. "I'm good, how are you doing?"

"Very good, but very tired. I do not know if you heard, but Nisha had twins last month. I have been awake every night with crying babies, so I volunteered for the nightshift. I figured that I had a better chance of getting some sleep." He chuckled and his hoarse laughter triggered my memory. It was Anand. He had helped me put up the tower on Dhonakulhi, but that was...what...almost eight years ago? He had been maybe twenty then.

I remembered how he had asked us for advice on how to convince Nisha's father to let him marry her. I don't remember what we told him, but it must have worked. And I remembered that he had played the sitar by the campfire at night. "Are you still playing the sitar, Anand?"

"Not as much as I'd like. Being a father takes up too much of my time. With the twins, I now have six children."

"Six! In eight years? You have been busy."

He laughed and said, "Yes. But children are a blessing and I would not have it any other way. How about you, Aron? Any special women in your life?"

An image of Shannon wearing that tight black dress sprang into my mind. "Nope. Life's too complicated as it is."

"Yes, that is true. But women bring such pleasure and peace to our lives, no?"

"I guess. Well, Anand, I've got a couple more radio checks to make. It was good catching up with you. Tell Nisha I said hello and congratulations on the twins."

"Thank you, my friend. Please do not be a stranger. You know that you are always welcome in our home."

"Thanks, but I think I'll wait until your babies are a little older. I was never very good with kids at that age. North Point, over and out."

"Over and out," he repeated.

I pressed the DISCONNECT icon and the video screen disappeared. The communications panel returned to the list, but the other two addresses that had been green, Iru Fushi and an MDF patrol boat, had turned red. Connections weren't that stable out here. North Point was just barely within range of the Dhonakulhi tower. Still, it was weird that the MDF patrol boat was now out of range. They usually kept a patrol running in this zone and those boats had some pretty powerful amplified antennas. Maybe it was interference from the storm that was moving in. Storms always played havoc with the VHF frequencies.

I thought about making a snack before bed, but I opted to sleep instead. No sooner had I laid my head on the makeshift sleeping bag than I fell asleep.

***

In my dream, the food dispenser was beeping. Kelly stood by the stove cooking some of her famous French toast. She was beautiful, exactly as I remembered her. As she reached out to silence the beeping dispenser, I tried to tell her not to do it. But no words came out of my mouth. I watched helplessly as she pushed the button and I woke up.

My eyes were met by darkness. I lay for a moment remembering where I was and trying to figure out where the beeping was coming from. It didn't take me long to remember. I rolled over and tapped my data mat. It displayed a ghostly green image of a boat with at least three men on board. They were headed straight for North Point. From the video, I could tell that they were only a few hundred feet out. I didn't have much time.

I overrode the alarm and switched to the communications panel. Dhonakulhi was still the only green name on the list. I pressed it. It showed CONNECTING.

"Come on, come on."

Finally, a sleepy Anand appeared on the screen.

"Anand, I need your help. There's a boat about to land on North Point and I can't connect to the MDF."

"What? Aron, is that you? You are breaking up. Can you repeat?"

"I said there is a boat heading straight for me. It's about to come ashore and I can't reach the MDF."

The screen flickered and Anand's image disappeared. The list reappeared and everything was red. I went over my options. There weren't many.

Option one was fighting them off. Unfortunately, the only weapon I had was the spear gun and it wasn't that effective unless you were really close. Besides, I'd only get one shot and there three of them.

Option two was swimming to Bandos, but that wasn't much of an option either. In these strong currents, chances were that I'd be swept out to sea or chopped up on the reef before I made it there.

The third and final option wasn't really an option: make some kind of deal with them. But the thought passed through my head faster than Mohammad's mango juice passed through my bowels. Others had tried to reason with them. Rick had tried. There was no way I would let them get their hands on me.

I checked the communications panel one last time, but all the addresses on the list were still red. Time was up. I selected for Option two, swim to Bandos.

I stripped down to my underwear, but kept my t-shirt on. Although hypothermia was a risk, I knew that the jeans would weigh me down.

I folded up my data mat and shoved it into the crotch of my underwear. It was uncomfortable, but I couldn't let them get ahold of it. With my data mat, they would know everything about everyone in the Maldives, including where they lived.

On the way out the door, I grabbed the spear gun and snorkeling equipment. Crouching down, I worked my way back to the flat rock in the dark. I prayed that I didn't land face down in the tide pool. That's all I needed, a swirly. I made it to the rock and stepped into the tide pool.

I walked out into the shallow water of the coral outcropping, When I reached the edge, I stopped and pulled the rubber swim fins over my cut up feet. Then, placing the mask over my eyes and nose, I grabbed my spear gun and stepped off of the reef.

I swam in the opposite direction from where the boat was coming. About twenty-five feet out, I could make out the roar of their diesel hybrid motor over the sound of the waves. It was hard to judge in the dark exactly where the sound came from. I swam as hard as I could. How far had I gone? I couldn't tell, so I stopped and turned around. Lifting the mask onto my forehead, I struggled to see if they had landed on the island. There was a half-moon in the sky, but it was hidden behind some clouds. I could barely make out the silhouette of the shack. But after a few minutes, my eyes adjusted to the light and I could make out two men up on the observation deck. The sound of the water made it impossible to hear what, if anything, they were saying. But I watched helplessly as they ripped the cameras off the posts.

Bastards!

One of the guys turned on a flashlight. The silvery blue light of the ULEDs washed over the island. They were looking for me. He pointed the light over the water and swept it back and forth. I watched the light glide over the waves farther away from me.

Bandos was behind me…at least I thought it was. There was no way I would know until I was much closer. There was also another reef or two between me and Bandos, so I'd have to swim through the narrow zigzag channel. If I miscalculated, I would be dragged across the reefs and ground into fish food. Of course if I went back to North Point, I would be tortured and killed. I decided to take my chances with the reefs.

I lowered my goggles back over my eyes and nose. Turning, I began to swim away. The current wasn't too bad yet, but it would be once I got around the next reef. I did the side stroke, since it was the only way to swim while holding on to the spear gun. This was nuts and my nerves were shot. I kept waiting to smash into a reef. My muscles burned, but I pushed on…stroke after stroke.

After a few minutes, I stopped again to catch my breath. My heart pounded wildly. I couldn't tell if it was from swimming or from the fear of being caught. Turning back, I saw the light on the boat. It was heading my way. They must've seen me.

I started to swim again, faster this time. I glanced over my shoulder after each stroke, keeping an eye on the boat. It turned away, so I stopped to see what they were doing. Someone in the boat panned a large floodlight over the water. Maybe they hadn't seen me. The boat was closer now, maybe a hundred feet away. Suddenly, it turned back towards me. I couldn't catch my breath. There was no point trying to outrun it. I floated there helpless, watching the boat as it closed in on me. It kept turning back and forth. Fifty feet away now. I could tell there was only one son of a bitch on board. The other two must still be on the island.

I could hear the engines clearly. A few more yards and he'd be on top of me.

I took three deep breaths and dove underwater.

It was completely black and I was completely disoriented. I decided to swim back to the reef. I pulled myself along with one arm, holding tight to the spear gun with the other hand. I felt the sonic vibrations of the propeller ripple around me. Surfacing just enough to bring my eyes above water, I saw a circle of light five feet to my right. The boat was only ten feet away. I dove under the surface again. My hand hit something sharp and pain shot up my arm. At first I thought I got clipped by the propeller, but it was the reef. I grabbed it. Then I surfaced, took a deep breath, and pulled myself down as deep as I could.

Looking up, I watched the boat pass right over me. It seemed to slow down. My lungs felt like they were on fire. I knew that I couldn't hold my breath any longer. Suddenly, the pitch of the engines increased. Looking up, I saw a vortex of bubbles and then nothing.

I let out some air, but it didn't help. I started to spasm.

So this is what drowning felt like. It wasn't nearly as peaceful a death as I had thought it would be.

I had no choice but to surface. My face cleared the water and I gulped in air. When I finally caught my breath, I lifted my goggles and looked around. The boat was heading back to the island. I waited, unsure of what was happening. The boat docked. After a few minutes, I heard the engines rev up again and I watched the boat as it sped away toward the east.

I waited until I was sure the boat wasn't coming back before I swam back to North Point. I reached the shallow reef shelf, took off my fins, and climbed out. As I walked, I had to use the spear gun to steady myself. The pain in my feet was excruciating. But somehow, I managed to limp out of the water.

When I finally reached the shore, I dropped the goggles and fins on the sand. Still using the spear gun as a cane, I hobbled back to the shack and collapsed on the ground, dropping the spear gun next to me. I don't know how long I laid there, but by the time I sat up I noticed that the sun was above the horizon.

I looked around. The food and water were gone and so was my lucky fishing pole. The ladder up to the observation deck lay smashed outside the door. At least they had left me the shack.

I looked at the palm of my left hand and saw a dozen black dots set in a concentric series of rings. Shit! I must have grabbed a sea urchin when I clutched the reef. The skin was already red and puffy. I took a quick assessment of the rest of my body. I noticed that my legs were scratched up, but not bad. I inspected the soles of my feet and saw a dozen scalpel-like incisions made by the coral. Thankfully, twelve years of going barefoot had provided me with tough feet so the coral didn't slice through to the bone. Everything else seemed okay.

I pulled the data mat out of my underwear and shook off the water. Then I tapped the screen twice until it came to life. Using my right hand, I opened the communications panel. There was one green dot; it was the MDF patrol boat. I tapped the icon and waited. The screen flickered. I worried that the salt water had damaged it, but the flickering stopped and two video windows opened up. One was labeled MDF Patrol 743 and the other was labeled Ahmed. The window labeled MDF Patrol 743 had the image of someone in an MDF uniform, but the other one had the image of a Somali pirate. His head was shaved like most of the pirates, but I knew who it was. The scar that ran from the edge of his right eye down to his chin gave him away. It was Jamal. I'd never seen him before, but everyone knew about that scar.

The MDF officer and Jamal stopped talking when they saw me on the net. None of us spoke; we just stared at each other. Talk about your awkward moments. Before I could think of something to say, they cut the channel and the video screen went blank. Well...that was it. They'd be coming back for sure now.

With my data mat still in hand, I walked outside to wait. A few minutes passed and then I heard it, the sound of engines.

That was it. Game over. The only thing left to decide was whether I'd let them kill me or I'd kill myself. It was an easy decision

The spear gun was still on the floor back in the shack where I'd left it. So I went inside, picked it up, and carried it out to the doorway. Holding it up, I wondered if it were even possible to kill yourself with a spear gun. Fifty-fifty odds, I figured. Best odds I'd had all day.

I stared off into the distance and saw the boat silhouetted by the morning sky. It was almost to the island.

Pulling a spear from the clip on the side of the gun, I pushed it back until I heard it click. It was cocked and ready.

The boat sped toward the small stone dock. It throttled into reverse and slid up to the stone.

I flipped the spear gun around so that the tip of the spear was against my chest. It was awkward, but I was able to get my thumb in front of the trigger. I tried my best to position the tip between two ribs. It would be embarrassing if it got stuck in my ribs.

Someone jumped out of the boat. I watched as he ran towards me.

It was time. My hand was swollen from urchin stings. It made it hard to hold the gun steady, but I did my best. As I began to apply pressure to the trigger, I heard the pirate say, "Aron! Aron! Are you okay?"

I must have lost my mind. The pirate sounded just like Anand.

"Put the spear gun down. It's me, Anand."

Anand stopped a few feet in front of me. I stared at him. I knew who he was, but my brain was having a hard time believing it.

"A pirate boat is about a mile to the west. We have to go."

I wondered if the urchin poison was a hallucinogenic.

Anand grabbed the spear gun out of my hands and led me back to his boat. We sped out of the harbor at full speed. I looked back and watched North Point shrink in to the distance.

Anand was talking to someone on the radio. I sat down on a cushioned seat in the back of the boat. A strong feeling swept over me, but I couldn't place it. What was it? Relief? Gratitude? No. It was disappointment. Definitely disappointment.

CHAPTER 8

The boat bucked against the waves and I found myself following its movements like a cobra follows a snake charmer's flute. Anand kept turning back to look at me, but he hadn't said a word to me since we left North Point.

My hand vibrated. I looked down to find the data mat still clutched in my hand. I stared at it and considered throwing it into the ocean. Instead, I touched the screen and opened the message.

SUBJECT: CHANGE NOTIFICATION

THIS AUTOMATED NOTIFICATION WAS SENT TO INFORM YOU OF A CHANGE TO THE EVACUATION ELIGIBILITY LIST. THE FOLLOWING INFORMATION WAS CHANGED:

NAME	ISLAND	CHANGE
ZHOU, JIN	ERIYADOO	STATUS-MISSING

I began to shake and I couldn't stop. I grabbed the blanket that Anand had given me, drawing it tightly around my shoulders. It didn't help.

Jin was missing. Missing was the status they used for people whose bodies were never found after a pirate raid. A ball of guilt rolled into my gut.

I frantically checked through my other messages, but there wasn't anything from Jin. He had said that he had a plan, but what was it?

Jin documented everything. If it wasn't for his insistence on writing down the location and configuration of every part of the IICN, we'd still be working on getting the network up and running. The information had to be in his data mat somewhere. It was as good a place as any to start looking.

I stood up and made my way up to Anand, my blanket flying behind me like a superhero's cape. Anand turned as I laid my hand on his shoulder.

I leaned in close and said, "Head east. We're not going to Lohifushi. I need to go to Eriyadoo."

"What? Why?"

"I just need to go there. Please."

He looked into my eyes and I could tell that he was trying to decide if I had blown another circuit. Finally, Anand nodded and wheeled the boat hard to starboard. I grabbed the railing to keep from falling over. After straightening out the wheel, he pointed to a worn, brown leather bag on the empty seat next to him. "I have some clothes in there. Grab a pair of pants. They will be a little small for you, but you cannot walk around Eriyadoo like that."

I followed his gaze and looked down. I was still in my underwear. I opened the bag and found a pair of khaki pants. Funny, but I didn't realize how cold I was until I put the pants on. I began to warm up a little, but I still couldn't stop shaking. The news about Jin must have triggered another release of adrenaline into my bloodstream. I wouldn't be surprised if I was overdosing on the shit.

***

I shielded my eyes from the glare of the rising sun, but its reflection off the water blinded me. I wondered how Anand could see. I guessed that after twelve years of running supplies around the atoll Anand could probably navigate these waters blindfolded. An hour later, we arrived at Eriyadoo.

Two bare-chested, middle-aged Chinese men met me on the pier. They wore traditional Maldivian sarongs and sandals. Their faces were vaguely familiar, but in my current frame of mind I couldn't remember where or when I had met them. They seemed to know me.

The shorter of the two said, "Li Jing said that you would come. She asked that you wait for her at her hut. We will show you the way."

I knew the way, but I didn't argue. From their somber expressions, I knew they were as upset about the news as I was.

Before I stepped off the boat, Anand asked, "Shall I wait here for you?"

"No. Go home. I don't know how long I'll be."

"Are you sure? I can wait."

I shook my head. "Go home to your family. They need you more than I do." He studied me for a moment and then nodded.

"And thanks," I said. It didn't come close to expressing how I felt. I couldn't figure out why he would risk everything, his wife and six children, for someone he barely knew. Whatever his reason, I owed him.

"Okay," he said. "Stay safe, my friend."

I stepped onto the pier and followed the men to Jin's hut.

Li Jing was Jin's wife. She wasn't there when I arrived, but his oldest son, Bohai, was. He sat in front of their hut with his back against a coconut tree. He was systematically peeling fibers off a coconut shell. He looked up, studied me for a second, and returned his attention to the coconut without saying a word. I wondered if it had been a mistake to come here.

Bohai had been five years old when Jin and Li Jing came to the island. Rambunctious and always eager to help, Jin used to bring him along on our work trips. Bohai had been a great little assistant. He climbed the scaffolding and brought us tools, food, and anything else we needed, always with a big smile on his face. But that smile was nowhere to be seen now.

Now he was seventeen years old and stood a good four inches taller than his dad. His hair must have driven Jin crazy. It was short and spiky all around except for the back where he maintained a long, single braid. He had the braid draped over his right shoulder and it was almost long enough to reach the ground. His face was stuck somewhere between a boy and a man. It didn't look like he was shaving yet, but I could make out a whisper of a mustache.

"Bohai," I said. "I just heard about..." I cleared my throat, "I'm sorry about your father. I'm sure they'll find him."

Bohai peeled another fiber off the shell and dropped it on to the pile next to him.

"Did you hear from him recently? I mean, did you get a message or..."

He finished peeling another fiber before he said, "No. He didn't have his data mat with him."

That was odd. Jin always had his data mat with him.

Bohai threw the coconut hard against the hut. It bounced and rolled back to his feet. He kicked it away and then looked up at me. There were tears in his eyes. He said, "You know my father. You know cautious he is. He would never go out on a boat at night."

"Is that what they told you?"

He nodded. "The MDF sent a message to my mom."

Bohai was right. Jin was a stickler for safety. I felt sick to my stomach and struggled for something to say. "So it happened last night?"

"That's what they said."

It didn't make sense. There wasn't a single time in the twelve years that we worked together that Jin travelled at night. He always insisted that we leave in the morning. There was no way he would do it…not unless he was running from someone or…going to North Point to find me. The ball in my stomach seemed to explode.

I didn't know what to say. "Your father was a good man, Bohai."

"He is a good man!"

"I'm sorry. That's what I meant."

I started to turn away.

"Wait." He got up, reached into his back pocket, and pulled out a data mat and handed to me. "This is my father's. Before leaving for Male, he gave it to me and told me that if anything should happen to him, I was to give this to you."

I stared at it, afraid to touch it. Unlike my data mat, Jin's was folded neatly. It even had the original elastic band that held it closed. My hand shook. I reached out and took it.

***

I waited for the helojumper on a small beach at the northern end of the island. Surrounded by a wall of soaring palm trees that reached out towards the ocean, the beach was only fifty feet wide, but it stretched nearly a hundred feet out into the water. It had probably once been a great beach back when this place was a resort, but now it was littered with dried seaweed and swarming with sand fleas and cracked crab shells.

My conversation with Li Jing had been brief, hardly a conversation at all. When I saw her approach the hut supported by two elderly Chinese women, I knew she wasn't in any condition to accept visitors, much less answer questions. So I didn't ask any. I just told her that I was sorry and that I would pray for Jin's safe return. Her response was a deep, mournful sob.

A glint of light in the sky caught my attention and pushed the memory from my mind. It was the helojumper and it was coming in for a landing.

I couldn't believe that I was actually going to get inside one of those contraptions. Helojumpers scared the shit out of me, but I had to get back to Male and this was the fastest way.

Twelve years ago when I had arrived at the Male airport, I was offered a seat in one of those flying, glass-bottomed boats. I had considered it, but politely refused when I saw one up close. It resembled a giant food processor with seats inside.

The fuselage was round except for a small beak-like protrusion in the front where the pilots sat. Everything except for the column in the center of the fuselage that housed the engine were made out of transparent carbon fibers. Even the damned passenger seats transparent.

Turbine blades sat inside two stacked airfoil rings perched directly above the fuselage. It was an accident waiting to happen.

I remembered looking at that thing and thinking that one hard landing was all that it would take to send those turbines crashing through the roof and into the fuselage. Those blades would chop up the passengers into salsa.

There had been several dozen helojumpers in the MDF fleet before the storm. Now there were only two. The carcasses of the others sat in a pile on the end of the runway, cannibalized to keep the remaining helojumpers in the air.

Helojumpers weren't used to ferry tourists to their islands anymore because there weren't any more tourists. The MDF used them for air patrols and to airlift the sick and injured from outlying islands to the clinic on Male. The only other exception was transportation for members of the Council of Thirteen. Another perk of the job, as Shannon would say. Some Council members abused this privilege, using the helojumpers as their own personal air limousines. I had never flown in one and I never planned to, but today changed that. I had to get to Male and figure out how Jin planned to crack the encryption.

I turned my head as a wash of mist kicked up from the descending helojumper. It came down about a hundred feet offshore and then switched to hovercraft mode. It hovered a few inches above the water and then skirted onto the beach. Before setting down, it turned itself around so that the beak-like cockpit pointed out to sea. I flinched as a set of transparent doors on the backside suddenly slid open.

Well…this was it. I ignored the primal instinct to run in the opposite direction. Instead, I ran with my head down straight through the doors. They shut behind me. Glancing up, I saw the blades slicing the air and I quickly looked away. The cabin was empty, so I picked a seat close to the cockpit, buckled in, and then gave the pilot a thumbs up.

The blades came back to life. It sounded like the pilot had pushed the puree button. I closed my eyes and felt the vehicle pop up off the ground and then move forward. The whine of the electric engines increased and I felt the queasy sensation of lift. After a few minutes I figured we were safely in the air, so I opened my eyes. I was wrong. We were just taking off. I watched the water falling out from under me through the transparent floor. A wave of panic swept over me. I grabbed the armrests and squeezed, willing the machine to stay in the air. The fuselage pitched forward and we began to fly. I tightened my seatbelt as gravity pushed me back into my seat.

After a few minutes, I released the armrests and glanced down through the floor. We were a lot higher than I had expected. Spread out across the bluish green ocean, I saw hundreds of tiny islands that made up a tiny part of the Maldivian atoll. From up here, each island looked like a fried egg with a green yolk.

I needed something to keep my mind off flying, so I turned my attention to Jin's data mat. After sliding the elastic band off, I gingerly unfolded it as if it were some kind of sacred artifact. I tapped the upper left corner and the screen came to life. Chinese script filled the screen. I double tapped in the lower left corner and selected English from the language menu. The script changed and a prompt asked for a password. I tried my password, but it didn't work.

Now what?

I tried a few other words: the name of his wife, his son, his hometown. None of them worked.

Why the hell would Jin give me his data mat without giving me his password? Christ! Why did he bother putting a password on it at all? But I knew the answer. Jin was a stickler for the rules.

It didn't matter what the rules were or whether they made sense, he followed them. And the rule was that all data mats with

IICN administrative access must be password protected. Nobody enforced the rule. Hell, I didn't have a password on my data mat. But a rule was a rule to Jin, so I shouldn't have been surprised that his was locked down.

I smiled as I remembered how Rick and I had once taken a shortcut during a test of the IICN message system. We had disabled encryption on the servers so we could run through the test faster. Jin had found out and he wasn't happy. He shouted at us like we were new recruits in boot camp, "You know better! Security is what?" We both knew the answer, but we had just stood there quietly. "Come on, what is security, gentlemen?" We looked at each other, knowing that he wouldn't let us off until we completed the phrase that he had drilled into our heads. I grinned as I recalled how we had jumped to attention in a mocking acknowledgment of his military background and yelled, "Security is paramount, sir!"

That's got to be it! I typed the word, "paramount" into the password field. The screen unlocked.

I quickly scanned the folders and was amazed at how many documents he had stored on his data mat. This was going to take a while. I leaned forward and opened a couple of documents. It was mostly technical reference material. I also found some island maps, schematics for the communications towers, and operations instructions for the main communications center. But I didn't see anything about the satellite or message decryption.

My ears popped and I looked out of the clear walls. My God! Whoever invented this thing clearly didn't have a fear of heights.

The helojumper had begun its descent. I looked up towards the cockpit and saw the airport ahead of us. The airport was nothing more than a tiny island with a single blacktop runway that consumed it. There was only room enough for a small terminal next to the runway.

I was about to put the data mat away when I saw a folder labeled Communications Map. Jin had everything organized using a meticulous folder structure and file organization schema. This folder wasn't in the right place.

I opened it, and found a spreadsheet and a link to an app. I opened the spreadsheet first. It contained five columns of data: Sender ID, Recipient ID, Sender Location, Sender Date and Time, Recipient Location, and Recipient Date and Time.

The Sender and Recipient ID columns contained numbers that I easily recognized. They were User IDs, the ones we had created for IICN users. The location columns looked like they contained latitude and longitude information. I scrolled down the sheet. There were thousands of rows of data. This had to be the SIGINT data that Jin had talked about. As excited as I was to finally find something, it wasn't enough to overcome the dread at having to figure out how it all fit together.

I closed the spreadsheet and clicked on the application link. It was a satellite image of the atoll. Scattered across the image were thousands of small dots, each color coded. I clicked the filter button and a drop-down list of User IDs appeared. I found my own and selected it. Then I set the date filter for the last two days. Most of the dots disappeared. Only a handful of light blue ones remained on the screen. They were positioned over Lohifushi and Male, but a few were over North Point and Eriyadoo. I zoomed in on Eriyadoo and clicked the dot. A small box appeared with the same data elements that I had seen in the spreadsheet.

Sender	Location	Date:Time	Recipient	Location
1537668/ Aron Atheron	4 37'23.69'N/ 73 24'52.94'E	10/10/2168: 1345	1577229/ MALE AIR OPS	4 10'30.00'N/ 73 30' 32.00' E

It was the call I had made to the Air Operations Center an hour ago to arrange the flight.

He had really done it! The son of a bitch had hacked into a satellite and had developed an application that could track IICN messages in near-real time. A hundred questions popped into my head, but Jin wasn't around to answer any of them.

The seatbelt saved me from hitting the ceiling when the helojumper landed. However the data mat flew out of my hands and on to the floor out of reach. I looked down and saw blacktop. Glancing up, I saw the twin turbines still slicing and dicing. I unbuckled my belt, picked up Jin's data mat, and ran like hell out of the open back doors.

As I ran across the tarmac, I did some quick calculations in my head. The Council wasn't scheduled to meet until after the holiday weekend. That gave me just under two days to dig into the data and discover Jin's plan to decrypt the messages.

CHAPTER 9

I glanced at my watch. It was five thirty, dinnertime. But for the practicing Muslims around the city it was Fajr, the last call to prayer for the day. I knew this because of the skull-shattering wail that emanated from the minaret speakers directly across from my hotel room. It was like an alarm clock from hell and it went off every few hours. God, how I wished there was a snooze button.

My stomach gurgled, reminding me that I had skipped lunch. I didn't skip it on purpose, I just got lost in the maze that was Jin's data mat and I forgot to eat. But even a rat needed food, even if it couldn't find the cheese at the end of the maze. It was time to feed this rat. Maybe when I got back, I'd get lucky and find the cheese.

It had been ten hours since I landed on Male. I'd spent most of it here, trying to find some clue about how Jin had planned to decrypt those messages. All I had done was confirm that the spreadsheet was SIGINT data streaming down from the satellite. I didn't know any more now than I did when I landed.

I leaned back in my chair and for the hundredth time today I cursed myself for leaving Jin and going to that Council meeting. Maybe I could have prevented his…no…I wasn't going to go there again. I needed to focus on figuring out his plan. The answer had to be somewhere in that goddammed data mat. Why else would he leave it to me?

I got up and walked to the window. I opened it, leaned out, and took a deep breath of the salty air. Puffs of white fog billowed from my mouth as I exhaled. I shivered. Son of a bitch, it was cold. It had to be in the low fifties, maybe even the forties. As far as I could recall, the temperature had never dropped this much or this fast before.

The people on the streets didn't seem bothered by the cold. They were too busy reflecting. After all, today was the Day of Reflection. I had tried to block out the sounds of people yelling out the names of family and friends who died after the storm all morning. The ritual was intended to honor the memory of those who died. I didn't need a special day to do that. I did it every fucking day of my life. It was a depressing tradition, but I knew that tomorrow would be worse.

Tomorrow was the Day of Joy, a celebration of life. The day culminated in a massive street party at night, kind of like Mardi Gras only no booze or tits. Still, things sometimes got a little crazy...at least by Male standards. There was music, singing, and dancing. My hotel room was in the heart of party central. Tomorrow was going to really suck.

I closed the window and looked around the room. My mind was wandering. I needed food to think straight. So I carefully folded up Jin's data mat and tucked it into my back pocket. Then I headed out to find something to eat.

I opened the door and found Ahmed's slimy cousin, Viyaja, standing in the doorway. His pungent odor bitch-slapped me. I involuntarily took a couple steps back. I wondered if he was allergic to coconut oil soap or if he was working on a new way to repel mosquitos.

"Jesus Christ, Viyaja...you scared the shit out of me."

He smiled. It seemed to cause him pain.

"*Assalamu Aleikom* , my friend. Peace be on you." He gave up trying to smile. "I am sorry if I startled you, but I would like a word if you have the time."

"Actually, I'm on my way down to grab some dinner." The sound of chanting from the street below filled the hallway. "And shouldn't you be praying or something?"

His eyes narrowed.

"I'll tell you what," I said. "Why don't you go and pray and I'll go and eat. We can meet in the lobby in about an hour. Does that work for you?"

"I am afraid this is urgent."

I ignored my instinct to slam the door and I let him inside.

Viyaja stepped forward.

"I do not think you will find food downstairs until after sunset. It is a day of fasting or have you forgotten?"

My stomach growled in response. "I'm sure I can find something. I can't be the only one who doesn't participate in these rituals."

He closed the door behind him. The invisible reeking cloud that surrounded him was now inside my room. I tried not to breathe through my nose. His stench was killing my appetite.

"Okay," I said, "make it quick."

"We think it is time that this childish squabble ends."

"What are you talking about?"

"The list. Time is running out."

"Let's talk about it on Tuesday. Okay? That's what the Council meetings are for."

"No, my friend. The time for talk is over. We are prepared to take the necessary actions to ensure that the list is approved. We have been very patient with you and your friends, but our patience is wearing thin."

I studied him for a second. He was skinny, probably malnourished as a kid, but the way that he carried himself told me that he could probably put up a good fight. If he kept going down this path, I guess I'd find out.

"That sounded like a threat, Viyaja."

His eyes narrowed even more. "You did not misunderstand me. We cannot allow the fate of our people to rest in the hands of a few foreigners."

My heart raced and I resisted the urge to punch him. "Don't you mean infidels? Look, if you think you can scare me then you're stupider than I thought." I took a step toward him and said, "In the last few weeks I carried the mutilated body of my best friend back to his family. A couple weeks later I watched two young men die right in front of me. And yesterday—" I took another step towards him. "Yesterday, the same bastards who killed them tried to kill me. So if you want to scare me, you're going to have to do better than that."

I took another step forward. I now stood inches from his face and his stench engulfed me. But I didn't give a shit.

"If you want me out of the picture, then you better kill me. Go ahead. I won't even try and stop you."

I shoved him in the chest and he stumbled back against the door.

"Just be sure to do it right the first time, because I swear to God if you fuck it up, I'm going to be really angry...and you don't want to see me angry."

I grabbed his shoulder and shoved him away from the door and with my other hand I opened it.

"Why don't you get the hell out of here and tell Ahmed what I told you. Okay?"

His jaw clenched. Then without turning his back on me, he sidestepped in front of the doorway and stepped backward into the hall. I moved forward and grabbed the door.

"And Viyaja..." I slammed the door in his face. " *Ma'a salama*, asshole!"

***

I didn't sleep much. Not because of Viyaja's threat, but because my brain wouldn't shut down. It was stuck in an endless loop, trying to figure out Jin's plan. I was exhausted, but I had picked up where I left off in the morning. Maybe it was the lack of sleep or maybe Viyaja had gotten into my head, but I was no closer to figuring out this out than I was yesterday. I needed to get out of here and clear my head.

I thought about borrowing a kayak and seeing if I could catch anything, but the temperature was even colder than it had been last night. Running was out of the question. There were too many people in the street being joyful. So I decided to go perform a few systems checks on the servers in the tower. Mindless diagnostics might be just the thing to clear the log jam in my brain.

The noise from the streets had already invaded my room, and it was only noon. By nightfall, I wouldn't be able to hear my own thoughts. I filled my backpack with the fish jerky and plantain pancakes that I had scrounged up last night. I wrapped my bottle of moonshine in some blankets and shoved it all into the backpack. If the blankets didn't keep me warm, the moonshine would.

I zipped up the pack and made sure that I had Jin's data mat before I headed down to the lobby. As I opened the front door to the hotel, I was assaulted by the sights and sounds of happy people and the smells of street food. I took a deep breath and then headed out into the chaos.

Throngs of people brushed past me, some dancing and singing. A few tried to get me to join them. That didn't happen.

This was so bizarre. Yesterday, these same people moped around crying and mourning the deaths of their loved ones. Now they were jumping around and singing like they were at a Synthetechnic Wave concert.

I pushed through the mob and ignored every wish for a "joyful tomorrow." There was nothing joyful about today, tomorrow, or the day after that. The atmosphere, what was left of it, was burning off. The oceans were cooling down and sea life was dying. In another few years, we'd all join the sea life. For the love of God, didn't they feel how cold it was?

Finally, I emerged from between two tall, stucco buildings and stepped out onto the beach road. Out here, along the shoreline, there were only a handful of people. Most of them were heading into the city center to join the party. And the salt air replaced the aroma of fried foods. I could finally feel my shoulders begin to loosen up.

I looked up. The clouds looked like they might open up any minute.

I walked faster, hoping to raise my body temperature. Goddamm it was cold!

Up ahead, at the farthest point from the city, stood the main communications tower. The stainless steel sheathing reflected the gray and white clouds. Up on the roof, I spotted a tall, omnidirectional antenna. It appeared to cut a gash in the clouds that floated by. I picked up my pace.

I entered the stairwell and began my climb up to the observation deck on the fifth floor. A young couple came down the stairs and squeezed past me on their way down. They avoided eye contact, but started to giggle as soon as they were flight below me. The observation deck was Male's version of Lover's Lane.

As I entered the observation deck, the musty smell of damp concrete mixed with the fresh scent of sex filled my nostrils. A flattened cardboard box was carefully laid out on the floor near the far wall. I noticed a few damp spots on the cardboard. I smiled.

I walked to the far side of the room and climbed the rusted ladder. Up on the next floor was the main data center for the IICN. I punched in the combination and heard a click. I turned the handle and lifted the hatch, After I climbed up, I closed the hatch behind me.

Evenly spaced along the data center walls were a dozen directional VHF antennas, positioned in front of the ventilation openings. A cable from each antenna snaked its way to the servers in the center of the room. My eye followed two thick wires from the servers up to the ceiling, where they disappeared through a small hole. The wires were connected to the two omni-directional antennas up on the roof.

Those antennas were used for voice and video communications. The ones down here were the backbone for the IICN message service. The six, bulky servers blinked silently as if to say welcome back.

I dropped my backpack on the floor and walked over to the servers. As I checked the display lights, I noticed something new, a white cable that snaked its way over to the corner and up through a hole in the ceiling. I walked over to another metal ladder on the fall wall. This one was in even worse shape than the one that led up this room. I climbed up and onto the roof. There were no railings up here. My knees felt wobbly the moment stood up.

It only took me a second to spot the white wire. It led to a small parabolic satellite dish in the center of the roof. I walked over to it and knelt down. I'd only seen this type of dish in text books back in college. This was a technology from the turn of the twenty first century. I remembered a professor once describing how these dishes were once used to communicate to satellites back in the late Twentieth and early Twenty First Centuries.

I knelt next to the dish and examined it like an archeologist would examine a sarcophagus. It was smooth and elegant in its simplicity. On the base, I spotted two green lights that blinked on and off. It was operational.

I felt the dish rotate slightly and I pulled my hands away. It was tracking something. Jin must have configured it to follow the satellite signal. Damn, he was good.

I felt tiny drops of water on my face. I thought that it was raining, but as I looked closer I noticed that the rain was falling much slower than usual. I held out my hand and watched in disbelief as tiny snowflakes landed in my palm. They melted as soon as they touched the skin, but it was definitely snow. Not the thick heavy stuff I remembered from our family ski trips to the Sierras, but a wet snow mixed with the drizzle.

I watched it for a few minutes and wondered what the crazy bastards who were partying in the streets thought about this. They probably thought it was a sign from whatever god they worshipped.

I looked at my hand again, but there weren't any more snowflakes. It was just sprinkling now.

I headed down the ladder into the data center and closed the hatch behind me. The patter of rain on the metal roof filled the room. I peeked through one of the many long, vertical ventilation slots along the wall and watched the rain fall for a little while. I didn't see any more snow. Maybe I had imagined it.

It didn't matter. The rain was coming down harder now. I could tell that it would last for another couple of hours. So I settled onto the floor, pulled out my blankets, and opened the data mat. It was time to get back to work.

"Aron? Aron, are you up there?"

Someone pounded on the hatch. It pulled me from my erotic dream about Shannon.

"Aron, come on! I know you're up there!"

It took me a second to realize that the voice I heard was the same one from the dream.

"Yeah, just a second." I crawled to the hatch and opened it. "How the hell did you find me up here?"

Shannon popped her head through the opening and climbed up without waiting for an invitation. "Where else would an antisocial techno-geek like you go during the only decent party this island ever throws?" She dusted herself off and looked around. "I like what you've done with the place. Very...postmodern shitty."

"If I knew you were coming I would have cleaned up," I said, smiling.

"I'd offer you a seat, but as you can see..."

"I wouldn't have taken you for minimalist. I figured you more the late twentieth century romantic type." She plopped down on the blankets that I had slept on. Then she patted the ground next to her. "Come on. Have a seat. I promise...I won't bite."

I sat down next to her and said, "That's not what I hear."

"Lies and rumors spread by my enemies." She spotted my backpack, reached over, and grabbed it without asking. She found my bottle of moonshine on the first try.

"What's this?" She said as she unscrewed the cap. She sniffed it before taking a swig. "Mmm. Just what I needed." Raising one eyebrow, she said, "Weren't you the one who criticized me for smuggling booze onto the island?"

I grabbed the bottle from her, took a drink, and then said, "I have a prescription for this stuff. It's for my blood pressure. Besides, it's keeping me warm."

"I know, can you believe it? Snow…in the Maldives. Everyone is talking about it. Some think it's a sign from a God, a new covenant that things will get better."

I knew it. Shaking my head, I asked, "And what do the others think?"

"You know…another sign that the end is near. I don't know, I just hope that this isn't a new trend. I hate the cold. That's one of the reasons I left Ireland."

"Well don't worry," I said. "A few more sips of this and you won't feel the cold anymore."

"I can think of better ways to stay warm," she said with a wink. "But it's a good thing that you brought it along," she said. "You're going to need it after I tell you the news."

"What news?"

She shook her head and motioned towards the bottle. "First you drink and then we'll talk."

I took a sip and savored the warmth that it spread down through my chest. I handed the bottle back to Shannon who gulped it like it was water. She wiped her mouth and said, "You drink like a girl."

"Just give me the bottle and tell me what you know," I said.

I drank while she spoke. "This morning, before the celebration kicked off, I saw Ahmed in the square. He called me over and told me that Michio had resigned."

I coughed. Booze filled my sinuses. I squeezed them shut, but managed to ask. "Resigned?"

"I know," she said. "I couldn't believe it either. I made him show me the letter of resignation. It was definitely from Michio."

I blinked a few times and could finally see again. "Goddammit! It was Viyaja."

"Viyaja?"

"Yeah. He came to my room yesterday and tried to scare me."

"He threatened you?"

I polished off the last of the bottle and said, "Yup. For a little guy, he has some big balls. He said they were going to take action if I didn't do what they wanted. I'll bet he threatened Michio too." I put the bottle down and looked over at her. "Did they threaten you?"

She shook her head and smiled. "No. Viyaja knows better. I'd kick his ass if he threatened me. And Ahmed…well, you know him.

He's too smart to get his hands dirty." Then she frowned. "Whatever they told Michio must have scared the shit of the poor guy. I sent him a dozen messages, but he hasn't replied to any of them. I don't know, Aron…" She looked away.

"You don't know what?"

"I think we should quit while we're ahead. You said it yourself…what's the point?"

"Hold on," I said as I got to my feet. "You're the one who talked me into joining that goddammed Council and now you want me to just give up?"

"I never said we have to give up," she looked up at me. "I'm just saying that they've finally given in a little. Did you see the latest list?"

I shook my head. I'd been completely obsessed with trying to figure out Jin's decryption plan. I never even glanced at the list.

She stood up and took my hands in hers. "Ahmed dropped over a hundred candidates from the list. My group of islands picked up sixty two seats and you gained over twenty."

"Really?"

"Really," she said. "And I have every reason to believe that we'll get more than that before the next vote."

"But why would they suddenly give in?"

Smiling, she said, "I may have suggested to Ahmed that some people might view Michio's resignation as suspicious. And I may have told him that if we don't get our fair share of people on the list then I might raise the suspicion myself…at the party tonight."

"You threatened Ahmed?"

"I wouldn't call it a threat. It was more of a promise."

"But you said that you hadn't heard from Michio. How do you know they actually threatened him?"

"I don't know." She laughed. "But Ahmed doesn't know that."

"Then let's really stick it to them. Let's—"

"Take it easy, Aron. One thing I learned back on the streets of Dublin is that you should never back your opponent into a corner. We got almost everything we asked for. Who cares if they still have a few people on the list who aren't qualified? As far as I'm concerned we won."

She leaned in and kissed me. The sweet scent of coconut and jasmine filled my nose and I felt the sting moonshine on her lips.

She pulled away.

"Wow," she said. "You really haven't been with anyone in twelve years, have you?"

"Where'd you hear that?"

"Rick may have mentioned it."

I smiled. "That bastard promised to keep that a secret."

"Don't blame him. Rick and I tied one on after the first Council meeting. The moonshine made him chatty."

I wasn't sure if it was the kiss or the thought that we got more people on the list, but suddenly I felt like a giant weight had been lifted from my shoulders. Shannon was right.

Why the hell should we fight to the death? So what if Ahmed had a few unqualified people on it?

Shannon stroked my arm, stopping when she came to the scar on my wrist. Without looking at it, she traced the outline with her thumb and kissed my neck.

"Is William on the list?" I asked.

She nodded.

"Okay." I said. "I give up…I mean…I agree. Tomorrow we throw in the towel."

She grabbed the bottom of her shirt, and pulled it up over her head. "And tonight?"

I smiled, "And tonight *I* throw in the towel."

***

I breathed in her aroma and was ready to go again. But I didn't want to move. I wanted to lay there next to her for a little while longer, soaking up the warmth of her naked body. Her head rested on my chest and I listened to her shallow breaths, grinning at the occasional soft snorts.

Why the hell did I wait so long to get back on the horse?

With my free hand, I stroked her short, soft hair. I let it wander down past her neckline and trace the wonderful contour of her back. I was about to explore further when a series of high-pitched beeps made us both sit up.

"What the hell is that?" she asked.

"It's my data mat. It beeps like that when I receive an urgent message. Probably just another communications server going down." I smiled. "Good thing we're here. It'll be a short commute."

I stood up and looked down at her. The blue evening light streaming through the ventilation slots and lit up her body in a silky light. She rolled over and reached for her clothes.

The beeping was driving me nuts. I reached down, grabbed the data mat, and acknowledged the alert. I read the message twice before throwing the data mat across the room.

"What's wrong?" Shannon asked. "I thought you said it was a bad server?"

"She's dead."

"Who's dead?"

"Sarah. Rick's wife."

She came over to me. "I'm so sorry, Aron."

She tried to hug me, but I stepped away and began to gather my stuff. We both finished dressing in silence.

When I was done, I lifted the hatch and said, "I've gotta go. I'll send Ahmed a message to let him know that I may not make the meeting."

"Don't worry about the Council. It'll take a couple days to find a replacement for Michio anyway. Go take care of William."

I climbed down through the hatch without another word.

CHAPTER 10

Helen was waiting for me on the dock when I arrived. Her usual bright, cheerful face was a red, blotchy mess. Fresh tears rolled down her cheeks when I stepped off the boat.

"Aron, thank God you're back. Sarah went so quickly that there just wasn't time to call you." She wrapped her arms around me and squeezed tightly.

I hugged her back and looked up at the sky. After clearing the lump from my throat, I asked, "Where's William?"

She released me and took a step back. "Up in his tree. You know the one. He won't come down and he won't talk to anyone... Not even me." She started to cry again.

I nodded and said, "When's the funeral?"

Sniffling back the sobs, she said, "Sundown. Some of the men are building the pyre now." More tears fell and then she said, "What are we going to do about William?"

"Don't worry. I'll talk to him." I paused and finally said, "Sarah asked me to—"

"I know," she said. "She told me."

I could tell that she wanted to say something else. Maybe she wanted to ask how the hell I was going to take care of him. Thankfully, she didn't ask, because I didn't have an answer.

I headed down the path, walking past thatched huts and ignoring the sympathetic stares of everyone I passed. In a clearing near the beach, some kids kicked a soccer ball back and forth seemingly oblivious to the drama unfolding.

As I approached Sarah's hut, I saw Mohamed standing at the base of the tall palm tree in front of the deck. He was looking up at the foliage.

"William, it's time to come down," Mohamed said. "Be a good boy. We need to talk about the ceremony."

I looked up and saw William's skinny legs poking down through the palm fronds. His dirty feet clenched the trunk like a vise. The rest of him was hidden somewhere up above. I switched my attention to Mohamed.

Shaking his head, Mohamed looked at me with sorrow-filled eyes. "Aron, I am so very glad that you are here."

That made one of us, I thought.

I nodded.

The palm fronds rustled and I looked up again. His legs were gone. In their place I found William's dirt-encrusted, angelic face peering down at me. Even from way down here, I could make out the trails of tears on his cheeks. His eyes were red, but he wasn't crying. He just stared at me. I held his gaze as I spoke to Mohamed.

"Why don't you give me and the kid a little time alone so we can talk, okay?"

"But of course, my friend," Mohamed said. "I will be in the infirmary if you need me." He hurried off.

On the boat ride out here I had tried to think of what I would say when I saw him. But what do you say to a ten-year-old kid who lost his mother so soon after his father was brutally slain?

I recounted all of the stupid platitudes that everyone had said to me after the storm. Things like, they're in a better place now and you're still young enough to start again. Their words didn't help. They stung like ocean water on a fresh cut. But the one comment that really pissed me off came from a guy who said that their death was all part of God's plan. I felt like strangling that son of a bitch.

No...I couldn't say anything like that to William, especially not with that look in his eyes. I knew that look. It was the same look that I had seen in my own reflection the morning that I had slit my wrists.

Rick had pulled me back from the brink that day and now I guess it was my turn to do the same for his kid. I just wished that I had something deeply profound or at least comforting to say to him, but I didn't. So I said, "I'm going fishing. Want to go?"

William studied my face for a few seconds and then said, "I thought that fishing was too dangerous? You said that I would get hurt on the reefs"

"Yeah, well...who gives a shit what I said? Do you want to fish or not?"

He studied me for another few seconds and then shimmied down the tree. He came up beside me and we walked in silence to the beach. We didn't speak at all. We had paddled a hundred yards off shore. William sat in the front seat of my kayak and I sat in the rear. I figured he would talk when he was ready, and an hour later he was ready.

"Won't they be mad?" he asked.

I set my paddle across my lap, grabbed my fishing pole, and baited the hook. "Probably. Helen's definitely going to be mad, but she'll only be mad at me."

Silence.

"Why?" I asked. "Do you want to go back?"

Shaking his head, he said, "No."

I handed him the pole and said, "Here. You can use my lucky rod. Just hang on to it, okay? If it goes overboard then you go overboard. Understand?"

He twisted around, took it from me, and nodded. I watched him play the reel and get used to the feel of the pole. He lifted it above his head and cast out the line. It was a good cast. Rick must have taught him how to do that. I readied the other fishing pole and cast out on the opposite side of the kayak.

We fished like that, in silence, for more than two hours. Out of the corner of my eye, I occasionally saw people watching us from the beach. Helen came out twice. The second time she brought a set of binoculars and tried to get our attention by waving her arms. When it appeared that she had finally given up, William asked, "So what's going to happen now?" His voice broke a little.

"I don't know. I guess you'll be staying with me. Your mom asked me to take care of you."

He set the pole on his lap and said, "I don't need anyone to take care of me. I can take care of myself."

"I know you can, but I can't break a promise I made to your mom," I said. "So what do you think we should do?"

William paused, "I don't know."

"Me neither." The tip of my pole jerked towards the water. I pulled back and set my line. William looked over his shoulder and watched as I reeled in a pretty good-sized squirrelfish. He picked up the net and scooped it up. After I unhooked the fish, I tossed it in to the bottom of the hull with the rest. Then I cast out again and said, "I'll tell you what...until we can figure it out, why don't you bunk with me for a little while?"

"I told you that I don't need you to take care of me."

"I didn't say I would take care of you. You take care of yourself and I'll take care of myself. We'll just do it under one roof, that's all. We'll be roommates."

William sat still for a few seconds and then said, "Okay. But you can't tell me what to do."

"Agreed, but we got to have some house rules. I don't want my hut ending up like my college dorm room."

He tilted his head as he looked at me with a puzzled expression.

"You know…house rules. My college roommate and I had three simple rules. Keep the room reasonably clean. Keep the noise down after lights out. And stay away if the other guy has a girlfriend over. You know, your run-of-the-mill house rules."

I thought I saw a brief smile, but it quickly disappeared. He reached back and held out his hand.

"Deal," he finally said.

We shook on it. "Deal," I said.

After a few minutes, he reeled in his line and said, "Aron?"

"Yeah."

"Let's go in. It's getting dark and…I want to say goodbye."

***

I sat up in bed and looked around. William was still asleep. We'd moved his bed over to my place the day after Sarah's funeral. It was a tight fit, but what the hell. It had only been two days and I realized that I was enjoying having him around. But he'd be leaving for Mars soon. It was for the best for both of us. At least that's what I kept telling myself.

The curtains were closed, but I could tell by the way the sunlight was trying to find its way in that it was already late morning. I ran my hand through my hair and it came away wet…really wet. I was soaked in sweat and so were my sheets.

I lay there for a moment. My thoughts returned to that satellite image on Jin's data mat, the one with the MDF boat docked alongside Jamal's mother ship. Something was going on, but I tried to tell myself that it didn't matter anymore.

A couple of times over the past few days I felt like looking through Jin's data mat. But I didn't. I reminded myself that by Saturday I'd be back on Male. Shannon and I would vote for the list and that would be that. The Mars ship would come and William, along with the others on the list, would be whisked away, far away from the pirates. So who what did it matter if I figured out what was in those messages? That little voice in my head, that's who. It wouldn't shut up about it.

I tried thinking about something else. William snored and turned to look at him. I wondered what it'd be like for him up there.

Maybe it wouldn't be as bad as I had first thought. I mean, at least there were no pirates up there. And if you pulled the pirate variable out of the equation, William's chances of reaching manhood probably increased exponentially. And then there was the weather around here. What the hell was going on with the weather?

After the storm the weather had gotten gradually worse, but only gradually. Each year brought more storms, fewer sunny days, and cooler temperatures. Rick had actually kept a log for a while, but I had stopped paying attention to it several years ago. Based on his data, he figured that we'd all die from starvation long before we died from the weather. But something new was happening. The temperature swings over the last few days weren't gradual shifts. Two days ago it snowed and now the hut felt like an oven.

I got up and walked over to the environmental control panel on the wall. I turned on the air conditioner, something I hadn't done in years.

Yeah, something had changed alright and I had a pretty good idea what had happened. The continual loss of the atmosphere must have reached a tipping point. The planetary pressure system that regulated weather patterns must be out of whack. If that was happening then Rick was wrong about how we'd all die. It looks like we'll either freeze to death or roast to death. Personally, I preferred freezing to death. I had read somewhere that hypothermia was a pretty painless way to check out.

I looked at my watch. It was Friday, the last day before my final Council meeting. God that sounded good…final Council meeting.

"Why's it so hot in here?" William asked as he rubbed his eyes.

"Because it's hot outside," I replied.

He stood up. Like me, he was covered in sweat. He stretched as he yawned. I chuckled as his boxer shorts almost slid off of him. He reached down with one hand and grabbed them before they fell. The shorts looked ten sizes too big for him. It was probably a pair of Rick's shorts. William had them bunched together at the waist and tied up with a string.

"So, what are doing today?"

"Let's go see if there is any breakfast left. Then we can head down to the pier. We need to clean out the kayak."

"Clean! Doesn't it get clean in the ocean?"

"Good try," I said smiling. "But you're not getting out of this that easily. You've been out in the boat. It reeks of dead fish."

Shrugging, he said, "It doesn't bother me."

"That's because you smell as bad as the boat. When was the last time you took a shower?"

He shrugged again.

"Well you're taking one today."

"Awe…I don't need a shower."

"Oh yes you do…trust me. If I bring you smelling like that over to Helen's for dinner tonight, she'll fillet me instead of the fish."

He frowned, grabbed his towel, and headed to the bathroom. Yeah. The sooner he left the better.

***

"Now don't you worry about a thing while you're gone, Aron," Helen said for the sixth time. She patted William on the shoulder and said, "William and I are going to be just fine. Aren't we William?"

Dinner with Helen always reminded me of the dinners we had at Kelly's grandmother's house. Like Helen, Kelly's grandmother had a loving way of embarrassing the kids.

William leaned out of her reach and said, "I still don't see why I can't go to Male with you?" He looked at me for help. "I'll stay in the hotel room and won't bother anyone. I promise."

"Not this time, William. But don't worry, this is going to be a short trip. I'll be back in a day or two."

Mohamed looked up from his nearly empty plate and said, "So are you that close to finalizing the list?"

I nodded. "Shannon and I talked and we feel that the list is probably as good as it's going to get. We plan to vote for the list when—"

My data mat beeped and I took it out to see who the message was from. "I'm sorry," I said. Helen glared at me. She had a strict 'no data mats at the table' rule. "I really need to read this."

I stood up and walked out onto the front porch. The message was from Michio. I opened it and it read:

Aron,

I am deeply sorry, but my resignation was necessary to ensure the protection of my family and friends.

Michio

Fuck! They had threatened him, and from the sound of it, they threatened his whole family. No wonder he resigned. I couldn't blame him, but I made a mental note to kick Viyaja's ass as soon as I got back to Male.

"What is it, Aron?" Helen asked from inside.

I read the message a second time and said, "Nothing."

Then I put the data mat back in my pocket and went back inside. I took my seat and looked around the table. From their inquisitive stares, I knew that they didn't believe me. "Really, it's nothing. Just some Council stuff."

"Did something change?" Mohamed looked worried. "Are you still going to vote for the list?"

"Nothing's changed. We're still planning to vote for the list."

"Oh, that is good news indeed!" Helen said. "Mrs. Johansen's boy, Erik, delivered some supplies two days ago and said there was a rumor that the captain of the Mars ship would decide who goes and who stays." Before I could say anything, she said, "I know, I know...I shouldn't spread rumors, but it got me all riled up, that's all."

"I did not hear this rumor." Mohamed looked at me and asked, "Is this true?"

"You know I'm not supposed to talk about what goes on in the Council." I ate a spoonful of fish-head soup and hoped they would drop it. I took a sip and peered around the table. I could tell that they weren't going to let it go. "Okay, but this stays between us."

They nodded.

"Seriously, you guys can't tell anyone." I looked at Helen and said, "Not even Erik Johansen...got it?"

They both nodded again.

"It's not exactly true," I said. "If the Council can't come up with a list before the ship arrives, then the captain will have to do it. But don't worry. Like I said, we're closing the deal tomorrow."

"I am very glad to hear that," Mohamed said. "Outsiders should not decide our fate. We need to make sure that nice young men, like William here, will go to Mars and help rebuild mankind's future."

William looked up in surprise. "I'm not going to Mars. I'm staying here...with Aron."

"William! Your mother, God rest her soul, wanted you to go," Helen said. "I know that Lohifushi is your home, but…" She turned to me with a look of desperation in her eyes. "Tell him why he has to go."

"You won't make me go, will you Aron? You said we were roommates. You said we would be fishing partners," William pleaded.

Goddammit! I had hoped to avoid this discussion until after the Mars shipped arrived.

"Look, let's worry about this after the list is finalized. Okay? There's no use getting all worked up over nothing."

I saw the fear reflected in both of their eyes. The taste of fish-head soup filled my mouth as it worked its way up the back of my throat.

***

I tossed and turned most of the night. It was no use. I couldn't get to sleep.

I sighed and slipped out of bed. Grabbing my data mat, I went outside. I stood on the front deck and tried the bullshit breathing exercises that I had learned in that couples yoga class Kelly had dragged me to a year before the storm. Breathe in through the nose and out through the mouth. I tried to clear my mind by listening to the chorus of insects who sang along to the rhythm of the waves. Nope, it was no use. The thoughts that had kept me awake were still bouncing around in my head. That hippie yoga crap didn't work back then. I don't know what made me think that it would work now.

I looked up to the stars. Goddammit! This didn't make any sense. I got William on the list. The kid was going to Mars just like

Rick and Sarah had wanted. So why the hell did I feel like something was wrong?

I sat down, opened my data mat, and read through the new list again.

See! There was nothing to be worried about. Shannon was right. Ahmed had dropped more of his candidates, one hundred and thirty-eight to be exact. Still, there was something wrong. I could feel it in my gut.

I reviewed the replacements on the list, checking their profiles against the selection criteria. They all met the criteria… all of them. I don't think I'd ever seen a list without at least one person who didn't meet at least one of the criteria. Maybe our constant bitching had gotten through to Ahmed. Maybe he and the others had decided to finally follow the rules. As much as I wanted to believe that, I didn't.

I sorted the list by name, age, religion…nothing. See, I was just imagining things. But when I sorted it by island, the little voice in my head returned and said, "I told you something was up!"

It wasn't a smoking gun, but this wasn't a normal distribution. Ninety-two of the one hundred and thirty-eight candidates came from the same island, Hanikada. I knew that island.

There had once been a tiny resort there before the storm, but the island was eventually abandoned. Something about an insufficient water supply, or water quality issue. I don't remember. But I remembered the island. Goose bumps popped up on my arms as I recalled how eerie that place was…really creepy.

Everything had been abandoned. I even found a table in the dining hut that hadn't been cleared after a meal. The whole time we were there erecting the communications tower, I felt like I was in an Old West ghost town. So unless the names on the list were ghosts—.

The door latch clicked and interrupted my thoughts. I turned and saw William peering through the door crack and rubbing the sleep out of his eyes. "What are you doing?"

"I couldn't sleep. I thought some fresh air might help," I said. "What are you doing up?"

Shrugging, he said, "I dunno."

I motioned to one of the plastic beach chairs and we sat down. After a minute of silence, I asked, "Are you still thinking about the conversation at dinner?"

"No," he said. "Not really."

I looked over at him and raised an eyebrow. He looked away. "I can tell something's bothering you. Why don't you tell me what it is. I used to tell my girls that the only way to get the bad feelings out of your head is to talk them out."

He kept quiet, so I tried a different approach, "A lot of people are scared about going up in space and living on Mars. Heck, I don't even like the idea of—"

Scowling at me, he shouted, "I'm not scared!"

"Whoa. I didn't say that you were scared. I said that a lot of other people were scared." I chuckled.

His hands clenched and his eyes narrowed. "Why are you laughing at me?"

"I'm not. I was just remembering that time your dad and I came back to the job site and found you all the way up in a communications tower with Jin's kid. You probably don't remember. You were only four years old at the time, but you..." I laughed again. "You had followed Bohai all the way up the ladder and sat on the edge of the platform, swinging your legs over the side and smiling from ear to ear."

His face softened and his hands relaxed. "Really? I don't remember that."

I nodded. "Yup. Your dad just about shit himself."

William smiled.

"That's how I know you're not scared, William. You've always been a tough kid."

We sat there silently for another few seconds before I said, "So out of curiosity, if you're not afraid of going to Mars, then why don't you want to go?"

He got up and looked out towards the sound of the waves. "Because this is my home."

"I know. Leaving home is hard, but you understand that things are getting worse around here, not better. Don't you?"

"Yeah...I guess," he said. "But some people say that it might get better."

I got up and walked over next to him. "I wish they were right...I really do. But the people who say that are scared and can't face reality. I don't blame them. The reality of what's going to happen to this place is hard to face. Do you know what I mean?"

He looked down at his feet. "Sort of. I guess…I guess it just feels like Helen and everyone wants to get rid of me."

I put my hands on his shoulders and turned him towards me. When he finally looked up into my eyes I said, "That's the last thing they want. Everyone here loves you. You were one of the first kids born on the island after the storm, so that makes you special."

"Special?"

"Yeah. When you were born, people began to have hope again. They just want you to go to Mars because they need to know that life will go on." He looked away, but I held his shoulders firmly. "They want you to go because everyone knows how smart you are, William. You'd make a difference up there." He looked at me unconvinced, so I said, "Your mom and dad believed it. That's why your dad volunteered to be on the Council. He wanted to make sure that you had a fair shot at a new life. More importantly, he knew that you'd give the colony a fighting chance to grow and thrive."

Tears formed in his eyes and he buried his head in my chest. I hugged him tightly so he wouldn't see the tears falling down my face.

After a while, he stepped back and said, "I'm tired. I'm going back to bed."

"Okay. I'll be in soon."

He went inside and closed the door. I looked up at the stars again. I thought about the new list. What were they up to?

My chest tightened as a fear took ahold of my heart. If Ahmed sent unqualified people up to the colony, it could threaten the survival of the colony. The fear clamped down harder as a worse thought worked its way into my head. What if he had made a deal with the pirates? I thought back to that night on North Point when I saw the faces of the MDF officer and Jamal on the data mat screen. What if Ahmed had agreed to send pirates up to the colony!

I couldn't let that happen. I wouldn't let that happen!

For the first time since the storm, I had a clear understanding of what I had to do. I had to delay the vote until I could decrypt those messages. I just hoped that Shannon would understand.

CHAPTER 11

I flew to Male in a helojumper, but once again it wasn't by choice. Kamish had gotten a message from a friend on another island. There were new sightings of pirates in and around the channels. I didn't want to take the chance of bumping into Jamal and his buddies.

When I called the MDF operations center to request the flight, the officer on duty refused my request. He said that he required twenty-four hours' advance notice. But I reminded him of my rights as a Council member, and after dropping my share of F-bombs, he reluctantly agreed to schedule the flight.

I don't know what that guy thought I was trying to do...go for a goddammed joy ride? Clearly he didn't understand my feelings for that machine. The only reason I opted for the helojumper was that my fear of grappling hooks had recently outweighed my fear of being chopped into tiny, bite-sized pieces by the turbo blades.

By the time I had arrived at the Male airport, it was already eleven o'clock and it was cold again...winter wonderland cold. There weren't any storm clouds in the sky, so at least I didn't have to worry about snow this time. However, my ears felt like they would snap off if someone flicked them.

Ahmed had called for a vote at noon, so I didn't have much time to find Shannon and explain everything.

I knew that Shannon was tired of the council. I could tell that she wanted it to end as much as I did. I just hoped that she'd understand why we can't vote for the list after I told her what I found. Of course there was always a chance that her Irish temper might flare up.

I had considered explaining everything to her in a message, but I had a hard enough time formulating what I would write. It would be easier to do in person.

As I walked to the hotel, I was surprised at how many people were on the streets. On an average day, I'd see a couple dozen people milling about. Today, I had to push my way through a large crowd. When I finally made it to the hotel, I understood why. Hung over the hotel door, I saw a giant, hand-painted banner welcoming the Mars rescue mission.

In a few days, the massive interplanetary cargo ship would arrive in orbit and start hauling a thousand people up there. William would be one of them. The thought unexpectedly brought a tear to my eye. I wiped it away.

What the hell was wrong with me? Mars was William's best shot at a future, so why was I acting like Helen? I blinked the tears away and went inside.

On the helojumper ride over, I had sent Shannon a message and asked her to meet me in the lobby. She didn't reply. And now, as I looked around the crowded lobby, I began to get an uneasy feeling. What if Ahmed had tried to get even for her blackmailing him? I ran up the stairs two at a time and sprinted down the hall to her door. My knocks went unanswered.

Where the hell was she? The Council session began in less than an hour.

I went to my room and dropped off my bag. Grabbing the data mat from the pouch, I ran to the Council chambers, but no one was there yet, just a few hotel workers setting up the refreshment table in the back.

I tried the café where she usually hung out. She wasn't there either. My frazzled nerves were on the verge of a meltdown. I searched the promenade and followed the narrow streets that crisscrossed the town, but there was no sign of her.

I looked at my watch. I was out of time. The meeting would start in less than ten minutes. I decided to search one last place before heading back. I ran up the stairs of the communications tower to the observation deck. It was deserted except for a young man who was rounding second base with his girlfriend. I apologized for interrupting and left.

That was it. I ran back to the hotel.

When I entered the Council chambers, I was greeted by expressions of surprise. They looked like they hadn't expected me to show up.

Now it was my turn to be surprised, but in a good way. Shannon was here and she was safe. I took a deep breath and exhaled slowly.

She stood at the head table arguing with Ahmed about something. Viyaja stood behind Ahmed intently watching the two of them go at each another. Ahmed looked up at me. Shannon turned and followed the direction of his gaze. She saw me and I watched her face change from surprise to a sad sort of happiness in a split second. It wasn't pity, not exactly. It reminded me of how Sarah had looked at me when we discussed William; sad about the circumstances, but happy that I had agreed to watch over him.

Shannon gave Ahmed one final glare before walking over to me. She took my hands and said, "I didn't think you would make it given...everything. How are you holding up?"

Her touch sent a warm current through my cold body. I couldn't remember the last time someone had made me feel like that. "I'm fine." I squeezed her hands and said, "Where've you been? Didn't you get my message to meet at the hotel?"

"No. I left my data mat in my room." She let go and patted her pockets. "I haven't had it on me all day."

There wasn't time to tell her everything, not the way I had rehearsed it in my head, so I cut to the chase. "We can't vote for the list."

Her smile vanished. "What are you talking about?"

"Look, I know the odds are against us, but listen to me... we can't vote for the list, not yet. There's something really screwy going on. Ahmed's up to something and I think it's bad...really bad."

"I don't understand." The pitch of her voice increased and her Irish accent got heavier. "Didn't you see the revised list? Ahmed removed over a hundred more candidates from the list, the ones who weren't eligible. Don't you see? We've won."

Nodding, I said, "Yeah, I saw it. But did you see who they added? There are people on the list that I've never heard of and they're listed as living on Hanikada." I waited to see her reaction, but she just stared at me. "Come on, you know Hanikada, it's in the Gan island chain. It's been uninhabited since the storm. Don't you see? They're trying to pull some kind of bait and switch."

"Aron, I know who those people are and you should too."

I stared at her, my brow furrowed. What the hell was she was talking about?

"They're the last group of refugees from Sri Lanka. They were given sanctuary on Hanikada after their flotilla was rescued three years ago." She sighed. "Ever since this Council began, I've been trying to get Ahmed to acknowledge that they are equal citizens and add them to the inhabitant list." Shaking her head, she said, "But then again, how could you have known? You've spent the last three years fishing and feeling sorry for yourself." She took a step away from me. "Take a good look in the mirror, Aron. You're not the only victim of the storm. There are a lot of people in that reflection with you."

Her comment hit me harder than that wave that almost capsized me. She was right. I hadn't paid much attention to what went on. After the IICN was completed, I disengaged from everyone and everything. It was the only way I knew to keep from getting hurt again. But that didn't explain what I saw on North Point, the MDF officer and Jamal. I knew in the pit of my stomach that something still wasn't right.

"I'm sorry, but listen to me." I said taking a step toward her.

She held up her hands and waved me off. "No. No! We're not changing the plan now. We had a deal."

"I know, but...look. There's more you need to know. Just help me block this vote and I'll explain everything. Okay? If I can't convince you, then—"

"Aron, you don't know what you're asking me to do. You don't understand what's at stake."

"I do know what's at stake. A ten-year-old's future is at stake and the future of the human race is at stake and all I'm asking for is a little goddammed time so I can explain what—"

The clack of Ahmed's gavel cut me off. I looked over at the head table and watched Ahmed pound it again before saying, "Lady and gentlemen. It is time to begin the meeting. Please take your seats."

Everyone returned to their seats and I looked over at Shannon begging with my eyes. She stared at me for a few seconds and then looked away.

Ahmed pounded his gavel one final time. "The Council of Thirteen is now called to order. Mr. Secretary, will you please take roll call?"

Viyaja apparently had taken Michio's place as the Council secretary because he called out each Council member by name and made a check mark on a sheet of paper as each person responded with "present." The last name he called was Michio, but Michio wasn't there and that bastard knew it. He called Michio again. What the hell was he up to? Why were they going through all of the theatrics. They knew he wasn't coming. They had made sure of it.

"Mr. President, all members are accounted for except for Mr. Shimizu."

"Thank you, Mr. Secretary. I have a letter of resignation from him that I will now read to the Council." Ahmed held up his data mat and ceremoniously read, "Mr. President, it is with much regret that I must resign my seat on the Council effective immediately. Sincerely, Mr. Michio Shimizu."

Ahmed looked around the room and then rested his gaze on me. "It is with equal regret that I have accepted his letter of resignation. Given our timeline, I believe we must dispense with the normal selection process. So I move that the Council authorize me to name a successor for the post. Do I have a second?"

Viyaja raised his hand before Ahmed finished his sentence and said, "I second the motion."

"Very well," Ahmed said. "Then I put the motion to the Council for vote. Will all those in favor of authorizing Ahmed to appoint a replacement please say aye."

Everyone said aye.

"All opposed?"

"Nay," I said.

"Very well then," Ahmed said. "With the new authority invested in me, I hereby appoint Mr. Ramdas Prasad to the Council."

I shot out of my seat. "Goddammit Ahmed! You said you would select a fair representative. Ramdas isn't from the same island chain as Michio. How can he fairly represent the people of those islands?"

"You are out of order, Mr. Atherton."

"Well, you're out of your fucking mind if you think you're going to get away with this."

He pounded his gavel and cut me off. "Mr. Atherton, I said you are out of order. If you wish to make a motion, please use the proper protocol."

I wanted to make a motion that he shove the gavel up his ass, but instead I said, "Mr. President, I propose a motion."

In an annoyed tone, he said, "Please precede, Mr. Atherton."

"I would like to propose that you appoint someone from the Huran island chain."

He smiled. "A motion is on the floor. Are there any seconds?"

I looked around the table. Everyone avoided making eye contact...even Shannon.

"If there is not a second, then I am afraid the motion is dropped from consideration." He brought the gavel down hard with a sharp crack, causing me to flinch. I sat down, stunned by Shannon's abandonment.

The chamber doors opened and Ahmed called his cousin, Ramdas, to enter. He walked in and took Michio's seat at the table. Ahmed applauded. Everyone joined in, everyone except me.

I stared at Shannon, but she wouldn't look my way. I racked my brain for an excuse to stall the vote. If I could just speak with her, I knew that I could convince her.

"The Council will now consider the next item of business," Ahmed said, "a vote on the revised list of candidates for relocation to the Mars colony."

If Michio had been here, he would know what to do. Michio had memorized the parliamentary procedure book and could recall obscure rules at the drop of a hat. He once told me that the key to winning any game was to understand the rules better than your opponent.

Wait. That was it. I suddenly remembered a story that Rick had told me of how Michio had made Ahmed read the entire list of candidates before the Council could vote on it. He had said that it was a stalling maneuver to give Shannon time to make the meeting. I could pull the same move. It wouldn't stop the vote, but it might give me the time I needed to talk to Shannon. I knocked my chair over as I jumped to my feet. "Mr. President, point of order."

Ahmed looked like he had run out of patience. "Yes, Mr. Atherton? What is it this time?"

The crash of the chair made Shannon finally look over at me. I locked eyes with her as I spoke. "Mr. President. Given the importance of this vote and since this will be the final action of the Council and given that we have plenty of time left today, I move that the list be read in its entirety prior to the vote in accordance with the rules of the Council."

I looked at Shannon in desperation.

"Mr. Atherton, reading the list will only slow down the proceedings, not stop them." Ahmed gave me a patronizing smile. "But I will open your motion to the Council. Is there a second for the motion?"

I kept my gaze glued to Shannon's face. For a second, I thought she would look away, but instead she brushed the bangs out of her eyes and raised her hand. It hung next to her head for a second. My heart pounded in my chest. Finally, arching her eyebrow, she raised her hand and said, "I second the motion."

"Very well," Ahmed said. From his tone, I knew that he was pissed off, but it didn't matter because Shannon had seconded the vote. "A motion was made. All in favor, please raise their hands."

I raised my hand and Shannon followed suit. I looked around the room. Everyone's eyes were on Shannon. Then I watched as hand after hand lifted into the air.

Holy shit! This might actually work.

Ahmed's face was the color of the pomegranate on the top of the fruit bowl in front of him. Viyaja looked more puzzled than angry, but even he raised his hand.

"Fine!" Ahmed spit the word out. "The motion is passed. Mr. Secretary, will you please read the names?"

Viyaja stood up and read from his data mat. "Mr. Hariaban Kapoor from the island of Male. Miss Anaka Olsen of..."

I got up and walked to the back of the room, where pitchers of water and plates of fruit were laid out on the refreshment table. Shannon got up and joined me. I poured a glass of water. She came up beside me and whispered, "What are you up to, Aron?"

In a hushed voice I said, "Thank you." She didn't say anything, so I continued. "We have to stop the vote. There's more going on here than you know."

"What are you talking about?"

"Remember what I told you about my friend Jin? The satellite? Do you remember that?"

She nodded again.

"Jin stumbled onto something. He found out that either Ahmed or someone using Ahmed's IICN user account was sending messages back and forth with the pirates."

She turned pale and asked, "Are you sure?"

"I'm positive. And when I was on North Point, I accidently interrupted a video conference between an MDF officer and Jamal."

Her lip trembled. "How do you know it was Jamal?"

"The scar. It was him. Trust me."

"What were they saying?"

"Nothing. They stopped talking when I joined the net. But look, it doesn't matter that I didn't hear what they were saying. What matters is that I have the messages that were sent and we know that someone from the MDF is talking to pirates."

Her shoulders slumped and she asked, "What do the messages say?"

"I don't know. They're encrypted. But Jin figured out a way to decrypt them."

"But...he's missing, Aron. If he hasn't turned up by now, you know what that means. So what good are the encrypted messages now? Did he tell you how to do decrypt them?"

I shook my head. "No, but I think the answer is somewhere on his data mat and I have it."

She studied my face as if she didn't quite believe me.

"Shannon, all I need is a couple of days to figure out how to decrypt the messages. So vote with me to block the list. Give me time to figure out what they're up to and then I promise...if there's nothing in the messages about the list then I'll vote for it. Hell, I'll even raise the motion myself."

She wrinkled her brow and said, "I don't know." I could tell she still didn't believe me. "How did Jin figure out what was happening?"

Viyaja's voice droned on in the background as he read name after name.

"It's complicated."

"Don't pull that shit on me. If you want me to trust you, then you need to trust me."

She was right. "He used the satellite to intercept emails from our network."

"I thought you said it was a reconnaissance satellite? How could he—"

"I said it was complicated. I'm not entirely sure how he did it, but he did. Before he could tell me how to break the encryption, he disappeared."

"And can you do it? Break the encryption, I mean."

I shrugged. "I don't know. Maybe."

Before returning to her seat, she said, "I need time to digest all of this."

What the hell was she digesting? It was clear that something was going on.

It took nearly an hour before all the names were read. The whole time I kept studying Shannon's face, searching for some sign, any sign, that she was with me. But her face was a closed book. When Viyaja finished, he turned the floor back to Ahmed.

"Thank you, Mr. Secretary." Ahmed paused and looked at me. "With no further objections we will now vote on the list. All in favor, please signify by—"

"I request a twenty-four hour recess," I said.

"Mr. Atherton, what reason could you possibly have for a recess?" Ahmed asked.

"I need time to certify the list and I'm sure our newest member, Mr. Prasad, needs time as well."

"I don't want to speak for Mr. Prasad, but I'm sure he is fine with the list." Ramdas smiled and nodded. "However, since you made a motion I'll ask…is there anyone who will second Mr. Atherton's request for a recess?"

Once again, I looked at Shannon, but she just stared at her hands.

"Any seconds?" Ahmed said.

What was she doing?

Ahmed clacked his gavel loudly and he said, "The motion is dropped. Now, can we continue with the vote?"

I didn't say anything. I just stared at Shannon.

"Alright. Will all those in favor of the list please raise your hands."

I watched as each person around the table raised their hands. Shannon looked at me with sad eyes and lifted her hand into the air. And just like that, it was over. The list was final.

CHAPTER 12

I didn't wait around to talk to Shannon or to see if she would come and talk to me. There wasn't enough time to deal with that bullshit. I had to get back to Lohifushi and deal with real problems.

I sent Kamish a message and he picked me up a couple hours later, around six. We raced against the dark clouds advancing from the east and reached Lohifushi just as the storm hit. Kamish ran for cover in the equipment shed next to the old bait shack, but I braved the pelting sleet and rain. The weather fit my mood.

William wasn't in the hut when I arrived, which was a good thing. I didn't want to talk to anyone. I changed into something dry and unpacked my bag. Reaching inside, I pulled out a mostly empty bottle of moonshine and poured myself a shot. If there was ever a time that I really needed a drink, it was now. I choked on the first sip, but drank through it, enjoying the warmth as it passed through me.

My mind circled a single question: what was I going to tell William? I couldn't convince Shannon to delay the vote, I couldn't decrypt the messages, and worst of all…I had let myself love that kid.

The realization of it all hit me with the impact of a helojumper slamming into the ocean. I guess I got what I deserved…a big stinking pile of shit to deal with.

The sound of beeping pulled me out of my dreams and into the conscious world that I had tried to escape. I opened my eyes and stared at the vaulted ceiling. It took me a moment to get my bearings. I was in my own bed. I reached for my data mat, but it wasn't beeping. The sound came from William's data mat. I looked over and saw him sitting cross-legged on his bed, acting like he didn't know that I was awake.

"How long have you been sitting there?" I asked.

He shrugged while keeping his eyes glued on the game.

"What time is it?"

"Lunch time," he said.

I rolled into a sitting position and put my hands on either side of my head. When the pain subsided, I said, "You're probably wondering why I'm back so soon."

"Nope."

"You're not even a little curious?"

"Nope," he repeated. "Everyone got the message from the Council. It said that the list was approved. I figured you'd be back." He tilted his data mat and tapped the screen, seemingly pleased with whatever results the move had netted.

"Did it say when the list would be released?"

"The day before the shuttle takes people up to the ship. Helen said it had something to do with maintaining public order and stuff."

That sounded like something Ahmed would say, but I knew the truth. That bastard didn't want people to look too closely at the list. If they did, he would have a full blown revolt on his hands. And by waiting until the day after the ship arrived, the captain wouldn't have any reason to suspect anything was wrong.

I stood up and almost fell back onto the bed as pain shot through my head. William continued to play his game, and I wondered if he knew something was wrong. If he did, then his acting was getting better.

I watched as he played the game. He chewed his lower lip. Rick used to do the same thing, usually when he faced a particularly difficult technical challenge. Rick loved challenges…the tougher the better.

"William?"

He scowled, paused the game, and looked up. "What?"

"Where's the data mat that I asked you to keep safe for me. Jin's data mat?"

"Outside."

"Can you get it for me?"

"Now? Can I finish this level first."

"Now…please."

He sighed, set his data mat on the bed and stomped outside. I walked over to the window and watched him shimmy up a palm tree. He scaled the tree as easily as most people walk down the street. He climbed down with the data mat clenched in his teeth. As he entered the room, he tossed it to me.

"Thanks," I said.

He was already playing his game again. I could tell that he was pissed. I couldn't blame him. I'd violated one of our new rules: never bother your roommate when he's playing a video game.

I went out onto the front deck and plopped down in a chair. I had three days before the list was made public, which wasn't much time. If I could prove that Ahmed was involved with the pirates, even if it didn't have anything to do with the list, it might give the ship's captain enough reason to take a good hard look at the list. At this point, I didn't care if the captain knew anyone on the list or not. At least he wasn't under Ahmed's thumb, and that was good enough for me.

***

I ran my hand thought my hair.

Five hours! Five hours and nothing. It had to be here.

My stomach growled. It wanted something to eat. I decided to take its suggestion.

Helen was in the kitchen preparing dinner when I arrived. She turned and smiled when she saw me.

"Well, well, well...you weren't kidding about coming back soon, now were you? Can I get you something to drink? How about some mango juice?"

"What is it with you and Mohamed? Why are you always pushing the mango juice?" I sat on a stool next to the butcher's block. "How about a hot cup of chicory? I could smell it brewing all the way down by the beach."

"Coming right up." She went to the stove and filled a mug. I took the mug and said, "Thanks." Then I took a sip. It wasn't like the coffee I used to drink every morning at the corner bakery back home, but it was hot and bitter. It did the trick.

"No worries, dear," she said. "So...the list is final, huh? I guess that means we'll be saying goodbye to William and a few others soon." Her voice cracked, "It'll be hard to say goodbye to him." She looked at me.

To hell with it. I had to tell her sooner or later. "He's not going."

She froze, teapot still in hand. "What? Not going? That can't be. But you said—."

"I know what I said, but I can't send him up there unless I know what's going on."

Tears began to spill down her cheeks. "I don't understand."

So I told Helen everything. I told her about the list, and how Ahmed used Viyaja to threaten everyone on the Council, including me. I told her about Jin and the messages he'd intercepted and how I believed that Ahmed was in cahoots with the pirates. And I told her about North Point and what had happened there, including the video conference where I saw Jamal.

"So now you understand, don't you? I can't send him up there...not without knowing what they're up to," I said.

I could tell she didn't fully understand, but at least she had stopped crying. She dried her eyes with her apron and stood up straight with her chest pushed out. "Well then...you better get cracking."

"I've been cracking ever since I got my hands on Jin's data mat. I'm just not finding anything useful. He was a clever guy...too clever."

She walked over and took my empty cup, stared me in the eyes, and said, "Poppy cock! You are just as clever as he was. I knew Jin too, you know. He used to come in here and have tea with me sometimes back when you boys were putting up that tower. Such a sweet man."

Raising my eyebrows, I said, "Sweet? Not exactly the adjective I would use to describe him. Smart, yes. Clinical, definitely. But sweet...no."

"Well I guess you didn't know him as well as you thought. All the man used to talk about was his family. He went on and on about them. Used to say how the only thing important in his life was his family. They meant everything to him, you know."

I knew that he was a family man, but he didn't talk about them much to me. Maybe he knew the pain that it would cause. The only time I remember him mentioning something about family was when he spouted off those stupid Chinese proverbs like 'A happy family is but an earlier heaven' and 'The strength of a nation derives from the integrity of the home.' His favorite was 'A man searches the world for what he needs and returns home to find it.'

I jumped to my feet and said, "That's it, Helen. It has to be. You're a genius!"

I kissed her on the cheek and ran out of the kitchen. As I ran past the tables in the dining room, I heard Helen say, "Glad to be of help."

William was still on his bed playing video games when I returned. He gave me a quizzical look as I grabbed Jin's data mat and sat down.

By now, I knew the folders and their contents better than the trail around this island. Every folder was meticulously labeled and all of them contained files related to the IICN or the satellite hacking project. The only exception was the one labeled 'Family.' It was the one I had barely examined. It only contained photos and videos of his family, some taken in China, but most on the island.

I created a new folder and then copied each picture into it. Then I searched through his apps until I found a pattern recognition tool.

It took the tool about ten minutes to analyze the first picture in the folder. After I finished running the tenth picture through the app and I received another negative match, I said, "Shit! It's gotta be here."

"What are you doing?" William asked.

"Huh," I said, looking up to find William peering over my shoulder. "Oh, it's kind of complicated."

"I'm not stupid, you know. I wrote that video game on my own."

"You're right. I'm sorry." I smiled. "It's a tool that your dad, Jin, and I had used to analyze signal patterns over the network. It's pretty basic, uses something called an SVN model. That stands for Support Vector Network."

He nodded as if he understood, but I could tell from the expression on his face that I had already lost him.

"The SVN model recognizes data patterns by using a non-probabilistic binary linear classifier regression algorithm."

"Oh." He nodded again. "So what kind of pattern are you looking for?"

"That's just it...I don't know. I think Jin left me some kind of message embedded in one or more of these photos."

His face brightened up. "I get it. It's like those holograms. The ones you stare at and then eventually you see a hidden picture inside?"

"That's right. But to find an embedded picture, you need to know how to look at it. It's not as easy as you'd think."

There was a whole academic field dedicated to it called steganography. I wasn't an expert in the field. Hell, I barely passed the class in college.

"So if you don't know how to look for it, how can you find it?" He said.

"I configured the app to look for any known patterns. Here, see?" I pointed to the screen. "I set the pattern probability to ninety nine percent. The tool analyzes the pixels that make up the picture."

A window popped up on the data mat to let me know that it didn't find any patterns. I selected the next photo in the list, a recent family shot taken in front of Jin's hut, and I let the tool do its thing.

"Is there anything I can do to help?" William asked.

"No. It just takes time. Probably be another few hours before—"

A window popped up again, but this time it read:

POSITIVE HIT: 99.999% CERTAINTY
PATTERN FOUND: RIEMANN ZETA-FUNCTION

"Holy shit!" I said.

William leaned over and read the screen. "What's a Riemann Zeta-Function?"

I shook my head. "I have no idea." Math wasn't my strong suit. "But whatever it is, it's the key to seeing the hidden picture."

After a few minutes of reconfiguring the tool, I had it pull out the bits that fell within the pattern and then reassemble them into a binary file. When it was done, I opened the file with a text editor.

"That sneaky son of a bitch!" Smiling, I turned and grabbed William by the shoulders. "We did it. Look, there's the message."

Stepping back out of my reach, he said, "You did it. I didn't do nothing. I just asked stupid questions, that's all."

I stood up. "What are you talking about? I wasn't getting anywhere until you jumped in. From now on, we're a team. We're going to solve this problem together. Deal?" I held out my hand.

He looked at it for a second and then shook it. "Deal."

CHAPTER 13

The morning sun illuminated the room. But it wasn't until I felt the rays pouring through the skylight that I realized it was well into the next day.

I hadn't pulled an all-nighter like that since I was back in college. I chuckled at the thought of how many gallons of soda and how many pounds of chips I'd consumed trying to meet a homework deadline. Only this deadline was different and the realization of it drained the smile from my face.

I looked over at William. He was staring intently at his data mat. I knew that look. It was the look of a seasoned coder in the zone, oblivious to the world around him.

Last night he'd come up with an idea to bootleg CPU cycles from inactive data mats around the islands. There were probably some pissed off people wondering why their data mats ran so slow, but I didn't care. His idea had cut the processing time from a few days to ten hours. For the first time since I had started looking through Jin's data mat, I actually believed that we might be able to decrypt those messages before the ship arrived. Scratch that. I was positive that we'd decrypt those messages. We had to. William belonged up there. I knew that now. After seeing what he was capable of last night and knowing what he could do for the colony…hell, I'd pack him in a box of plantains if that's what it took to get him up there.

My data mat beeped. It was another message from Shannon. I deleted it. I didn't have time for her bullshit now.

"It's done!" William said without looking up. "The last picture is done."

I got up, went over to his bed, and looked over his shoulder. "Did you find any more hidden files?"

He tapped the window to display another screen. "Two more files." He tapped the screen a few more times and said, "There you go...I just sent them to you."

My data mat beeped, but before I could open the files, there was a knock at the door.

"Hello? Anybody home?" Helen asked before knocking again.

I walked over and opened the door. "Good morning, Helen."

"More like good afternoon. I've been worried sick about you two. You missed breakfast." She walked in with a tray full of food and set it down on the small table in the corner. "Well, come on then. You must be hungry. I can tell that you've both been up all night. You have the same look my old Bob had when he crawled home from the pubs at five in the morning."

She lifted a cloth, unleashing the smell of sweet bread. My stomach woke up and grumbled. William must have had the same reaction, because he grabbed a piece and gobbled it down before I reached the plate.

"We were working on that thing that I told you about yesterday. You know the—"

"Aron Atherton, didn't your mother teach you not to talk with your mouth full?"

"Sorry." I swallowed and took a drink of mango juice before continuing. "We found the information that Jin left behind, thanks in large part to William here."

William rolled his eyes and took another bite of bread.

"I told you he was smart, didn't I, Aron?" Helen said. "Well then, what is it? What did you boys figure out?"

I paused before taking another bite and said, "We don't know yet."

"But I thought you said you found some information."

I nodded and said, "We did. Now we have to figure out what it means. From what I've seen so far, it isn't so much a plan as it is pieces of a plan. I've just got to—" William looked up at me. "I mean *we've* got to figure out what Jin planned to do with this stuff."

"I'll leave you two at it, then," she said, turning toward the door. Before leaving, she looked back and added, "Try to get some sleep. You two look like road-kill wallabies that have been lying in the sun too long." She smiled and closed the door behind her.

"She's right," I said. "We should get some sleep."

"But I'm not tired. Let's keep going?"

I shook my head. "Trust me. I learned a long time ago that brains don't function very well without sleep. Let's take a power nap and pick up where we left off."

"I'll lie down," William said. "But I'm not taking a nap. I told you...I'm not tired."

"Suit yourself."

After finishing the food, I laid down. My mind was still spinning and I was having a hard time slowing it down. What did Jin have in mind? Most of the files didn't make any sense, at least not on the surface. One of them contained a spreadsheet with the names of Chinese cities with some kind of number sequence next to them. The numbers appeared random, but at the same time they seemed familiar. Other files contained information like communications equipment inventories.

I yawned. Before I closed my eyes, I turned my head and glanced over at William. I smiled. He was already snoring.

***

I slept but my brain kept working on the problem. The number sequences turned into snake-like creatures. They surrounded me and formed themselves into a web-like cocoon, trapping me within the shell. A giant spider was about to plunge its fangs into my neck when my eyes flew open and I found Shannon caressing my cheek with the back of her hand.

"What are you doing here?" I blinked to make sure this wasn't just another part of the dream.

"What do you think I'm doing here? You wouldn't answer my messages. I came to see if you were alright." She traced her fingers down my arm and stopped at my wrist. I shook her off and sat up. William mumbled something in his sleep and rolled over.

"Come on," I whispered. I got out of bed and motioned for her to follow. We went out onto the front porch, and I quietly closed the door behind me.

Turning to face her, I said, "I'm serious, Shannon. What the hell do you want?"

"Most men I sleep with wait a few months before they avoid me." She smiled, but I didn't.

I didn't need this and I didn't need her. My heart knew I was lying, but I ignored it like I ignored the little voice in my head. First she popped into my life after three years without a word. Then she suckered me into joining the Council, convincing me that I could make a difference. And just when we had chance to make that difference, she fucked me over in front of the entire Council. What does she want? Does she think I'm going to forget all about that so we could play kissy face again?

She shrugged and went on, "I wanted to make sure you were okay, that's all. You took off so fast after the Council meeting that I didn't have time to talk to you about your crazy stunt."

"My crazy stunt? Jesus H. Christ! Are you shitting me? I told you what I was trying to do. I needed time...time to figure out what was going on, but you couldn't wait, so what is there to talk about?"

"Come on, Aron. You weren't making any sense. You sounded like some kind of lunatic conspiracy theorist. What did you expect me to do? Block the vote so you could go off on a snipe hunt while we risk having an outsider decide the list for us?" She took a step toward me and said in a soft voice, "Listen, I know that you're dealing with a lot right now." She nodded toward the door. "I get it. It's a big change for you."

"You don't know anything about what I'm dealing with. Did you have three close friends die over the past month? Huh? Did one of your friends disappear in the middle of the night? Did you wake up one morning to find yourself the parent of a ten-year-old boy? No! So don't tell me that you know what I'm going through." I turned to walk away, but she grabbed my sleeve and stopped me.

"Rick and Jin were my friends too, you know. But you're wrong." She let go of my sleeve and turned to face the ocean. "I know what it's like to be a parent. Saravan and I had a baby. I never told you that, but we did. That's why I didn't come to see you after I got back from that walkabout."

"You have a child?"

"Had," she said turning her back on me. "We lost her." Her shoulders slumped and she began to cry.

"I didn't know," I said walking to her and put my hands around.

She stopped crying, pulled herself up straight, and turned to face me. Her face was a mix of embarrassment and anger. "Well screw you, Aron Atherton!" She pushed me away. "You're not the only one who goes to bed every night and wakes up every morning with a broken heart,. Every person who survived the goddammed storm lives with the same pain you have. Your problem is that you'd rather feel sorry for yourself than enjoy what little time you have left."

"Listen, Shannon...I'm sorry about what I said. It's just—"

"Save your apology for someone who wants it. I offered you the most precious thing I have left on this planet, my time. Time I wanted to spend with you. But you would rather spend your time trying to prove that Ahmed is a crook. Well here's a news flash for you...he is a crook. Everyone knows it, but nobody cares. Don't you get it? The list is final and nothing you dig up now is going to change that. Why can't you just let it go?"

"Because," I said softly, pointing to the hut. "There's a boy in there that deserves a chance to grow up and become the man that I know he will be. But he's not going to get that chance unless I find out what's going on."

I placed my hands on her shoulders again. "And you're right. I did spend too much time feeling sorry for myself, but you're wrong if you think that's what I'm doing now. For the first time in a really long time, I care about what's going to happen to someone besides me. And I'm not just talking about William. I mean everyone. I don't think I actually understood how big a deal the list was until it was finalized. It's not about who gets to go and who stays behind. It's about whether or not the human race survives. I know how grandiose this sounds. But it's how I feel. Do you understand?"

Her face softened. "Yes. I get it." She looked down. "But we'll never get a perfect list of candidates together. The only thing we can do now is hope that whoever goes up there can make it work." Then she took my hand and said, "And all we can do down here is enjoy the time we have left. Do you understand *that*, Aron? It's time to let this go and start living again."

I wanted to let it go. But I couldn't give up. Not yet.

I shook my head. "I can't. I gotta try."

Rage flashed across her face and she threw my hand back at me. "You're a fucking idiot, Aron! A goddammed fucking idiot! You have no idea what you just gave up." She turned and stormed off towards the dock. I just stood there and watched her go.

After a few minutes, I heard, "Aron?"

I turned and saw William looking through the half-opened door.

"Yeah?" I said.

"Are you okay?"

"I don't know."

"She was pretty mad, wasn't she?"

I nodded.

"Why?"

I rubbed the back of my neck and shrugged. "It's complicated."

He tilted his head and said, "Is it boyfriend-girlfriend stuff?"

I grinned and said, "Sort of, but we don't have time to worry about boyfriend-girlfriend stuff, do we?"

He shook his head.

"We have work to do. Right?"

He opened the door the rest of the way and said, "Right."

"Then let's get to it."

***

It was painstaking work, but little by little, we pieced together the information we had found. By the time we had finished the food that Helen brought us for dinner, William and I probably knew more about the Chinese military communication infrastructure than anyone else left on the planet.

I found a map of Asia and had William plot the location of the equipment we found on one of the lists. It didn't take him long to figure out how to do it. He drew lines between the symbols he placed on the map using the information from the spreadsheet. With him doing that, I had time to focus on the big question. What did it all mean? So far, all we had was a pretty map and we were already through most of the files.

I scratched my head and ran my hand through my hair. I felt like we were going down another rabbit hole. It was just a bunch of communications equipment: hubs, routers, laser uplink stations, and radio towers. Maybe Jin thought he could build something out of all this stuff, but there was no way in hell that I could. He had been a Cyber Ace in the Chinese Cyber Force. I had managed communications contracts. Even if he did plan to build something, how did he plan to get the stuff from China to the Maldives? Perhaps he had some other secret up his sleeve, like an SF296 fighter jet hidden in a mango grove somewhere.

"I'm done."

I looked over and saw William sitting cross-legged on the bed, leaning back on his elbows. If I sat like that, I'd crack in half like a dry crab shell.

"Did you plot everything?" I looked over his shoulder and pretended to understand the intricate web of communication pathways laid out on the map.

"Yup." He nodded. "So, what does it mean?"

I stood up straight, interlaced my fingers behind my head and said, "I don't have a clue. Are you sure that's everything?"

He nodded again. "Everything that you told me to plot. The only thing I didn't use were the numbers in the hidden column."

My hands dropped to my side and I grabbed his data mat. "What hidden column?"

"Right there, between the seventh and eighth column. There's a column of numbers that was minimized. I thought you hid it so I wouldn't mess up."

He was right. There was another column. Each cell contained a one or a zero. I selected the column title, hit the translate button and then watched as the Chinese symbols turned into four letters: EMPH.

"What's an emph?"

"It's not an emph, it's an acronym. EMPH stands for Electro Magnetic Pulse Hardened. Do you know what that means?"

He shook his head.

I began to get that same excited feeling that I used to get back in school when my brain managed to finally wrap itself around a really tough math problem. "It means that some of this equipment might have survived the storm. These ones." I pointed at column. "The cells with a number one in them."

"I don't get it."

☐ "Do you remember what your dad told you about the storm?"

"A little." He shrugged. "He said a big solar flare hit the earth and burned up most of the atmosphere."

I nodded, "Right. A solar flare burned up most of the atmosphere, but solar flares also do something else." I began to pace the room. "See, solar flares are huge clouds of charged solar plasma…energy like electricity. Anyway, when the sun shoots out a flare. The flare flies through space really, really fast."

William looked at me, his head tilted to the side.

"Have you ever shocked yourself? You know, touch something and get zapped?"

He nodded.

"Well, a solar flare has a lot of stored energy and when that energy touches the earth…Pow! It zaps it just like when you get shocked. That energy comes in through the planet's magnetic poles."

William said, "That's what I said. A solar flare burned up the atmosphere."

"Yeah, but it did something else. That energy spawned massive geomagnetic storms and those storms fried most of the electronics in the world."

His brow furrowed. "Is that why you and dad had to build all the stuff for the IICN from all that spare junk?"

I smiled. "Exactly. Some bits and pieces of equipment didn't get fried, but that was just luck. EMPH equipment wouldn't have been damaged at all."

"So some of this stuff," he said, pointing to the map, "might still work?"

I sat down on the edge of the bed and said, "It's possible. But the only way to know for sure would be to go there and check it out or—"

William stared at me for a half second before saying, "Or what?"

"William, I need you to go through that list again."

"Again?" he whined.

"Yup. All of it. For every piece of equipment that has a one in the EMPH column, I want you to color the equipment icon blue. Got it? How long do you think that will take?"

"About thirty seconds," he said, smiling. "I linked each icon to the spreadsheet, so all I have to do is write a script to change the color based on the value in the column. Come on…I did harder stuff when I was five."

I ruffled his hair. He ducked out of my reach and flashed me an annoyed look. It was the kind of look my girls had given Kelly when she would dress them up in the same outfits.

It actually took him closer to three minutes to finish the script, but I wasn't complaining. All real coders underestimated schedules. He handed me the data mat and I overlaid the position of the Indian reconnaissance satellite on it.

"There," I said, pointing at an icon located in the southwestern part of China. "See that?"

He nodded.

"If that laser uplink station is still operational, we might be able to communicate with it through the Indian satellite that Jin hacked."

"I don't get it. How is that uplink station going to decrypt the messages?"

I folded my arms across my chest, leaned back, and smiled. "Jin really was a genius."

William shook my shoulders and said, "How is that going to help?"

I looked at him and smiled. "Do you know how those laser uplink systems work?"

He shook his head.

"They shoot a laser through a liquid lens that automatically morphs itself to adjust for the scintillation of the upper atmosphere." I could tell from the puzzled expression on his face that I had lost him. "You know how on a really hot, sunny day when you look out over the dock and everything looks all wavy?"

He nodded.

"That's scintillation. Same thing happens in the upper atmosphere. If you shoot a laser through the distortion without adjusting for the scintillation then the information the laser sends gets all messed up."

Looking even more puzzled, he asked, "But how does the uplink know what the scin-till-ation will be like up in the sky?"

"It uses a quantum computer to figure that out."

He still didn't get it, but I did. I finally understood Jin's plan. He planned to use the quantum computer at the laser uplink station to decrypt the messages. All we had to do now was—

The door flew open and Mohamed charged into the room. He was out of breath. "Aron, you must come quickly."

I stood up. "Take it easy. What's going on?" I knew from the sound of his voice and the fear in his eyes that it wasn't good.

"The pirates just attacked the Tari island chain."

That was only three islands to the south of us.

"Is it still under attack?" I asked.

Mohamed shook his head and tried to catch his breath. "No, but we just got a call for assistance. They have several hundred wounded and a few—" He paused and looked at William as if deciding whether he wanted to finish the sentence. "And there are some dead too."

"Well come on," I said. "Let's go."

I snatched my backpack from the floor and hurried past him, but he grabbed my arm and stopped me.

"There's more."

"Well...what is it?"

Mohamed didn't speak.

"Come on...if there are people hurt, we've got to move."

"The pirates attacked three boats near the island, and there are reports that they killed the men on board and kidnapped the women." His gaze fell to the floor before he said, "Your friend Shannon was on one of those boats."

CHAPTER 14

Our boat approached Tari from the east and I looked out at the plumes of black smoke rising into the early evening sky. Swarming around the smoldering island, a ragtag armada from nearby islands rushed in to help. I grabbed the binoculars from Mohamed and scanned the boats. There wasn't a single MDF patrol boat in the mix. I searched the sky and didn't see any helojumpers either. It didn't really surprise me, but it pissed me off.

The main pier was overflowing with boats, so Kamish pulled around to the south side of the island. He docked next to a hut that sat on stilts over the shallow water. I didn't wait for Kamish to tie the boat to the moorings. Grabbing my bag from the deck, I slung it over my shoulder and sprinted down the narrow boardwalk and out on to the beach.

I had only made it twenty feet before I came across a young girl lying face up in a grotesque heap over a small boulder. Her eyes were open, but they already clouding over. I knew from her blood-stained, naked legs how she met her fate, but I pushed the thought away. Seared on her forehead was the seal of Jamal. I didn't bother to stop. There wasn't any point. Her throat was cut so deep that I could make out the ridges of her trachea.

I passed a dozen more victims. My hatred for Jamal and his pirates grew with each crescent moon and star that I saw branded on their bodies.

I could make out the roofline of the community center up ahead. I stopped and took a few deep breaths before going on. I decided that throwing up in front of the wounded wouldn't instill a sense of confidence. Best to let my stomach do what it wanted out here.

When my stomach was empty, I straightened up and headed for the community center. As I approached the building, I tried to make sense of what was going on outside. The scene that unfolded was pure chaos.

Laid alongside the open-air hut were rows of bodies covered in blood-soaked sheets. A boy, maybe four, sat next to one of the corpses. He wailed as he shook an uncovered foot. A two-man team carrying a body almost tripped on the boy. They dumped their load a few feet from the kid and hurried off. I stood

133

there and watched as body after body was brought in and dropped to the ground, I had to get out of here, so I walked inside the community center. What I found in there was worse.

Screams filled the air. Those unlucky enough to have survived the attack were sprawled out on every inch of open ground. I passed by a woman in her thirties. She sat cross-legged on a thatched mat holding a makeshift tourniquet on the stump of her right arm. I tried not to make eye contact. I failed. Her eyes locked on to mine. I saw her mouth open and close as if she was trying to speak, but nothing came out. I closed my eyes to break her hold on me and kept going.

As I moved through the hut, I scanned the faces looking for Shannon. But all I saw were the faces of people on the verge of death. A woman carrying towels rushed past me. There were others like her, people moving from patient to patient trying to prevent the inevitable. Their clothes were covered in as much blood as their patients.

I felt a hand on my shoulder. I jumped and turned to find Mohamed standing behind me. His warm smile and laughing eyes were replaced by a somber, resolute expression. He had seen this before, the insanity and horror of an emergency medical ward. But I hadn't. After other raids, I had helped carry the bodies to the makeshift morgues. Dealing with the dead was far easier than dealing with the dying.

"Follow me, Aron. I need your help."

"Me? I can't help here. I'll go out there and see if they need help bringing people in."

"These people need us. Just do what I say and stay calm."

I nodded, but I had lost my calm back on the beach next to that girl on the boulder.

I followed him through the ward. We stopped next to a large group of tables that were pushed together. Linens, buckets of water, and bottles of various medicines were spread out across the table. Next to the tables I watched as an elderly woman sang gospel songs, cried, and washed bloody utensils.

A tall, skinny man with a large crooked nose and a shaved head came up to Mohamed and said, "Thank God you're here, old friend."

Mohamed reached out and clasped the man's bloodstained hand. "Hans. Who else is here? Victoria, Raj?"

Hans shook his head. "You and I are the only doctors here so far. Perhaps others will come." The look on his face told me that he didn't hold out much hope of that.

"So this is it?" Mohamed motioned towards the tables. "Is this all we have to work with?"

"I'm afraid so. I've instructed everyone to send the uninjured straight down to the main pier. Everyone else is out there, trying to stabilize the patients." He pointed toward the paved pavilion behind the hut. "What I really need is someone to triage the wounded, so I can focus on helping the most seriously injured."

Mohamed nodded.

"Place a mark on their foreheads...you know the drill. Just like we did with the refugees."

Mohamed nodded again and grabbed me by the arm. He led me out onto the pavilion. There, sprawled across the ground, were men, women and children. They rolled around on the ground and rocked back and forth. They shrieked, mumbled, and cried. There had to be at least a hundred. I looked out towards the jungle and saw more being carried in or staggering in on their own.

Reaching into his shirt pocket, Mohamed pulled out a pencil made out of tree resin. He handed it to me and said, "I'll tell you what to write. Try to write it clearly on their foreheads. Do you understand?"

I nodded and followed him. He examined each person and then yelled out a letter. I wrote the letter on their foreheads. It took several minutes before I finally had the courage to ask, what the letters stood for.

Mohamed examined a deep laceration on the shoulder of an old man and said, "Mark this one with a D." He stood up and walked toward the next patient, but paused to say, "The letter D stands for delay. That means the patient can wait. The letter I stands for Immediate. Those patients need to be seen at once. And M stands for Minor. Those people can be taken straight to the pier for transport off the island."

He bent over the next patient, an unconscious woman in her late twenties. He lifted her eyelid and placed two fingers on her neck to check her pulse. "Mark her with an X." He got up and walked over to a small girl who was missing a leg. She looked like Taylor, my youngest daughter. I marked her forehead an X and quickly looked away.

"What does the X mean?" I asked.

He looked up at me and I saw the answer in his eyes.

***

It was dark before the stream of casualties had finally slowed down. I had no idea what time it was, but it was late…probably early morning.

After the last patient had been stabilized, I walked outside and slumped to the ground against the building. Pulling my knees up to my chest, I encircled them with my arms, closed my eyes, and rested my head on my knees. The smell of death hung in the air.

All night long I looked for Shannon, but she had never come through the triage area. Before I came out here, I had walked through the morgue. I lifted the sheet off of each body and looked at each face. With every sheet I lifted, I prayed that it wouldn't be her. I guess my prayers were answered, but it didn't make me feel any better. I was so numb and so tired that I couldn't feel anything.

"You did well today, my friend," Mohamed said.

I heard him plop to the ground next to me. I leaned my head back against the wall and looked at him through one opened eye. "It didn't make much of a difference. I stopped counting the Xs when I reached sixty."

He patted my arm and said, "It is not about the ones we couldn't save. It is about the ones we did save. Here…this will help."

He dangled a small flask in front of my face. "No thanks. Not tonight. That shit gives me bad dreams."

He opened the flask and took a swig before saying, "I understand. I felt the same way after that first wave of refugees arrived on the islands. Do you remember? I spent weeks on Male helping to treat them. They were all so sick from radiation. I felt helpless because all I could do was make them comfortable before they died. A terrible thing, radiation poisoning."

He took another drink and then motioned towards the jungle canopy with the flask, "Look, the sky is starting to lighten up. The sun will be up soon. Kamish said that he'd be back for us around sunrise."

I looked towards the east and saw the first light of dawn filtering through the leaves. "I guess we should head down to the main dock."

He nodded, but neither of us moved. We just sat there, lost in our own thoughts for a few minutes. Finally, I got up. Then I pulled Mohamed to his feet and we headed toward the main pier.

I counted six boats tied up at the pier. It was a big difference from the day before. Around the pier there looked to be about forty people. Some sat on the beach alone. Others huddled together in small groups. Like us, they were probably waiting for rides.

As we walked past the first group of people, I did a double take. Standing there, smoking a coconut-fiber cigarette. It was Michio. He looked as exhausted as I felt.

"Michio!"

He turned his head and saw me. I heard him apologize to a man who was talking to him and then he walked over to me.

"Aron, I did not realize that you were here."

"I spent the night in the triage area. Have you been here the whole time?"

He nodded. "We were one of the first boats to arrive." He shook his head. "It was very bad. I spent most of the night out there," he nodded towards the water, "We pulled victims out and then kept watch against another attack."

We stared into each other's eyes and an awkward silence enveloped us. I knew that he wouldn't mention it, so I did.

"What happened...with the Council, I mean?"

He bowed his head and said, "I hope that you can forgive me. There was no other way."

"No other way to do what?"

"To save my son, Kazuki." He looked up and said, "They took him. They sent me a message and threatened to kill him if I did not vote for the list. I knew that I could not do it, but I also could not risk having my son…" He cleared his throat and said, "So I resigned and he accepted my resignation."

"Who? Ahmed?"

Michio shook his head. "No, Viyaja."

"I knew it!" I felt the rage begin to build, but a thought flashed through my mind transforming the rage to excitement. "Wait a minute. You have proof!"

"I do not understand. What proof?"

"The message. It's proof that Ahmed and Viyaja blackmailed you. They tried the same with me, but Viyaja threatened me face-to-face."

"I do not understand."

"Don't you see? All we have to do is tell the ship's captain that they coerced a member of the Council. The captain will have no choice but to scrap the list and start from scratch. They'll be here—"

"No! We cannot tell anyone!" He grabbed my arm and said, "Viyaja said that he would kill my boy if I said anything to anyone. I told you, Aron, because I know that I can trust you."

I ran my hand through my hair. I felt like grabbing a clump and pulling it out. "Yeah...of course. I won't tell anyone." I kicked the sand and said, "Those fucking bastards!"

Mohamed interrupted, "You still have the other messages, Aron. Once you decrypt them, you will have the proof that you need."

"What messages?" Michio asked.

I'd forgotten that Michio didn't know about the messages, so I went over the whole story, beginning when Jin came to see me in Male and ending with our breakthrough yesterday.

"That is incredible," Michio said. "Do you really think that you can decrypt the messages in time?"

I shrugged. "If I remember enough of my quantum programming class, then decrypting it will be the easy part. The hard part is figuring out how to connect to the computer. I've never actually operated a satellite before and I have no idea how to make a connection without going through a laser uplink station."

Mohamed patted me on the back and said, "You will do it."

Michio nodded, but then said, "Aron, can I speak with you in private?"

Before I could say anything, Mohamed said, "I will go wait for Kamish over there." He pointed to the pier. "You two talk."

When Mohamed was far enough away, Michio motioned for me to follow and we walked away from the crowd. He looked from side to side. Then, in a hushed tone, he said, "I was the first to arrive here."

It took me a few seconds to realize what he was trying to tell me. Then it hit me. He must have found Shannon's boat. I wasn't sure if I wanted to hear what he had to say, but I said, "Was she—"

He shook his head. "She was not on the boat, but I found this." He pulled out a data mat from his pocket. "It is hers." He paused as if he wanted to give me time to process what he had just said. Finally, he said, "There is some blood on it, but I did not find her body. I think they took her."

I reached out, took the data mat, and held it up to my face. The faded scent of jasmine and mangos was still perceptible.

"Aron," he said.

I looked at him.

"I believe that I know where they have taken her. It is probably the same place where they took my son."

"How do you know where they took them?"

"Before they forced me from the Council, I was researching some of the names that had been added. The sudden addition of such a large number of names from the same island seemed very strange."

"Hanikada!"

He looked at me and furrowed his brow. "Yes. That is correct."

I nodded. "I saw the same thing. Hanikada used to be abandoned. I know, because Jin, Rick, and I put a tower up on that island. But Shannon said that they put some refugees there a few years ago."

"That is correct. But I made some inquiries about Hanikada from a friend who delivers supplies there. My friend told me that over the last several months, the people on that island became very secretive. They never let outsiders past the dock…not even my friend. I suspect that the island has been taken over by the pirates."

My heart began to pound.

Michio continued, "I was preparing to go there last night in search of Kazuki, but that is when I received word that this happened. So I am going tonight instead. If you want to find Shannon, you can come with me."

I stared at him for a moment before saying, "Michio, listen. I understand that you want to get your boy back, really…I do. I want to get Shannon back too. But if the pirates are in control of that island…" I wasn't sure how to say this. "Come on, Michio. You're a bureaucrat, not a samurai."

Michio said, "I can handle myself in a fight."

"I'm sure you can, but how are you going to get on the island without being seen?"

"Tonight is the last night of a new moon, so I believe that we can get onto the island undetected."

I studied him for another moment. "I hope you know karate or something, because I don't."

He smiled and said, "You will make a fine addition to our team."

"Team?"

"My youngest son, Yoshirou, is coming with us."

This was suicide, but what choice did I have. If those bastards had Shannon then I had to try.

"I will come to Lohifushi tonight," Michio said. "Meet me at the pier after sunset."

I held out my hands and said, "Whoa. Tell me about your plan first. How are going to get there? How are we going to find them?"

"I will tell you everything tonight." He reached out, grabbed one of my hands and shook it. "It is said that a single arrow is easily broken, but we will be three. Together, we will have the strength to succeed."

Before I could ask him what that proverbial mumbo jumbo meant, the sound of a helojumper cut through the air. I turned and looked up

It had crept up behind us, flying low over the island. It stopped, hovering thirty or forty feet off shore. A minute later it descended toward the water. The engine whined as it flipped into hovercraft mode and skirted above the water to the shoreline. It rotated around and stopped when the door faced the beach. The engines cut and it settled on to the sand. A moment later, the doors slid open and Ahmed and Viyaja stepped out.

Ahmed whispered something to Viyaja who nodded. Then Viyaja walked briskly over to Hans, who stood next to the pier. Ahmed worked his way through the crowd, shaking hands, patting people on their shoulders, and looking unconvincingly dismayed. I pushed my way over and stepped in front of him. He looked at me and I slugged him. He fell to the ground like a sack of plantains.

Viyaja must have heard the commotion. He sprinted to Ahmed's defense, positioning himself between me and my victim.

"Stop! What do you think you are doing?" Viyaja shouted.

"I'm going to do to him what he did to these people," I replied.

Ahmed rubbed his nose and surveyed the blood on his hand.

"You are crazy!" Viyaja said. "Ahmed has done nothing. You have no right accusing the prime minister of such atrocities."

"If the atrocities fit—"

I took a step towards Ahmed, but Viyaja pushed me back. I swept his arms away with a swift uppercut. I was about to send him into the sand, but stopped when Ahmed yelled, "Enough!"

He crawled up to a kneeling position and repeated, "Enough. There has been enough violence for one day." With a grunt, he stood up and said, "I have done no harm to you or these people. I came here, at great risk to myself, so that I could see what those barbarians have done. Viyaja tried to persuade me to stay in the capital, but a leader's place is with his people...even when there is danger."

For the first time since I met him, Ahmed sounded like a real leader. But I wasn't going to let that stop me from kicking his ass.

"You want to see what they've done? Come on, I'll show you. Just up that path over there are over a hundred bodies. Yesterday they were people going about their daily lives and now they're dead. They didn't deserve to die. The only person on this island that deserves to die is you."

Ahmed confused..

"I know what you've done, so don't try to act innocent with me," I said. "I've seen the messages between you and the pirates."

"What messages?" he demanded.

That son of a bitch actually looked surprised. Years of being a politician must have given him a lot of acting practice.

"You know what I'm talking about. The messages sent from your data mat in Male to the pirate mother ship that's anchored south of here."

"Preposterous!" Viyaja interjected.

Michio grabbed my shoulder and pulled me back. "Aron, this is not the time."

I brushed his hand off and glared at Viyaja. "I've seen the message traffic, you spineless prick." I looked back at Ahmed. "Go ahead, Ahmed. Deny that you sent those messages."

People began to gather in a circle around us.

Ahmed said, "Of course I deny it. It is a lie. I have never sent a message to any pirate."

"You cannot accuse a prime minister without evidence," Viyaja added. "Show us the messages that you claim are from Ahmed."

"I'll show them to the captain of the Mars ship when he gets here."

Viyaja looked as if he was about to come at me. I was ready for him, but Ahmed intervened. Putting his hand on Viyaja's shoulder, Ahmed said, "My cousin, we do not have time for this. He is angry and upset. We will deal with him later. Right now I need you to collect the names of those killed."

"You fucking vultures!" I yelled. "The bodies aren't even cold and all you can think about is replacing the dead people that might be on the list?"

The crowd closed in and for the first time, I noticed their faces. They seethed with hatred and rage. It wasn't going to take much to turn this crowd into a lynch mob.

Ahmed must have sensed it too, because he said, "Go Viyaja, gather the information that I asked you for. The MDF patrol will be here soon. You can return with them. I must go back to the capital now and prepare for the arrival of the Mars ship."

He turned and ran for the helojumper. As soon as he was on board, the doors shut and it took off. I watched it lift straight up, hover for a moment, tilt forward, and then fly away. I turned away, disgusted. I was thinking about going after Viyaja when the energy wave of the explosion punched me in the back and pushed me into the sand.

I rolled over and looked up in time to see flames and a billowing black cloud of smoke in the sky as pieces of helojumper splashed into the ocean.

CHAPTER 15

I felt like a hundred-pound coconut had fallen on my head. I could barely hear the screams and shouts of people over the high-pitched ringing in my ears.

I struggled to make sense of what had just happened. I pushed myself up into a sitting position and looked back out to the water. The boats that were tied up at the pier were now coming back from the area where I spotted wreckage floating on the water. How did they get underway so quickly? Maybe I had blacked out. The part of my brain that kept track of time wasn't back online yet.

The ringing in my ears began to go away, but the pain in my head was at full throttle. I stood up, holding my arms straight out to keep my balance. When I felt like I wouldn't fall, I dropped my arms and surveyed the scene.

A few people ran to the safety of the jungle. Most of the others had moved onto the pier, awaiting the return of the boats. Some, like me, just stood there transfixed by whole fiasco.

I still couldn't wrap my brain around it. A helojumper had just exploded. Electric turbine engines just don't explode like that. If it twisted itself inside out and fell apart, I could understand it. Hell, I'd always expected that to happen.

The first boat reached the pier. I watched as the crew handed pieces of helojumper to the people on the pier. Suddenly a woman on the pier screamed and dropped whatever she was holding. A man came over and picked it up. I squinted and saw that it was an arm.

It was hard to make out everything that was unloaded. But occasionally, I saw things that made my skin crawl, things like an upper torso without arms, legs, or a head.

Viyaja ran to where they were unloading the boats. He started yelling at the men and women on the dock. A middle-aged woman took off running into the jungle. The others frantically created two smaller piles from the one big pile they had started…body parts in one, everything else in the other.

A few minutes later, the woman who had taken off had returned with a bloodstained sheet. She must have borrowed it from one of the corpses up by the hut. I was sure that the corpse didn't mind, but it seemed to really bother Viyaja. He threw the sheet into the harbor, slapped the woman, and continued screaming. He was out of control.

I don't know why I walked over there, but I did. Others from the beach followed me. When I got within a few feet of Viyaja, I said, "Settle down. They're doing the best they can."

Wild eyed and visibly shaking, he turned on me and yelled, "Don't you tell me to settle down! They killed the leader of the Maldives!"

"What are you talking about? Nobody here killed anybody."

"Yes they did, yes they did. They did it!" He pointed at the crowd that had gathered to watch the spectacle. "One of them must have planted a bomb on the helojumper. How else do you explain what happened?"

"Look, you're upset and you're not thinking straight."

"Don't you tell me I am not thinking straight!" he yelled. He looked out at the crowd and asked, "Which one of you did this? Tell me!"

Everyone began to back away. I wanted to slap him. I didn't think that it would calm him down, but it'd make me feel better. Just as I was about to try, the high-pitched whine of twin electric engines filled the air.

Everyone turned and watched an MDF patrol boat made a high-speed entrance into the harbor. I recognized the hull number. It was the same one that I saw on the satellite photo that Jin took. The engines slammed into reverse and the boat skidded sideways up to the pier.

Uniformed men with their guns drawn jumped onto the dock. I turned and saw Michio and Mohamed in the crowd. I worked my way over.

"We've gotta get out of here," I said as I reached them.

"What is the matter, Aron?" Mohamed asked.

I pointed at the boat without looking, "That's the boat, the one in the satellite photo."

Michio looked at me and said, "There is no place to go. They can chase down any boat here. Besides, if we flee it will look like we are guilty."

I looked back over my shoulder and saw an MDF officer talking with Viyaja. Two other men stood behind him.

"Aron," Michio said. "If they came here to harm us, wouldn't they have done it by now?"

"I don't know. I guess. But there are dozens of MDF patrol boats in the fleet. What are the odds that the one in that photo would arrive here first?"

"Pirates!" Mohamed said. "You think they are—"

"Shhh." I put my hand up to Mohamed's face. "Keep your voice down. I didn't say they were pirates. Just give me a minute to think."

Michio was probably right. If they were here to kill us, they would have opened up the heavy machine guns that were mounted on their boat. From this distance and with the aid of their auto targeting system, they could wipe out ninety-nine percent of the crowd in a few seconds. But I didn't think they were here to kill everyone...just me.

I looked back and saw Viyaja pointing at me. Yup, I was right. The MDF officer nodded, called for a couple of his men, and they headed straight towards me. The two smaller guards held their rifles across their chests at the ready. The officer kept his pistol in his holster, but hand hovered next to it. He didn't look like he needed a weapon.

The officer was as big as a sumo wrestler, only with less of a gut. At first I thought he might be Samoan, but his facial features weren't right.

Hanging from his wide black belt was a short, curved sword with a silver ornamental handle. It was a Khukuri. I'd seen them in India. Son of a bitch...he was a Gurkha!

I'd heard way too many stories about Gurkha exploits, how they went berserk in battle and how they could kill twenty men at a time. I'm sure some of it was overblown hype, legends, myths. But standing there in front of him, I suddenly believed every story I'd ever heard. This wasn't going to be a fair fight. He had a Khukuri. I had a data mat.

I stepped out in front of Michio and Mohamed and faced them. My legs shook. I tried to convince myself that it was the adrenaline pouring into my bloodstream. Of course, that wouldn't explain why I needed to piss...fear would.

They stopped in front of me. He was even bigger than I had thought. He stared down at me through his large, dark eyes.

Holding his stare as best I could, I waited for him to pull out his sword and disembowel me. But he didn't move. The sound of Viyaja's voice broke the trance.

"I know that you had something to do with the helojumper. Save us all the trouble of a trial and confess."

"You have got to be kidding me," I said, looking over a Viyaja, who now stood next to the Gurkha. "I was right there with you and Ahmed from the time you landed to the time that thing took off. I never stepped near it. Do you think I made a bomb out of thin air and magically put it on the helojumper?"

If I could do that, I'd have a grenade in my hand right now.

"You may not have done it yourself," Viyaja said, "Perhaps you had one of your friends here do it while you distracted me."

I glared at him. Gurkha or no Gurkha, I was ready to slug that son of a bitch. I took a deep breath to calm down. "If you want to come after me for something I didn't do…fine." I took a step towards him and said, "But keep my friends out of this."

The Gurkha stepped in front of Viyaja and pulled his sword out of his belt. I took two steps back.

"So what are you going to do, Viyaja?" I asked "Huh? Have your bodyguard execute me right here in front of all these people without a trial?"

I pointed at the sword and addressed the Gurkha whose expression was still a steely mask. "Well…what are you waiting for? Go ahead, tough guy." I'd heard that every time a Gurkha draws his sword that he must feed it with blood. I figured it was just a fairytale to scare young children. I was wrong. Young children weren't the only ones scared by the tale.

I looked around and raised my voice so everyone who had gathered around could hear me. "When word of this gets to the captain of the Mars ship, he might have second thoughts about this being the last civilized human settlement on the planet. He might have to make his own list."

I saw the conflict in Viyaja's face, but it was short lived. He smiled and said, "You will get your fair trial, but it will be after the ship departs."

Then, addressing the Gurkha he said, "Escort Mr. Atherton and his friends to Lohifushi. Stay with him…as his guest." His smile widened and he continued. "And be sure to inform the MDF patrols that Mr. Atherton is not to step foot on Male until after the last shuttle for the Mars ship leaves. Do you understand?"

The Gurkha nodded. Viyaja turned to leave but stopped, looked back at the Gurkha and said, "Feed your Khukuri."

The Gurkha raised his sword, the morning sun reflected off of it and blinded me. I tensed in for the blow. But I wasn't on the sword's menu. The Gurkha held out his other hand and sliced the palm wide open. Blood oozed from the wound onto the sand, forming small red craters.

***

The MDF patrol boat followed us back. I couldn't understand why. It wasn't like we could go anywhere, not with the goddammed Gurkha onboard. Mohamed, Kamish, and I didn't say a word on the way back. The Gurkha just stared at us. I avoided looking at him by staring out at the ocean, and soon my thoughts drifted to Shannon.

I wondered if she were alive or dead. The pain of not knowing brought back memories of the days after the storm when I had wondered the same thing about Kelly and the girls. Part of me hoped that she had died, because the thought of what those bastards would do to her if they took her was almost too much to bear.

Just before twelve o'clock, we reached Lohifushi. As we entered the harbor, I turned in my seat and faced the Gurkha. His eyes were glued to me.

"So...what do I call you?"

Nothing. Just the stare.

"Come on. Viyaja said that you are my guest. What kind of host would I be if I didn't know the name of my guests?"

"Captain Pun Narbahadur, Maldivian Defense Force," he said.

"Alright if I call you Pun?"

No response. Just the stare.

"Pun it is," I said. "So look, my place is a bit crowded. I'm sharing my hut with a kid. His name is William. So the first of the guest rules that we should talk about is that you don't look at, talk to, or in any way upset him. His father died a few weeks back and a few days ago his mother passed away. So leave him out of this. Got it?"

Silence. But this time I saw an almost imperceptible nod. It could have been from the rocking of the boat, but I decided to take it as an agreement to the rule.

"Good. The second rule is that you have to figure out where you will stay. There are plenty of open huts. I'll have Helen help you find one if you'd like."

And we're back to staring. Great.

We pulled up along the pier and for once, William wasn't there to meet me. I felt relief. I didn't want to explain what was going on, not out here.

As I stepped off the boat, I felt a few raindrops on my arm. I looked up; the partly cloudy skies that had covered us during most of the trip back had turned into black rainclouds.

By the time I reached my hut, the rain was coming down in sheets. Dripping wet, I pushed open the door and turned to face Pun.

"Sorry. As you can see, the inn is full. Give me a few minutes and I'll send Helen a message so we can find you some place to dry off."

Water cascaded down his granite face. He looked at me and didn't say a word.

I shrugged and closed the door.

Dropping my bag to the floor, I shook the water from my hair and clothes. If only I could shake off the feeling of doom about tonight's raid this easily.

"Hey, quit it!" William said. "You're getting water all over my screen."

I looked over to find William in his familiar position, cross-legged on the bed and huddled over his data mat.

"So what? They're waterproof."

"It makes the screen look all weird." He wiped his data mat against his t-shirt, examined it, and repeated the process until it seemed to meet his approval. "Who's that?" he asked.

"He's going to be with us for a few days."

"Why?"

"It's a long story. But in a nutshell, somebody thinks that I blew up a helojumper."

William looked up, eyes wide. "Did you?"

"Come on," I said. "You know me well enough to know I wouldn't do something like that. I don't know what happened to that helojumper."

He seemed to relax a little.

"But until I can clear it up, our friend out there will hanging around."

"That's creepy."

"Tell me about it," I said.

I peeled off my wet clothes and dropped them onto the floor. Then I rummaged through the small dresser for something dry to wear. When I finished changing, I sent Helen a message asking her about which hut she would recommend for our guest. She sent back two recommendations that were nearby.

I opened the door and faced the back of a very wet Gurkha. He turned and looked at me.

"There are two huts nearby. One is just three huts down. I can take you there now if you want."

"I will remain here," he said.

"I can tell this rain isn't going to let up for a while. Are you sure? I promise I won't go anywhere without letting you know first."

He just stared at me and then did an about face. I shrugged and closed the door. Looking at William, I said, "He must like the view from the front deck."

William shrugged without looking up from his data mat.

I walked over and leaned over his shoulder to see what he was working on.

"Is that what it looks like?" I asked.

He shrugged. "I don't know. What do you think it looks like?"

"Like a decryption algorithm. More specifically, like the decryption algorithm that I told you about yesterday before I left. How the hell did you figure out how to code one?" I snatched the data mat from his hands.

"It's not as hard as you made it sound." He grabbed the data mat back . "It reminded me of an app that I saw my dad use once. I found it on his data mat. I started playing around with it and well...."

Shit, I forgot about that tool. When we were still in the early stages of designing the network, Rick had built a quick-n-dirty utility to decrypt test messages so we could see if they showed up on the distant end properly.

"But that tool only works if you have both sets of encryption keys," I said.

He looked up at me as if I was an idiot, and to be honest, I was beginning to feel like one.

"What I meant was," I said, "how did you figure out how to write a quantum decryption algorithm?"

"I didn't," he said. "See?" He pointed to a section in the code. "I stubbed out a place for it. You said you knew quantum programming. Besides, I had to leave something for you to do." He smiled.

"Very funny." I said, "And don't be putting words into my mouth. I didn't say that I knew quantum programming. I said that I took a class once. If you keep up with the wise cracks I'll let you figure that part out too."

We ended up working on the code together while the storm raged outside. Struggling to remember quantum coding actually helped keep my mind off Shannon and the raid tonight. Twice, I got up to check on our guest. He hadn't moved an inch.

By dinnertime, we had completed the first version of the decryption algorithm. Now the only problem was testing it. But to test it, we first had to establish a connection with the Chinese computer through the satellite. There was no way we'd be able to connect now, not with these storm clouds. We decided to take a break and headed over to the dining hut. Pun followed. I couldn't wait to introduce him to Helen.

***

"Hey Helen, any food left?"

William and I entered the kitchen followed by a rain-soaked Gurkha. Helen turned and I watched her cheerful smile dissolve.

"Who's this then?" She asked.

"This is Pun, he's the *guest* that I mentioned in the message."

She looked from me to Pun to me and then back to Pun again. Her hands rested on her hips and she said, "Bless me, you're soaking wet...Pun is it?"

He didn't respond. He just stood there.

"Well, I can see that Aron didn't do a very good job of caring for his guest. Let's get you some towels." She went over to a cabinet, opened the door, and pulled out a stack of towels.

"I tried," I said. "But he preferred hanging out in the rain."

"Nonsense," Helen said bringing the towels to the Gurkha. "Here, dry yourself off before you catch a cold."

I looked at Pun. He stared at Helen and then at the towels. He seemed conflicted.

"Come on. Start drying off or I'll dry you off myself. I can do it. I had six boys you know, all of them bigger than you." She pushed the towels into his arms.

He took them, but didn't move. So Helen grabbed the towel on the top of the stack and started to dry his face. "Honestly," she said. "A grown man like you acting like a child."

He reached out and grabbed her by the wrist. The stack of towels wobbled in his other hand. I looked around the kitchen. My eyes fell on the meat cleaver hanging on the side of the butcher's block. I was just about to make a move for it when Pun said, "Thank you, miss. It is very kind of you, but I will dry myself." He took the towel from her and started to mop his face.

I took several breaths to calm myself.

"That's a good boy," Helen said, giving me a sideways glance. "And I'll go pour a nice cup of soup for each of you. That's the trick for a rainy day…hot soup."

We ate at the small table in the kitchen. I tried telling myself that he was just following orders, but it was hard…especially with him staring at me all the time.

Helen did most of the talking. We listened. Helen asked Pun a few questions. At first he didn't talk, but he was smart enough to answer when she repeated her questions. Helen was a force of nature equal to or greater than the mountain of a man sitting next to her.

She got him to tell her where he was from. I was right. He was from Malaysia. He'd been a Gurkha since he was in his twenties. He was part of an elite team that protected a Sri Lankan government minister. He came to the Maldives with the group of refugees that had settled on Hanikada. The minister died and so Pun joined the MDF and took a vow to protect the inhabitants of the Maldives. That was pretty much all the information she got out of him.

When we finished our meal, we thanked Helen and walked back to the hut. Pun transformed back into his old quiet self. We passed one of the empty huts that Helen had recommended for Pun. I pointed it out, but he followed us back to my hut. William and I went inside. Pun took his post in front of the door.

I checked my watch. It read 8:00 p.m. Michio would be here soon. I had to figure out some way to ditch Pun. It would come to me. But until it did, William and I kept trying to connect to the Chinese satellite.

The storm had subsided, but the clouds were still pretty thick. Even if the clouds weren't blocking our signal, there was no guarantee that we could connect to the computer. It was a long shot at best.

I looked over at William. He was lying flat on his back and staring up at the ceiling. I could tell that he was frustrated.

"Let's try the sequence again," I said.

"Why? It's still raining."

I switched screens on the data mat, pulled up the satellite console, and clicked on the tab titled Communications. A new screen appeared with a window that listed the available communication channels. There were only two. One was the Single Frequency Laser (SFL) channel, which had been the industry standard for all satellite communication channels since 2037. The other was the Advanced Extremely High Frequency (AEHF) channel, the one that Jin had used to hack into the satellite.

TYPE	FREQ	INCOMING	OUTGOING	STATUS
SFL	100KHz	25Gb	27Gb	INACTIVE
AEHF	250GHz	150K	256K	ACTIVE

I clicked on the AEHF channel and another window opened. It displayed more detail. At the top of the screen was a SCAN button. I pressed it for the twentieth time tonight and was presented with the same data entry screen. By now, I had the latitude and longitude of the Chinese quantum computer memorized. I entered the data into the respective fields and pressed the button. As I waited for the CANNOT CONNECT error, I thought about Shannon again. I wondered how she was holding up.

Suddenly, a message appeared.

CONNECTION ESTABLISHED.

"Holy shit, we're in."

"Really?" William jumped up from his bed and looked over my shoulder.

"Well, that's what it says." I pinged the satellite from my data mat and watched as successful data packets scrolled down the screen. "Yup, we're in."

William reached for my data mat, but I pulled it away. "Hold on, cowboy. Go and get your data mat and give me the name of the quantum computer so we can see if we can connect to it too."

He jumped off my bed and grabbed his data mat. A few seconds later he said, "Weishan. It's spelled W-E-I-S-H-A-N."

I used the satellite to scan for available nodes and the only one that appeared was WEISHAN. This was a lot easier than I thought it would be. I pressed the CONNECT button and waited. A second later, the following message appeared on my screen:

UNABLE TO CONNECT

"I don't get it," William said. "Why can't you connect to the computer? It's right there."

I ran my hand through my hair and said, "I don't know. The computer isn't recognizing the commands that I'm sending. I think it's using some weird kind of command language that I don't know. Here, watch."

I clicked WEISHAN and a new screen opened. It had a user name and password field, so I entered the ones that were next to WEISHAN on the Jin spreadsheet. Below that were four other fields without any labels. "These fields are the problem. I think it wants routing strings, but the fields won't accept IPPR network routes."

"What's that?" William asked.

"IPPR? It stands for Intelligent Prioritized Packet Routing. It was the standard network protocol before the storm. The one we use for the IICN is similar, but it's not as sophisticated. The standard routing strings for the IPPR are twenty-four characters and these fields only accept sixteen." I tossed the data mat onto the bed next to me. "We're so goddammed close."

Why the hell would Jin leave us all the login credentials for the computer, but not for the fucking routing strings?

I got up and walked to the window. Water rippled on the glass against a backdrop of blackness. Somewhere out there Shannon was—no! I slammed my hand against the wall. I wasn't going there.

"Don't worry, Aron. We'll figure out how to connect to the computer."

I turned my head and saw the concern in William's eyes. He still didn't know about Shannon or what I'd promised to do tonight.

"Sorry. It's not about the computer."

He looked puzzled and said, "Then what is it?"

"Do you remember that girl, the one that came over that day?"

He smiled and said, "You mean your *girlfriend*?"

"I told you she wasn't...yeah okay...my girlfriend. After she left that day, her boat was—"

I swallowed hard and he finished the sentence for me.

"Her boat was attacked by the pirates, wasn't it? I heard Mohamed say something when he came for you yesterday."

I nodded and cleared my throat.

"Is she...dead?" he asked.

"I don't know, but I don't think so. A friend found her data mat on the boat and he thinks he knows where they took her."

William looked worried and said, "You're going after her, aren't you?"

I nodded. "I have to. I can't just leave her with them. But I'm not going alone. My friend's son might be there too. We're going together."

William's eyes began to tear up. I walked over to him, laid a hand on his shoulder, and said, "It's okay. I'm not going to do anything stupid. Look at me." I lifted his chin until his eyes met mine. "I'm no warrior, I'm a geek." I smiled, but he still looked worried. "My friend and I aren't going to fight anyone, we're just going to sneak onto the island, get Shannon and his son, and then sneak off before anyone knows we're there. That's it. I promise." The lie almost got stuck in my throat.

Tears fell freely down his cheeks and he shouted, "My dad said the same thing before he left! He said that he'd watch out for the bad guys and now he's dead and mom's dead and you're going to die too!"

He jumped off the bed and ran to the door. I reached out and grabbed his arm.

"Look. I have to go, okay? And I need your help."

He tried to pull away, but I held firm. Finally, he looked up and said, "Help with what?"

"With getting away. That guy out there, Pun, he won't let me go. I'm not supposed to leave the island."

Sniffling, he said, "So? What can I do?"

I let go of his arm and smiled. "I need a diversion. Do you know what that means?"

He shook his head.

"I need you to distract the guard long enough for me to get to the pier."

William wiped his eyes with the back of his hand and said, "Okay. How?"

I told him the plan. He smiled. That kid really was fearless. I wouldn't have had the guts to do what I had just asked him to do...not at his age.

I sent a message to Mohamed and waited for the reply. When it came, I asked, "Ready?"

He nodded.

"Okay, do it just like before, but louder."

William and I stood a few steps from the door. I nodded and William yelled, "That's not fair. I hate you. I really hate you." Then he ran to the door and opened it. Pun turned to look. William pushed him, but Pun didn't budge. William squeezed by him and started to run, but fell as he jumped off the deck.

"Ow!" William screamed. "My leg, my leg."

I pushed Pun out of the way and ran to William.

"It's okay, William. Let me see." I pretended to examine his leg and looked up at Pun. "I think it's broken. I need your help to get him over to the infirmary."

Pun looked down at us. That look of conflict returned to his face again.

"Come on. You're going to follow me over there anyway. I'm just asking you to carry him for me. I can't lift him with this hand." I held up my hand, which was still covered in scabs from the close call in the kayak. "It's broken," I lied. "I can't lift him."

Pun hesitated, but finally came over, bent down, and gently picked up William. William screamed out in pain. Damn, that kid was a good actor.

I motioned with my other hand. "This way."

We walked quickly over to the infirmary. I knocked and Mohamed opened the door.

Looking first at Pun, who held William, and then at me, he asked, "What is it? What is wrong?"

"It's William. I think he broke his ankle," I said.

"Come in, quickly," Mohamed said.

Pun went in first and I followed.

"Over there. Put him on the table," Mohamed ordered. "Gently."

Pun did as he was ordered.

"Good," Mohamed said. "Now hold him firmly by the shoulders. I don't want him to fall off the table when I examine his leg." Then looking up at me, he said. "Aron, I need you to bring me some extra gauze. It's out on the deck, in the big box marked Emergency Supplies."

Pun looked at me. William gave another award-winning scream. Pun looked back at him. I did too. I winked and went outside.

I ran to the pier without stopping. Michio was waiting for me on his friend's boat.

CHAPTER 16

The vibration of the ship's diesel hybrid engines resonated through my body. I stared into the mug that I cradled in my hands and watched the chicory dance to its rhythm. I was buying time. Michio had just gone over the plan. Everyone was waiting for me to say something. But what could I say?

I glanced at the scars on my wrists and realized that this plan wasn't that much different from what I had attempted twelve years ago. The only difference was that this would be a mass suicide. But that wasn't the sort of pep talk that this ragtag group needed. Unfortunately, I couldn't bring myself to lie and tell them that it was a great plan. It wasn't.

"Aron?" Nisha asked softly near my ear. I looked up. Her almond-shaped eyes sparkled like they did eight years ago when I first met her on Dhonakulhi. Even her round, dark-skinned face hadn't changed much. It was easy to see why Anand fought so hard to marry her. Sure, she was a little plumper, but anyone who squeezed out six kids in eight years earned the right to carry around a little extra weight.

"Yeah?" I said.

"Would you like another cup? Yours looks cold."

Her smile was infectious. I smiled back. "Sure, thanks, Nisha."

She took the cup, inched past Michio, and smiled at Anand before walking down the stairs into the galley. I still couldn't believe that Anand was the friend that Michio had talked about.

When I had boarded the ship and saw Anand standing at the top of the gangplank, I almost ran up and hugged him. After he saved my ass on North Point, there was nobody I trusted more on a mission like this. But after we had gotten underway, I saw a group of kids playing ball in the cargo hold. Anand had brought his entire family along. I begged him to go back and drop them off.

He had tried to assure me that it was okay. His family always traveled with him on long supply runs. But this wasn't a normal supply run and we both knew it. In the end, he finally confessed that he didn't want to leave his family alone and unprotected. I couldn't blame him.

Nisha returned a minute later with a steaming mug. She bowed slightly as she offered it to me.

"Thanks," I said with a nod. She smiled and returned to the galley. When she was gone, I looked around the bridge. Anand stood at the helm, one hand on the wheel and the other on the throttles. Michio leaned against the outer bulkhead on my right. His son, Yoshirou, stood beside him. Both wore black, loose fitting clothes that looked like martial arts uniforms. Michio had never mentioned that he knew martial arts, but then again I had never asked him. I just assumed that a bureaucrat like him collected stamps or butterflies. It never dawned on me that he might know how to break a concrete block with his forehead.

Yoshirou looked to be in his late teens. He had wide, glossy eyes and straight black hair. Like his father, he walked like a panther stalking its prey. Unlike his father, Yoshirou had a goatee, or at least what I assumed was supposed to be a goatee. It was faint and patchy; the kind of facial hair that makes a kid think that he looks like a man. I thought he looked like a kid who had just finished eating a chocolate ice cream cone.

Kamish stood to my left, hunched slightly so his head didn't bump against the ceiling. Before we left Lohifushi, Michio had raised concerns about Kamish coming along, because he didn't know him. He had said that he wanted to keep the group small. But I had insisted. What kind of chance did we have against an island full of bloodthirsty pirates? With Kamish along, at least we had a little muscle on our side. Besides, Kamish wouldn't take no for an answer, not after what the pirates did to his brothers.

When he saw me running to the pier he stopped me and asked where I was going. As I told him, I saw the flash of vengeance in his eyes. He didn't say a word. He just followed me on board.

I took another sip of chicory and finally spoke. "I don't know what you want me to say, Michio. If you want me to say that it's a good plan...well, I'm not going to do that. I think the plan gives us almost no chance of getting out of there alive."

"Do you see, father?" Yoshirou said, throwing his hands up in the air. "I told you that we should have done this alone. He will only hinder us and I—"

"Silence," Michio said. His eyes narrowed and jaw clenched as he stared down his son. Yoshirou averted his eyes and Michio continued, "Aron is a good man and you disrespect him and me with your childish words. Remain silent and allow him to finish his thoughts." Michio looked at me and said, "I apologize for my son. Please...continue."

"Michio, the kid has a right to say what he thinks," I said. "He's putting his neck on the line too. Besides, I'd rather know what he really thinks now, before we get there. We all have to be honest with each other if this is going to work." I swallowed hard. "So I'm telling you what I really think because that's what you asked for. I think that plan is way too risky...but I'm in."

I looked over at Kamish and asked, "How about you?"

He looked at each one of us before responding, "They will pay for what they did to my brothers."

The hairs on the back of my neck stood on end.

"Okay, so we're all in. Now let's go over the first part of the plan again," I said. "I'm not quite sure how we're supposed to paddle in on surf boards from that far off shore on a moonless night."

Michio walked back over to the map that was laid out on the table. He placed his finger on the map and said, "You see these large outcroppings just to the north of the island."

Everyone except Anand huddled around the map to see what he was pointing at. Anand probably had the map memorized. But I looked. I saw two tiny dots on the map that marked the location of the outcroppings. They looked to be about a quarter mile apart from one another.

"So?" I said.

"So, we use this to help us find the island."

"That'd be great if we could see them."

Michio looked at me with the hint of a smile. "We will see with our ears," he said.

I cocked my head to one side and waited for him to explain.

"All we have to do is listen to the sound of waves crashing on either side of us. As long as we hear that, we know we are moving south toward the island."

I looked closer at the map and said, "I'm pretty sure my surfing guide brought a group of us down here twelve years ago. And if I remember right, he called those outcroppings the Razors or the Razor's edge or something. I'm guessing they called it that for a reason?"

Michio nodded.

I continued, "So it would probably be a bad thing if we got too close?"

The smile disappeared and Michio said, "We will be alright as long as we stay in the middle and we stay close to one another."

I nodded and said, "Okay. I don't like it, but okay. We paddle in between the outcroppings. But why don't we leave the same way we go in? Wouldn't it be easier?"

He shook his head. "No. The prevailing winds are currently blowing from the north, so instead of fighting the wind, we will use it to help us get off the island." He stabbed his finger on the map again and said, "Here on the south side."

Kamish said, "That is close to the main pier. You said that it will be guarded."

"That is true," Anand said without looking over. "And they have snipers in at least two places on either side of the pier."

"How do you know that?" I asked.

"I've been delivering supplies there ever since the refugees arrived."

"So you saw the pirates up close?"

Anand shook his head. "No. Up until a few months ago, there was nothing unusual about the island. But then things began to change."

I set my mug on the table. "Change how?"

"The people who normally met me at the pier for deliveries were replaced by men I had never seen before. They dressed like the refugees, but they looked like middle easterners. Others had very dark skin, like Africans." He continued to look out the front window and said, "One day, I arrived and they would not allow me to get off the boat or talk to anyone. They said it was a new security rule. Occasionally, when I would drop off supplies, I would see familiar faces, but when I waved to them they hurried off. I mentioned this to an MDF patrol once."

"What did they say?" I asked.

Anand looked at me and said, "They said they would check it out, but I never heard anything more about it. That was a few weeks ago. So when Michio asked me if I had seen anything strange during my supply runs, I told him about the island. He asked me to keep a closer eye out for anything unusual. That's when I noticed the snipers hidden in the bushes near the pier."

Michio walked over and put a hand on Anand's shoulder. "Thanks to Anand, we now have a much better chance for success."

I don't know whether it was Anand's story or the smell of the diesel exhaust, but I felt nauseous. "So how do we get the surf boards from the north side of the island to the south side?" I asked.

"Yoshirou will take care of that. He will tie the boards together and swim around the island and then wait for us."

"But father," Yoshirou said, "You know that I can fight better than him," he said, pointing at me. "He should take the surf boards around the—"

"Enough, Yoshirou!" Michio said. "We have had this discussion and I will not have it again. You will do as you are told."

Yoshirou looked like he was about to say something, but looked away.

The kid was probably right, but if anyone was going to risk his life to get Shannon back, it was going to be me. After the fight we had on Lohifushi, I didn't know how she felt about me anymore. But I knew how I felt about her. The feeling had been there ever since I saw her on the day of Rick's funeral. And the feeling had grown. At some point, it broke through the wall I had built around my heart, the wall I had built to protect me from the pain I felt after my family died. She rescued me from that prison and now it was my turn to rescue her.

Yoshirou stormed out of the bridge.

"I apologize for my son," Michio said. "He is young and rash, but he is a good boy."

We all nodded.

"Please excuse me," he said and went after Yoshirou.

I was about to go out on the deck for some air, but Kamish came over to me and pulled out an eight-inch curved blade from his belt. It was still in its sheath.

"Here," he said.

"I've never been very good with knifes," I said.

"Take it." He held it out in front of me. "It belonged to Senil." His eyes gleamed with fresh tears as he said the name of his brother.

I took it and felt the weight of it in my hands. I didn't know what to say. So all I said was, "Thanks."

***

I laid on the long board, paddling toward the island. I had to admit that Michio's plan to hear our way to the island was actually working. In fact, it had worked so well that after a half an hour I closed my eyes. With no moon, I couldn't see anything anyway. Even with the ghostly glow of the floating bioluminescence, there wasn't enough light for me to see more than five or six feet in front of me.

My other senses quickly kicked in. I could gauge the distance between the outcroppings from the sound of the waves that crashed into them. I felt the chill of the water that engulfed my arms with each stroke. I tasted the salt from the water that dripped down my face and onto my lips. Even my sense of time was keener. Somehow, I was able to anticipate the swells that passed underneath me. Like I said, the plan worked pretty well. Right up until it didn't.

My first inkling that something was wrong was when the sound of the waves went from either side of me to all around me. I opened my eyes to get my bearings, but all I could make out was the ghostly white surface of my surfboard. The bioluminescence was gone. There was no way to tell how close I was to the island, but I sensed that it was close. The plan called for strict silence, so I didn't call out to anyone.

My heart began to pound against the board. I stopped paddling, hoping to hear the sound of the others. They should be near me.

Nothing.

The sound of waves seemed louder to my right, but it extended out in front of me now. I swung up to a sitting position, desperate to see anything. My left foot scraped against something. Pain shot up my leg. It felt like I'd been stung or bitten by something. I pulled it back, but then my other foot smashed into something. It had to be a rock or coral. I could tell that the toenail on my big toe was gone. Water this shallow meant that I was either over a reef or close to shore. I silently prayed for the latter. Either way, I was about to find out.

I grabbed the board with both hands and lifted myself into a kneeling position. The sound of the waves was deafening now and I still couldn't tell which direction to go. I had to decide or else those bitches, the Fates, would decide for me. If I was going to die, I preferred that it was on my terms.

Leaning forward, I paddled to the left. When the sound of the waves seemed to be in front of me, I paddled as hard and fast as I could. My board scraped against the bottom and I struggled to stay upright. In the back of my mind, I knew what would happen if I fell. A wave would drag me across the bottom. I wasn't about to let that happen.

It was time to find out where I was.

I grabbed my board once again and set my feet down in the water on either side.

Sand! I felt sand.

A wave hit me from behind, knocking me forward. But my feet remained anchored to the bottom. Water rushed around me. Moving as quickly as I could, I pulled the board through my legs and hoisted it above my head. Another wave hit me. I managed to keep my balance. I still couldn't see anything except for the surfboard hanging over my head. Another wave crashed against me, this one stronger. I kept moving forward. Finally, I found beach. I set the surfboard down, took a few more steps, and crouched down beside it. I heard leaves rustling in the wind and could just make out the silhouette of the tree line.

I'd made it, but I was alone.

CHAPTER 17

I looked at my watch. It was too dark to read it. I pressed the button on the side. The watch face lit up and cast a ghostly teal glow. I quickly let go. It was almost two thirty in the morning.

On Lohifushi, very few people would be awake at this hour. There wasn't much to do at night ever since they stopped playing karaoke at the bar. They didn't stop because people didn't come, they stopped because there wasn't a bar anymore. It had been converted to a school room for the kids. I hoped that it would be quiet here as well. Somehow, I doubted it.

Someone grabbed my arm. I turned and took a swing. Kamish caught my fist in his hand. Then in a hushed voice, he said, "Aron, it is me."

Relief swept over me and I got to my feet. "Thank God. I thought—"

"Shh. There are guards patrolling nearby."

Whispering, I said, "Where is everyone?"

"Down at the beach, at the rally point." Kamish whispered. "Grab your board. We must go."

I knew it. I had gotten lost, not them.

I picked up my surfboard and followed him about a hundred yards down the beach. Kamish's arm shot out in front of me like a crossing road guards. I stopped. Then he whistled. It sounded like the call of the Koel, a migratory bird from India. They had been all over Lohifushi when I had first arrived. I hated them. Their mating calls woke me up every morning. Thankfully, there weren't many around anymore.

His call was answered by another bird call. Kamish motioned for me to follow. We moved cautiously another twenty feet. Michio and his son crouched behind a large boulder.

Yoshirou came over and took my surfboard. Even in the dark, I could tell that he was scowling. I watched him carry it back to the water's edge, where I could just make out the silhouette of him tying it to another board. It looked like he had daisy-chained all the boards together.

"Aron, are you alright?" Michio whispered.

"Yeah. Sorry."

"We were worried."

"I'm fine. I thought you guys were still out there. I can't believe we made it."

"That was the easy part. There is no room for mistakes going forward."

I nodded.

Michio ran over to Yoshirou and whispered something to him. Yoshirou nodded and waded out into the surf, pulling the first board with him. I watched the rest of the boards follow behind him like a train. Once he was out of sight, Michio ran back to us and said, "Let's go."

We entered the jungle following a narrow path that seemed to lead towards the interior. Unlike Lohifushi, branches and palm fronds covered the ground. It was hard to move without stepping on something. Luckily, the wind was pretty strong. The noise from the canopy masked our movement.

Michio led the way, I was in the middle, and Kamish stayed in the rear. We moved fast. Within a few minutes, we came upon a clearing. There were six huts set next to each other in a semi-circle. They looked deserted, except for the one on the far end. The light from its window was enough to illuminate the area.

Michio turned and motioned for Kamish and me to wait. Then he ran, hunched over, to the closest hut. He opened the door and went inside. My heart beat so fast that I was afraid that somebody might hear it.

I looked back at Kamish. He scanned the area around us. I wondered how long we should wait. I didn't have to wonder for very long. He came out of the hut and closed the door. Then he repeated the process four more times, moving from one hut to the next. Kamish and I moved along the tree line, staying out of sight.

When he had cleared the fifth hut, I readied myself. I pulled out the blade that Kamish had given me on the boat.

Come on, Senil…bring me luck.

I watched Michio, bent low at the waist, move to the last hut. He maneuvered himself below the window. He looked out towards us. I wondered if he could see us from there, but there was no way…not in this light. He nodded in our direction, turned, and then peeked into the window. He looked in for a few seconds and then crouched down again. He sprinted back to the bushes. I called out in a whisper, "Michio, over here."

He found us easily.

"What did you see?" I asked.

"There were six of them. Definitely pirates. Four were playing a game at the table and two looked like they were passed out on the beds. There were a lot of empty bottles on the floor."

"So what do we do? Go in and take them out?"

He shook his head. "No. We leave them. We must stay focused on our objective."

I nodded and looked over at Kamish. Anger flashed in his eyes. It didn't surprise me. I knew that he wanted to spill some pirate blood. But we moved on.

We stayed inside the tree line moving in short, rapid bursts. We stopped anytime we heard anything out of the ordinary. Just before we reached another clearing with another grouping of huts, I heard men talking. We all stopped and ducked down. A few seconds later, a two-man patrol walked up the path. I thought they would pass us by, but they stopped right in front of us. They were backlit by the light from one of the huts. I didn't understand their language, but they seemed to be joking with one another. One of the guards, a tall skinny guy with a large assault rifle slung over his shoulder, lit a cigarette with a cigarette that the other guy had given him. When the cigarette was lit, he threw the other butt into the bushes. It landed a few feet from where I crouched.

The other guy, a medium built African who carried his rifle across his chest, started yelling at the skinny guy. He kept pointing into the bushes. The skinny guy laughed. That seemed to make the other guy angry. They began to argue. Finally, the skinny guy grudgingly walked into the bushes, pushing branches out of his way in search of the cigarette butt.

It wouldn't be hard to find. It had landed in an open spot three feet from me. The red glow from the tip stood out like a beacon. He kept coming. I tried to press myself closer to the ground, but my body would only go so low. Maybe I should have stuck with those yoga classes.

The skinny guy stopped in front of the cigarette. I held my knife tight. He bent over, picked it up, and started walking back to the path mumbling to himself. I let out a breath that I'd been holding. Then he stopped and fell silent. A second later, he dropped to the ground. I saw Kamish's head pop up for a second, but he disappeared back into the bushes.

The other guy called out to his friend. He mumbled something and then walked into the bushes. He only made it a few steps before he fell flat on his back. I stood up to see what had happened. Kamish was on top of him. He slit his throat from ear to ear, but not before the guard managed to squeeze off a single shot. The crack of the rifle echoed into the night.

I looked at Kamish, worried that he'd been shot. But he got up and dragged the guard into the bushes. Michio moved over by me and a few seconds later Kamish joined us. We waited for a rush of guards. After a few minutes, Michio said, "I think it is okay. But we should go."

I nodded and got up to go. A shot rang out from nearby. We all ducked down. Then I heard a small child scream followed by men laughing. Michio and I looked at each other. I heard branches snap and looked over to where Kamish had been. He was sprinting toward the sound of the child.

We followed. A minute later, we reached the edge of a clearing. I looked out and what I saw made my stomach turn. A small child was climbing frantically over a huge pile of rubble, desperately trying to get away from three pirates who were laughing and pointing at him. The pirates stood on the deck of one of the huts. Torches affixed to railing of the deck illuminated them with a hellish glow. One of the pirates held a pistol. They exchanged something; it looked like cigarettes. It was hard to tell. The one who collected them pointed at the boy. The other one spun the guy with the pistol around in circles. It looked like they were playing some kind of children's game. When he stopped spinning, the guy with the pistol staggered to the left, caught himself, staggered to the right, and caught himself again. Then he brought up the pistol, took aim, and fired. The screaming stopped. I turned and saw the child fall face first onto the pile.

There was more laughter followed by a payout to the guy with the pistol. I looked over in the direction where Kamish had run, but he wasn't there. I pulled on Michio's sleeve. He pointed to the three men. They were now passing around a bottle and taking turns drinking from it.

I wondered if Michio meant for me to charge the pirates. But then, out of nowhere, Kamish popped up behind the first guy and slit his throat. The guy collapsed on the deck. The second guy took too long to figure out what had happened. Kamish was on him. As

Kamish buried his knife into the guy's chest, Michio sprinted out of the bushes and sprang into the air, landing a flying kick into the face of the third pirate. They both fell. I heard the bottle smash. Then I watched as Michio bent over him and punched him twice in the throat.

I ran to the pile of rubble to see if the child was still alive. As I began climbing, I was overcome by the putrid smell of death. I looked down and saw that I wasn't climbing on a pile of rubble. It was bones and decaying flesh. I tried to reach the child, but I began to throw up and I couldn't stop.

Michio reached me and helped me off the pile. He held my shoulders as I continued to puke. When I finally stopped, I looked up. Kamish threw the last of the pirates onto the pile.

"Is the child...?" I asked.

Michio looked down and shook his head.

Those bastards! Those goddammed fucking bastards! I reeled as something occurred to me.

"What if Shannon's there?" I asked.

"She isn't," Kamish said.

"How do you know?"

He didn't answer, but the look on his face told me what I knew in my gut. They wouldn't have killed a woman like Shannon, not right away. They would get as much use out of her as possible first.

Kamish looked at me and then Michio. "I heard more laughter coming from there." He pointed towards the center of the island.

Michio nodded. "Okay, but this time nobody takes off by themselves." He looked at Kamish, who held his stare. "If we are to save my son and Shannon, we must work as a team."

Kamish nodded, and we moved toward the center of the island.

We followed the sound of laughter and the occasional scream. It led us to what must have once been the main reception hut. A large bonfire on the brick patio beside the hut cast plenty of light for us to see what was happening. We hunkered down watched as about three dozen pirates, dressed in ragged T-shirts and long, colorful, wrap-around sarongs, sat around the bonfire. Most of them wore embroidered hats called Koofiyads, the metallic threads reflecting the firelight like a disco ball.

A few of them danced. Some sat in small groups. The rest were passed out on the ground.

I saw four young women mixed in with the pirates. My heart skipped a beat when I mistook one of them for Shannon. But it wasn't her.

The women looked terrified. They screamed every time a pirate grabbed them. They fought to get away only to find themselves caught by another pirate. I watched a young woman, maybe sixteen or seventeen, slap an exceptionally ugly guy who tried to kiss her. He rewarded her with a punch that sent her flying. She landed next to the bonfire. When she got up I saw blood streaming from her mouth.

I clenched my jaw as I watched another girl stand motionless while two pirates ripped off her clothes. One of them held her breasts like trophies. It seemed to amuse his friends. She just stared out into the darkness.

"What do we do?" I asked.

Michio said, "We look for my son and Shannon. They must be held somewhere nearby. Let's go."

I looked at Kamish and he followed Michio. I took up the rear.

We stopped and peeked into a few huts. Most were empty or filled with sleeping pirates.

I could tell we were getting closer to the ocean from the sound of the waves. A small shack stood next to the ruins of a dock. A single torch cast a wavering puddle of light on a pirate who sat watch in front of the door. His head hung down and I could hear his snores above the surf.

Michio locked eyes with Kamish and motioned for him to go ahead. Kamish took off. He worked his way around to the right and up along the water's edge until I lost him behind the hut. The pirate snored one last time before Kamish cut his throat. Then Kamish waved us over.

By the time we got to the shack, Kamish had opened the door. Michio pushed him aside and went in. A few seconds later, Michio emerged with a skinny Japanese kid. From the way Michio wrapped his arms around him, I knew that it was his son. The boy looked confused. He stared at his father and then at me and then back at his father. He seemed to be afraid to say anything.

A minute later, three other boys emerged from the shack like zombies, wide eyed and moving slow. I tried not to think about the hell they must have gone through, but I couldn't stop myself. I'd heard the stories of how Jamal tortured boys and brainwashed them to become soldiers in his holy crusade. The more I thought about it, the madder I got.

"You must all keep absolutely quiet," Michio said to the boys. "We are here to take you home. So do as I say."

The boys looked like they were in pretty bad shape. Michio's kid had only been held captive for a couple weeks and even he looked bad. The other boys looked like they had been there a lot longer. What clothes they wore were ripped and full of holes. Two of them were shirtless. Their skin was pulled taut over their rib cages. I flinched when I saw the scars that covered their bodies like some kind of sick roadmap.

I hoped that none of these boys was too far gone. I didn't know what I'd do if they started to call to the pirates for help. But they stayed quiet and seemed to understand Michio's directions.

Michio looked at me. "I will take them to Yoshirou. You two continue in this direction." He pointed along the coastline. "I will meet you at the rendezvous point."

Kamish and I both nodded.

"Don't worry, Aron," Michio said. "We will find Shannon."

I nodded. But after what I saw back by the bonfire, I wan't sure that I could handle finding Shannon in this condition.

Kamish and I zigzagged back and forth along the coastline. We slowly worked our way towards the rally point. Another patrol walked down the beach. We took cover behind some rocks. Kamish kept his eyes glued on the patrol. I kept my eyes glued to Kamish. The last thing I needed now was him taking off on another pirate killing spree.

There were two of them, a man and a woman. They stopped about twenty-five yards from our position. The man looked towards the tree line and waived. Then they continued down the beach.

When they were out of sight, I looked up ahead and could make out some light. It was the main pier. A half dozen pirates wandered in and out of the circles of light created by the torches that lined the pier. The red smoldering glow of their cigarettes gave away their positions.

Kamish put his hand on my shoulder and I turned to look. He had his finger up to his lips and he nodded in the direction of the tree line. He must have seen something else.

He motioned for me to stay where I was. I nodded. He turned and went back in the direction we had come from. I waited. At least ten minutes passed. I didn't see or hear anything. The waves crashed on the shore and the jungle canopy swayed wildly with the wind. I was getting worried. Kamish was taking a long time.

I heard something up ahead. It was the sound of branches breaking. I crouched down, but kept my eyes focused on the tree line. My heart began to race. I pulled the knife from my belt and almost dropped it.

Then, just as quickly as the noise began, it stopped. My heart beat faster. I felt like I had to do something. I took off towards the trees. The knife felt light in my hand. Just as I was about to enter the brush, Kamish stepped out. I almost stabbed him.

We both crouched down in the bushes.

"Where'd you go."

"I saw a sniper," he whispered. "But he is no longer a problem."

I noticed fresh bloodstains on his shirt. One of the stains appeared to be growing bigger.

"Are you okay?"

"I am fine." He nodded towards the jungle. "I heard a woman cry out over there."

He took off. I followed. We worked our way through the thick mash of branches. Kamish stopped at the edge of another clearing. I came up beside him and saw a single hut with a light coming from a window. We waited. I strained to hear whatever it was that Kamish had heard, but I didn't hear anything.

"Are you sure—" The subdued cries of a woman cut me off. It sounded like Shannon, but I didn't trust my own ears. My nerves were shot.

Two pirates walked around from the back and stood on the front deck. They smiled and joked with one another.

I heard it again. This time, it sounded like she was in pain. The guards chuckled. My anger boiled inside of me. I had to help her.

Kamish must have sensed that I was about to charge, because he placed his big hand on my shoulder and held me firmly in place. I glared at him, but he shook his head and then calmly motioned towards the hut. It only took me a second to understand what he wanted me to do. I pulled out Senil's knife and nodded.

Kamish moved to the right and I took off towards the left. We each circled around to opposite sides of the hut. I listened to the pirates talking. The talking stopped. I heard a scuffle. Kamish must have struck. I ran around the corner.

Kamish knelt next to a dead pirate. The other pirate brought his rifle up. He aimed it at Kamish who smiled and nodded. The pirate turned. I lunged and thrust my knife up into in his gut. He started to step back, but I reached around with my free arm and pulled him in close. Eyes wide, he tried to speak. I twisted the knife and lifted the blade. I felt a gush of warm liquid soak through my t-shirt and run down my legs. His eyes rolled up into his head. Then I felt his full weight. I let go of him and pulled the knife out. His body slumped on to the deck.

Kamish got up and motioned toward the door.

I nodded.

A scream from inside the hut triggered something in me, something that I'd been trying to keep in check. It was a dark and mindless hatred. I went to the window and looked inside. It was Shannon. She was pinned on the bed under a naked, dark skinned man. He bucked her like a wild beast. Her head moved from side to side and she cried out over and over again.

The man had a tattoo on his back. It was a circle inscribed with a crescent moon and a single star. He flung his head back in a primal display of ecstasy. I saw the scar on his cheek. It was Jamal and he was raping Shannon!

CHAPTER 18

Everything moved in slow motion. I felt like I was watching the horrific scene unfold from a distance.

I don't remember barging through the door, but I remembered burying my knife into Jamal's back. I don't remember skinning the tattoo from him, but I remembered the look on Kamish's face as I held the bloody swath of skin in my hand. He proud, like a father who had just witnessed his son take down his first deer.

Suddenly I was back in my body. I looked at Shannon. She was trapped under the bloody corpse. She screamed and cried out as she fought to get out from under him.

I dropped the skin on the floor and ran to her side. I flipped Jamal off of her. His body fell to floor with a loud thud.

"Shannon, it's okay," I said. "I'm here. I'm going to get you out."

Eyes wide and panting, she looked back and forth from me to Kamish. She kept repeating, "No! No! No!" I tried to hold her, but she whimpered and pushed herself back until she sat up against the backboard. Her knees were up against her chest and she cradled herself with her arms. "No! No! No!"

I knelt down on the floor next to her. I placed my hands on her shoulders. She pulled away and buried her head in between her arms. Then she let out a primal groan.

"Shannon, it's me, Aron. Look at me."

She looked up. I saw recognition in her eyes.

"What are you...how did you find...?" Her mouth quivered as she spoke.

"I'll explain everything, but right now we need to go."

She looked at Jamal and began to cry. Her tears washed lines through the blood that was smeared on her face. She looked at me and nodded. I grabbed a sheet from the floor and draped it around her.

Kamish said, "Come on."

I looked over and nodded. Kamish went out first. He waived us on and we followed. I kept one arm around Shannon's shoulders as we worked our way back to the shore. On the far side of the pier, I saw a row of huts along a boardwalk that stretched out over the water. It was the rendezvous point. Michio would be waiting for us underneath the boardwalk.

We stopped and made sure the coast was clear before crossing the wide path that led to the pier. Once on the other side, we moved fast. It wasn't much farther now, just a few hundred feet. All we had to do was get to the far side of the huts and work our way under the boardwalk. But as we approached the huts, Shannon suddenly stopped.

"I can't," she cried.

"Of course you can. We're almost there," I said. "See? It's right over there, under the huts." I pointed and she looked.

Shaking her head, she said. "I can't leave. Not without her."

"Without who?" Kamish asked.

"The girl. She was on the boat with me. She doesn't have anyone to help her." She pleaded and looked into my eyes. "They took us into that hut there, the one on the end. I can't leave her there." She looked up at me with pitiful eyes.

I looked at Kamish. He shook his head, but I said, "Okay. Let's go."

The boardwalk was unguarded. We ran up to the hut.

"Is this the one?" I whispered.

She nodded.

"Is there anyone else in there with her?"

"No," she said. "They tied her up to the bed before they took me away."

Kamish opened the door and we followed him in. An emaciated woman in her mid-forties stood on the far side of the room. She held a rifle tight up against her shoulder, her cheek glued to the butt of the rifle. Staring at us with one eye through the sight, she moved the barrel back and forth between me and Kamish.

I'd never seen a woman with a face like that before, so hard and callused. She had the face of a deep-earth miner. Her head was shaved, except for a shock of red hair that ran down the middle of her skull. At first I thought it was a man, but then I saw her flabby tits swing freely beneath a dirty white tank top.

"If you move," she said in a thick, Russian accent, "I will shoot you between the eyes."

I wasn't about to move. But without warning, Shannon ran past me, straight for the woman.

"Shannon, no…stop!"

I tried to grab her, but Kamish held me back.

"I said do not move!" the woman with the Mohawk shouted.

I froze and waited for her to shoot Shannon, but Shannon brushed right past her. Then she stopped, and turned around. A thin smile stretched across her face, a smile that sent a chill up my spine. Her eyes were wide and darted back and forth between Kamish and me.

Why didn't the woman shoot her? She didn't even look at Shannon, she just kept her eyes locked on me and Kamish.

Like a computer program choking on unexpected data, my brain couldn't process what had happened. I felt like I needed a reboot.

"Shannon," was all that I managed to say.

Shannon laughed.

She must be in shock. What else could explain her wide-eyed stare and the way she panted like an overheated dog? But shock didn't explain why she wasn't dead on the floor. I wasn't ready to face the truth, but the truth refused to be ignored. It pushed its way up through the layers of my consciousness and exploded in my head.

"You're…" I couldn't finish the sentence.

"You're what? With them?" A maniacal cackle escaped her mouth. "That's right, Aron…I'm with them. I thought for sure you had figured it out back there…when you broke into our hut." Tears began to fall from her eyes. "When you murdered Jamal!"

"No," I said. "He was raping you. I…I saved you!"

"He wasn't raping me, you stupid bastard! He was making love to me." Her voice cracked. "And now he's dead."

As I watched, her face transformed. The sadness disappeared and was replaced with a calm and cool expression. Pulling the sheet from her shoulders, she tied it off just above her breasts. Then standing up straight and pulling her shoulders back, she said, "You killed a great man, the man that I loved." Her last words cut through me like a machete through a banana leaf.

"Great man? How can you say that? He was a murderer, a fanatic!"

Shaking her head she said, "He was no fanatic. He was a genius. After the storm, when everyone else huddled together in their towns and villages, he built an army. Societies collapsed, but his army grew. He understood what it took to survive in the new world. You call it murder, he called it what it was, thinning the weak from the herd"

I heard a low guttural growl and looked over at Kamish. He glared at Shannon, seething with fury. I spoke up before he did something that would get him killed.

Looking back at Shannon, I said, "I don't know what he did to you or what they did to you after they kidnapped you yesterday, but you're not thinking straight."

She laughed that cruel laugh again. "Yesterday? I've been with Jamal for nearly three years. Do you really think that I went for a walkabout?" She laughed again. "I was on a supply run when they took me prisoner. Nobody came looking for me. So I did what I had to do to stay alive. It wasn't easy, but then I met Jamal" She closed her eyes and took a deep breath before continuing. "You want to know what he did to me? I'll tell you. He opened my eyes. He saw within me the spark of a survivor. He reminded me of the lessons I had learned growing up in the slums of Dublin. Fists, Aron…fists. You fight for what you want or you get nothing."

"That's not what Islam teaches," I said.

"You're such a dolt. Jamal didn't care about Islam or any religion. He used religion to build the army. His army gave him strength, the strength he needed to take the resources so we could all survive."

"He didn't just take resources. He killed innocent men, women, and children."

"I don't have time to explain this to you. You'd never understand anyway."

She looked at the woman with the rifle "Nika. Give me the weapon and tie them up."

Nika handed Shannon the rifle. Shannon pointed the barrel at Kamish. "Start with him, the big one. He looks like he might try something stupid."

"What should I use?" Nika asked.

Motioning with her head toward the window, she said, "Use the cord from the curtains. And be sure to tie his hands tightly. Don't worry about cutting off the blood supply. He won't have need for blood when I'm done with him."

Nika nodded and went over to the curtains.

"No!" I said. "If you're going to kill anyone, then you kill me. I'm the one who cut up your boyfriend."

I saw rage flash in her eyes, but she remained calm. "Trust me. You will die. But first, you must tell me a few things."

"I'm not telling you anything, you bitch!"

"Is that any way to talk to the woman who rescued your heart?" She laughed. I felt the darkness rising within me. It took every ounce of willpower to keep it in check. I had to stay in control. I had to think of a way out of this.

"Once I start to cut up your friend like I cut up Rick, you'll tell me everything I want to know."

I couldn't breathe. It felt like I'd been kicked in the stomach. "You killed Rick?"

I closed my eyes and let the darkness sweep over me. My whole body began to shake, not with fear, but with adrenaline.

"And if you still won't talk," Shannon said, "then we'll bring Jin out here and start cutting him up…what's left of him anyway."

"Jin's alive? Where is he?"

She motioned with her head, "Next door. I've been trying to get him to talk, but he hasn't been very cooperative." She smiled. "I'm actually glad that you came out here, because we were about to give up on him and come pay you and William a visit. From what you told me at the Council meeting, you and the boy were pretty close to figuring out how to control the satellite."

My fists clenched and my heart raced. Nobody, not this psychotic bitch, not anyone, threatened William! I was about to charge when Nika turned to face us. I stopped and watched her coil the cord in her hand. I prepared to make my move.

"Put your hands behind your back," she said to Kamish.

I looked at Kamish. I could tell that he was about to make his own move, so I readied myself. He glared at her, but he put his arms behind his back.

As she walked behind him, Kamish turned on her. In one smooth sweeping motion, he pulled a knife from the back of his belt and stabbed her. Nika cried out, but her voice was drowned out by the blood that began pouring from her mouth.

Shannon yelled, "Nika!" Then she lowered her cheek on to the butt of the rifle, aimed, and fired. The sound of the shot was deafening. Kamish let go of Nika and she fell to the floor. Blood oozed from a small hole in his shoulder. He charged at Shannon. Another shot, this one to the head. Kamish fell back on top of Nika, the knife flying out of his hand and sliding across the floor.

I went to him, but stopped when Shannon yelled, "I'll shoot you too, Aron. Don't think that I won't."

"Go ahead. Shoot me. When I'm dead, you'll never get the information you want."

"Oh I don't know about that. William's a smart kid. He can probably tell me what I want to know."

Just before an ocean of darkness engulfed me, I saw a little girl walk out from a back bedroom.

"Mama," the dark-haired toddler said. "I heard a scary noise." She began to cry.

Shannon looked over at her, "It's okay, dear. Mama is here."

She had barely finished her sentence when I buried my shoulder into her stomach. The rifle flew out of her arms. The little girl screamed, "Mama!" I slammed Shannon into the wall. She collapsed onto the floor, but immediately crawled towards the rifle. I scrambled to get it before she did, but she stuck her leg out and tripped me. I fell hard. Pain shot up my elbow as I hit the floor. She pounced on me, clawing my face. I ignored the pain and rolled over on top of her. I slugged her in the face…again and again. Blood spouted from her nose.

The little girl screamed.

I reached for the gun, but Shannon grabbed my ankle. I fell next to the girl. Without thinking, I scooped her up and rolled over.

"Let go!" I said kicking her hand from my ankle. I sat up facing Shannon. Holding her daughter in one arm, I used my free hand to scoot backwards. My hand landed on something. It was Kamish's knife.

Shannon rolled towards the rifle and I yelled, "I'll kill her! I swear to God, if you touch that rifle, I will slit her throat!"

Shannon stopped and I saw fear in her eyes. Then she screamed, "Put her down!"

I moved the blade a few inches closer to the girl's throat. "Move and she dies."

Shannon stayed where she was. I stood. The little girl cried and struggled to get free.

Holding her brought back memories of my own girls. I knew there was no way I could hurt her. My face must have given away my thoughts.

"You won't do it, Aron," Shannon said. "I know you." She got up on her knees. "You don't have what it takes to harm a child. You're pathetic." Spit flew from her lips. "You're like the rest of them. None of you have the strength to do what it takes to survive."

The girl leaned forward, squirming to get away. I almost dropped her. I managed to hold on, but the child shrieked. I looked down. Blood dripped from her arm. I had accidently cut her with my knife.

"No!" Shannon screamed. She moved toward me, but stopped. "Okay, I'm sorry. Just don't hurt her. She's all that I have left of Jamal."

I looked at the cut. Thankfully it wasn't deep, but it was still bleeding. I adjusted my grip on the girl by placing my hand over her arm and holding it tight against her body.

I didn't mean to cut her, but Shannon didn't know that. Now I was in control.

"I'll let her go, but first you're going to tell me something, like what the hell is going on."

She glared at me, but kept silent. I shook the girl, not a lot, just enough to make her cry louder.

"Okay, okay. I'll tell you." She looked at her daughter as she spoke. "I was on the Council so I could gather information about the inhabitants of the Maldives."

"But what about the list? Who are those people you put on the list at the last minute?"

"The crazies…the religious nuts." she said.

"I don't understand."

She shook her head. "Jamal started his army with Islamic fundamentalists from across the horn of Africa. He professed to be a prophet of Allah and they believed him. As his legend grew, his army grew with it. But they were becoming a liability. Like you said, Islam teaches something different than what we were doing. So Jamal recruited and trained others, survivors like me. Once he had enough people to carry on his mission, he told the crazies that Allah had spoken to him. He said that Allah wanted to send them to Mars where they would establish a new paradise, free from infidels."

I felt my stomach tighten. If those fanatics made it to Mars, they'd kill William and everyone else up there.

"What did he plan to do with the rest of his army?" I asked.

She looked at me like I was an idiot. "We plan to use this place as a base camp so we can launch missions across the equatorial zone."

"That's why you want the satellite, isn't it? You want to use it to see where other people are."

A hint of that evil smile returned and she said, "You're not as dumb as I thought. With the satellite, we'll be able to crush the other bands of pirates and we won't have to search for resources like a needle in a hay stack anymore."

"Well, you're not getting the satellite or anything else from me. You're finished...all of you."

She laughed and said, "You're so cute when you're trying to save mankind. But it's too late, Aron. Even if we don't get the salellite, we'll take the islands in a few weeks. We have the list, remember? We know where everyone lives and who they are. And we have a few men inside the MDF, which you already know. So when the MDF responds to the attacks, we'll be waiting for them."

If not everyone in the MDF worked for the pirates, we still had a chance.

"Tell me who they are...the ones in the MDF," I said.

"I don't know. Viyaja was taking care of that part." She laughed. "The dumb bastard actually thinks that he's going to become their supreme leader on Mars. They'll kill him on the trip out there, I guarantee it."

I had to get back to the boat so I could warn everyone. But how? If I left her here, she'd warn the pirates. Anand's ship was fast, but it couldn't outrun their fast attack boats. And I couldn't kill her... not in front of her daughter. Goddammit!

I glanced down and saw the curtain cord still coiled up in Nika's hand. Keeping my eye on Shannon, I squatted and picked up the cable.

"I'm getting out of here," I said. "So turn around."

"You're never going to get off this island."

"You let me worry about that. You just do as I say and you'll get your daughter back."

She sneered and then turned around. "I'm going to enjoy killing you, Aron. I'm going to take my time and savor every second that you suffer."

"Shut up and put your hands behind your back!"

She did as I demanded. Now the tricky part.

I walked over, stopping a foot from her. "If you move, your daughter's death is on your hands…not mine."

I set the girl on the floor and then grabbed Shannon's arms at the wrist. She tensed, but didn't struggle. The girl clung to Shannon's leg, crying. I slid the knife into my belt. Then just as I started to wrap the cord around her wrists, she spun around and I lost my grip. One of her arms swept out and hit me in the head. The room began to go dark. I took a step back, but she was already on me.

Her daughter screamed and fell backwards. Shannon let out a roar like a mother bear whose cub was under attack. She grabbed for the knife in my belt. My hands wrapped over hers, but she managed to pull it free. We struggled. Then I felt a sharp pain in my side.

I looked down and saw the blade. The top two or three inches were in my side and she was trying to push it in deeper.

Drawing on a reserve of strength I didn't know that I had, I pulled the knife out. I brought my knee up, slamming it into her arm. I heard the snap of her bone. The knife dropped. She screamed and punched me with her other hand. I brought up my elbow and clocked her in the side of her head. She took a step back. Then I watched her eyes roll up into her head just before she fell on to the floor. Her daughter crawled to her and called out, "Mama, mama, mama."

I headed to the door, holding my side. I felt the sticky warmth of my blood on my hand. When I reached the door, I turned. I looked at the little girl. I thought about my own daughters.

"Mama! Mama!"

The room began to spin. I thought about saving the girl, but knew I had to get out of there. I turned and left.

Somehow, I found my way beneath the boardwalk and called out for Michio. My legs were getting shaky. I sensed that I didn't have much time before I passed out.

"Michio," I called out again.

"Aron, over here."

I looked, but it was too dark.

"I need help. Come here."

A few seconds later, Michio appeared.

He must have seen how I was holding my side. "You're hurt. Come on. We'll get you back to the boat. Where's Kamish?"

Shaking my head, I said, "Dead. But we can't go back, not without Jin."

"What are you talking about?"

"They have Jin in the hut, the second one on the boardwalk. You need to get him."

Yoshirou ran over to us. "Come on, father. We must go."

"Get Aron to the boat, but leave two boards behind. I will join you soon."

I saw the concern on Yoshirou's face, but he nodded and led me to the water.

CHAPTER 19

I don't remember how I got to Anand's boat, whether I swam on my own or Yoshirou towed me. Everything was a blur. I remembered being helped onto the boat and seeing the scared faces of the kids we had saved. And I remembered hearing the distant crack of gun fire. But that was it. The next thing I knew I was looking up into Nisha's eyes as she wiped my face with a cloth. I tried to talk, but I could only manage a groan.

"Shhh, Aron. It's all right." Nisha then looked over at someone, and I followed her gaze. I was in a cabin on the boat, Anand's cabin. The portal on the wall was opened, allowing the cool, early morning breeze to flow inside. It felt good. Over by the door was one of Anand's kids, a small boy about seven years old. I tried to remember his name, but the my head felt like it was going implode, so I stopped trying.

"Go and get your father. Tell him that Mr. Atherton is awake."

The boy left and I looked up at Nisha again. She lifted the back of my head and held a glass of water to my lips. I took a sip, but started coughing. Each cough sent a sharp pain into my side.

She lowered my head to the pillow and said, "That's enough for now." She smiled. "You gave us all a scare, Aron. But you are going to be fine. We are almost there."

"Where?" I managed a croak.

"Lohifushi. Mohamed is waiting for you and will fix you right up."

I reached for my side and felt the bandages that covered the wound.

Anand and Michio came in and walked over to the bed. Michio spoke first. "It is good to see you awake."

I grunted.

"I know that you are in pain, but can you tell me what happened?"

"Lying bitch!" I coughed words out and it triggered another coughing fit. The pain was so bad I thought I would pass out. When the coughing stopped, Nisha held the glass to my lips again. I took a sip. This time I didn't cough.

Anand and Michio looked at each other. I knew that look. It was the same look that I saw on Kelly's face when we found her mom wandering around the front yard in a nightgown, talking to her dead brother. They thought I had lost it.

"Aron, I don't understand," Anand said.

"She is one of them...the pirates," I said, feeling tears begin to well up in my eyes.

They looked at me in disbelief.

"She was behind it...all of it...Rick, Senil, Lanka, Kamish, Jin."

I suddenly remembered what Shannon said about Jin being in the next hut.

"Jin! Did you find him?"

Michio nodded. "He is in the other cabin. I am afraid that he is not well. They...they tortured him. He is missing all of the fingers on one hand and he is badly beaten up."

I squeezed my eyes shut and clenched my fists. If I ever saw her again, I'd do to her what she did to Jin.

Anand asked, "Are you sure? I thought she was abducted?"

I shook my head and opened my eyes. "No. She was part of the raid. She told me that she had been with Jamal for three years. She thought they were the winning team, so she switched sides."

I saw the look of disbelief on their faces.

"She's still alive. I couldn't kill her." More tears fell. "She had a young daughter. I couldn't kill her in front of her daughter."

"It is okay, Aron," Nisha said. "You did the right thing."

"Did I?" I asked. "Everyone is now at risk and I put them there. She said she was going to pay us a visit. I think she's planning to attack Lohifushi."

"They could not attack Lohifushi without going past Male," Anand said. "If they tried that, the MDF would stop them."

I shook my head. "They have people on the inside. Spies who are in the MDF." I looked at Michio. "She's coming for us...for me...for William. We have to evacuate everyone off of Lohifushi."

Michio studied my face and then said, "How many people are on the island?"

"Less than a hundred and fifty," I answered.

"Anand," Michio said. "Can we fit everyone from the island onto your boat?"

Anand thought about it for a second and then said, "Yes. We should be able to handle the load. But where would we take them?"

"Male," Michio said.

"No!" I said. "Viyaja is mixed up with them too. Male isn't safe."

"Then where?" Michio asked.

I looked at them through a tunnel of blackness. I tried to answer, but the tunnel closed in on me.

***

When I opened my eyes, I was in a strange hut lying in bed.

Helen was sitting in the chair next to me. She smiled.

"Well, then. Mohamed said that you'd be asleep for a while, but I was beginning to get worried. You've been asleep for a whole day."

My tongue felt like fly paper. "Water," I said.

"Let's get you comfortable first. I'm going to put a couple pillows behind your head, okay?"

She placed a hand under my shoulder and helped me sit up. My side still hurt, but the pain wasn't anywhere close to what it had been on the boat. With her free hand, she placed two pillows under my back and gently lowered me onto them. Then she handed me a glass. Her hand hovered near mine as I drank.

The water tasted amazing. I tried to drink the whole glass, but Helen took it away from me. "I know you're thirsty, but drink slowly. Okay?"

I nodded and took the glass back. Then I sipped the water more slowly.

Mohamed entered the hut and said, "It looks like my patient is awake and doing well. How do you feel?"

"Like I lost a bull fight."

Mohamed laughed.

The memory of the rescue mission was like a fading bad dream, but it hung around the edges of my memory.

"So do you feel like having visitors?" Mohamed asked. "There is a very anxious young man out here who would like to see you."

I nodded and Mohamed opened the door the rest of the way. William stood on the front deck. He started to come in, but hesitated when he saw me. I must have really looked like shit.

"Come on, William. I feel much better than I look."

Tentatively, he entered the room and walked over to the other bed. He sat cross-legged and stared at me.

"Come on, Helen," Mohamed said. "Let's leave these two alone for a while." Then, looking at me, Mohamed added, "No roughhousing, okay?"

I smiled and said, "I don't think you have anything to worry about."

They left and I looked at William. I had almost forgotten that he was only a ten-year-old boy. All the work that we had done to decrypt the messages made me think that he was older.

"I told you that I wouldn't get myself killed," I said.

"But you got stabbed." I saw the fear in his eyes. "Did it hurt?"

"Yeah. It hurt a lot." I saw the concern in his eyes and added, "But it doesn't hurt too much now. Well, a little."

He looked around the room and then said, "So what about your girlfriend? Did you find her?"

"No." I lied. How in the hell could I tell him the truth? How could I tell him that she was responsible for his dad's death?

I needed to change the subject.

"Where are we?" I asked.

"Embudu," he said.

I don't know who came up with the idea to come here, but it was genius. The island had been left uninhabited after the raid. The pirates wouldn't think to go back to an island that they already raided.

"So everyone is here now?"

He nodded. "Everyone except for Pun. He left the island right after you did. You should have seen him. He was really mad."

"Any idea where he went?"

"Nope. A helojumper came for him. I think he went looking for you."

"Well, don't worry. He didn't find me. By the way, you did a great job with the diversion."

"Yeah, well...I had to keep that cast on until the boat came for us. Mohamed was worried that Pun might return and see me without it. It was so itchy."

I smiled. "Well thanks for taking one for the team. ."

"Oh yeah!" His face suddenly lit up. "I almost forgot. I got a surprise for you."

He reached into his back pocket and pulled out his data mat. Sliding off the bed, he brought it over and held it out in front of me. "I did some coding while you were gone."

I took the data mat and said, "Did you write a new game?"

He smiled and said, "Nope. I fixed your code." I looked at him, puzzled, as he explained. "You remember how you couldn't figure out how to connect to the computer because the routing strings wouldn't fit in the fields?"

I nodded.

His smile got wider. "Well, I got it to work."

I looked at the screen and opened the communications console. I tried to connect to the quantum computer. A message popped up, followed a second later by a command line prompt.

CONNECTION ESTABLISHED >

He had actually done it.

I looked at him and asked, "How did you do it?"

His smile was from ear to ear now. "Remember that hidden column? The one with the four strings of numbers that we couldn't figure out?"

He didn't need to finish because I suddenly understood.

"Of course. TCP/IP."

"What's that?" he asked.

"An old protocol for something called the Internet. It was before your time and it doesn't matter. What matters is that you figured it out. Now all we have to do is see if that code we wrote works."

"Already did," he said. "That's the surprise. At first I couldn't get it to work. So I played around with your code and...well...it took me about six hours but I got it working. Look in there, the folder marked MESSAGES. I ran the algorithm against all of the ones that Jin had collected." He pointed to the folder. "I put them in there."

I opened the folder and started reading the messages. He'd done it. This was the evidence that we needed to stop them from sending pirates to Mars. Most of the messages were between Shannon and Jamal. Shannon had sent him the entire inhabitant spreadsheet, piece by piece. She also gave him reports on everything that went on in the Council meetings. That bitch! She even sent him reports about me, how she had me wrapped around her finger.

As I read the messages, everything came together. Shannon had used Viyaja just like she had used me, only she leveraged his political ambition to get him to overthrow Ahmed. She even smuggled him the bomb to blow up the helojumper. All I needed to do now was make sure this evidence got to the ship's captain.

The door opened. It was Mohamed. "Glad to see that you two aren't wrestling."

"Mohamed, what day is it?" I asked.

Looking a little concerned, Mohamed said, "Saturday, why?"

"And the ship, the Mars ship...it's here?"

Mohamed nodded. "Yes. It arrived yesterday night around seven. Viyaja sent out a message to everyone. It said a delegation from the ship had arrived in Male and they were finalizing arrangements for the transport of passengers."

"I've got to get there," I said.

I started to sit up, but the pain punched me back down. "You're not going anywhere," he said. You have a very serious wound. It needs time to heal. Besides, the message said that they have heightened security around Male. Only authorized ships are allowed to dock and even then, they're not letting anyone on or off the island."

"What? Why?"

"It said that it was to prevent disorder and disruptions to the transfer process."

I tossed William's data mat on to the bed. "Shit."

"What is it?" William asked.

"Nothing. Wait! Is Anand still here?"

Mohamed nodded. "Yes, but he is getting ready to depart. He said that he must continue his supply deliveries before the MDF becomes suspicious."

"I need to see him. Can you get him for me?"

"He may have already left, but I'll go check."

Mohamed left and William asked, "What do you want to see Anand for?"

He had the same worried expression that he did the night I left for the rescue mission. I couldn't do this to him again, but I had to get to Male.

"William, do you remember the diversion?"

He nodded.

I continued. "I need you to do it again, but this time we're going to trick Helen and Mohamed. Okay?"

"But why?"

"I think I know how we can stop the pirates from getting on that ship."

"You're going to Male, aren't you?"

I nodded.

"Then I'm going too."

"Absolutely. I can't do this without you. But you have to do exactly what I say, okay?"

He nodded and said, "So what's the plan?"

"I'll tell you while you help me get dressed."

CHAPTER 20

Anand tried to talk me out of going to Male. But in the end, he agreed to take me. I think he realized that I was going with or without his help. He probably figured that I had a better chance of making it there on his boat instead of, say, on my kayak.

Convincing Anand was one thing, but I knew that I wouldn't be able to convince Mohamed and Helen. That's where William came in. While Anand helped me walk to his boat, William pretended that he had hurt his leg jumping out of the palm tree. It had worked once, so we decided to try it again. Thankfully, it worked again. But this time William joined me. He told me how he had climbed out Mohamed's window after Helen had taken him to the clinic.

On the trip to Male, I explained to William what I planned to do. The kid seemed up for it. Rick would have been proud.

Just as I finished going over the details, I felt the vibrations from the engines decrease and then stop all together.

"Something's up," I said. I looked at my watch. "We're still fifteen minutes away."

Nisha came into the room a few seconds later and said, "We must go."

"Go? Where? What's going on?" I asked.

"Quickly, into the cargo hold. We have been stopped by an MDF patrol and they are boarding us." She looked worried. "Come, we haven't much time."

We followed her to the hold. I managed to walk without assistance, but each step brought a fresh surge of pain.

"Go in there," she pointed to a large cube in the center of the room. It was a carbon fiber bin filled with crushed coral powder. The bin was fifteen feet by fifteen feet and almost ten feet tall.

"In there?" I asked.

"Yes, please hurry. They rarely check the powder bin. It is too messy." She went over to the wall and brought back a ladder. William climbed up quickly. I followed, one rung at a time. Each step felt like someone punched me in the gut. Finally, I managed to get into the bin. As I laid down next to William, I saw the top of the ladder disappear.

The bin was filled almost to capacity and a fine power hung in the air around us like smoke. I tried to keep my mouth shut so that I wouldn't cough. Ten minutes passed and I thought that maybe they wouldn't inspect the hold after all, but then I heard the metallic clink of the hatch. I listened as people entered.

"You see, sir, just as I said. We are delivering fruits, vegetables, and some coral powder." It was Anand's voice.

An unfamiliar voice said, "Open that so I can see inside."

"But it is just plantains," Anand said.

"Open it."

The pop of a carbon fiber lid echoed across the cargo hold.

"You see, just plantains. Go ahead, take some."

The voice said. "And what's in there?"

"Just coral powder."

"I would like to see for myself."

"Okay, but it is very messy. The powder sticks to everything and is hard to get out."

I heard the sound of footsteps coming towards us. A few seconds later I looked up and saw the top of the ladder. My heart raced. If the MDF inspector looked in here, it would be all over. I felt a hand on my shoulder and turned towards William. He looked as scared as I felt. I put a finger up to my lips and then looked back at the ladder.

"Here, let me show you." Anand said. A minute later, I saw his smiling face looking down as me. We exchanged a quick glance before he reached into the bin, pulled out a handful of powder and said, "See, coral powder."

"Yes, but I'd like to see for myself."

"Of course," Anand said. He started to climb down and I heard him fumble on the ladder.

"Stop," the inspector said. "Look what you are doing!"

"I am so sorry. I told you that the powder was very messy. Oh my, you are all white, please, forgive me. Here, come with me. My wife, Nisha, will help clean you up."

I smiled as I listened to the inspector continued to complain all the way out of the cargo hold.

When I heard the hatch close, I peeked over the edge. They were gone. I motioned for William to climb down and then I followed him. Once I reached the deck, we looked at each other and laughed. We both looked like ghosts.

"Come on," I finally said. "We have to get this shit off of us."

We took our clothes off and beat them against the side of the bin for a while. A cloud of dust enveloped us.

"This isn't working," William said. "I think it's getting worse." He began to cough.

"You're right. Grab your stuff and let's—" I felt the engines start up. "Come on. Let's go find Nisha. She'll know what to do."

We found Nisha up on the bridge. She laughed when she saw us. "You look like spirits," she said.

"Yeah," I said. "I know. Can you help us get the powder out of our clothes?"

She shook her head and said, "Coral powder is difficult to get out. I'll go get you some of Anand's clothes."

She returned a few minutes later with a stack of t-shirts and sarongs.

"Thanks," I said, as I reached for the clothes, but she pulled them away.

"Not yet, first you better get that dust off of your skin." She motioned for us to follow her. She led us upstairs to a room with a tiny shower stall. "Be quick. We are entering the port now."

William showered first, and while he dressed, I got in. As I washed the powder off, I inspected the stitches on my side. The gash was only two or three inches long. There was a little seepage, but not much.

By the time I finished with my shower and got dressed, Anand showed up and said, "Come with me." We followed him back up to the bridge.

The dock was busier that I had seen it in a while. There were four ships unloading their cargo. There was no place for us to dock.

"When that ship is finished, they will start to unload our cargo. The dock workers are already on board getting ready." Anand pointed down at four dockworkers near the bow. Two were opening the large cargo hatch on the deck.

"So how can we get out of here?" I asked.

"That is going to be the tricky part. Viyaja has imposed security restrictions on all crews. We are not supposed to leave our ships. Only dockworkers are permitted to come and go. See over there?" He pointed at a gate along the perimeter fence. Two MDF guards were checking workers as they entered and left the area.

"Yeah, I see it. Is that the only way in and out?"

Anand nodded. "I am afraid so."

"I suppose that swimming isn't an option?" I said.

Anand shook his head. "No. They will spot you for sure."

"Shit. So how are we going to get past the guards?"

Anand smiled and said, "I have an idea."

I raised my eyebrows and waited.

"I thought that I could try the same trick that I pulled on that MDF inspector."

"Huh?"

"You two just go down by the gate and wait. Act like dock workers. You'll know what to do when the time comes."

I looked at William. He looked as puzzled as I felt. We shrugged and thanked Anand before we slipped off the boat.

With all the activity on the dock, it wasn't too hard for William and me to go unnoticed. We walked toward the gate and stopped by a stack of boxes. We pretended to look them over. I kept looking up at Anand's boat, waiting for something to happen.

William asked, "What do you think he is going to do?"

"I'm not sure, but whatever it is we have to be ready to move. Okay?"

He nodded.

A small cargo crane was welded onto the deck of Anand's ship. I'd seen Anand use it to load and unload large cargo at Lohifushi. He was up in the cab now, getting ready to unload something from the cargo hold. He lowered the hook into the hold, and a few minutes later, I watched it emerge with the giant bin of coral powder. When the bin was about ten feet above the deck, Anand swung the crane arm around. The bin now hung in the air over the dock. A worker directed Anand to lower the bin. It started to descend, but stopped. A loud metallic clang echoed out from the crane. Suddenly the bin lurched hard to the right. Some powder spilled. A dust cloud drifted down over the dock workers. They turned and ran. Others noticed it. People began to yell and run. A second later, two of the four chains that held the bin broke free and the bin toppled completely over, swinging from the two remaining chains.

A massive white cloud rolled out over the dock. People ran past us toward the gate.

"Now, William. Go!"

We ran with the crowd. We fell into the mass of people who swarmed the gate. The guards tried to control the crowd, but when the cloud reached the gate, everyone, including the guards, ran out of the dock area. William and I followed the crowd for a while, but then I grabbed him and we peeled off towards the communications tower.

Anand's diversion drew everyone's attention, including people from across the island. People began to fill the streets to see what was going on. Everyone was so focused on the docks that William and I were able to get into the tower unnoticed.

When we reached the observation deck, my side burned like someone had stuck me with a hot poker. I looked down and saw a baseball-sized bloodstain on my shirt. William saw it too.

"You're bleeding. What should we do?" he asked.

"Nothing, I'm fine. It's just some seepage." I didn't want to worry him with the truth. "It must have squeezed out when we ran through the gate."

He didn't look convinced. "Maybe we should send Mohamed a message and ask what to do."

I shook my head. "Don't worry, it's okay. Besides, it's time to kick off the plan. Do you remember what you need to do?"

He nodded and said, "I wait outside the hotel."

"Right. And then?"

"And then I find someone who looks like they're from the Mars ship and I give them Jin's data mat."

"Perfect," I said.

"But how will I know who is from the Mars ship?"

"I don't know exactly, but they're not going to be dressed like anyone around here. I guarantee it."

"Will they have space suits on?"

I laughed, "Probably not, but their clothes will look different."

"I still don't understand why I can't help you here first, and then we can find the Mars people together."

"Because when those messages go out, the bad guys will try to disconnect the servers remotely. I have to keep them from doing that. When I reconfigure the servers, someone will notice and come to the tower. Luckily, the guys that I taught to operate systems are about as sharp as a coconut, so I'll have plenty of time to get out and join you."

William smiled.

"Once I'm done, the only way they can stop the messages from going out is by powering down the servers."

"What will happen if they shut down the servers?"

"The whole IICN will go down. But don't worry...they won't do that, because I'm the only one who knows how to bring it back up."

"What if they catch you before you finish?"

I put my hands on his shoulders and said, "William, we don't have a lot of time for 'what if' questions. If we stick to the plan, everything should turn out fine. Now get going. The sooner I get started, the sooner I can get the hell out of here. I'll see you in front of the hotel. Just wait for me there."

He nodded, but he studied me for another few seconds before he turned and ran down the stairs. Before climbing the ladder up to the data center, I sent a quick note to Helen and Mohamed telling them where they could find William.

I climbed into the data center. The pain in my side was getting worse.

Once inside, I disabled the electronic lock on the hatch and went to work. It took me half an hour to reconfigure the servers. Besides shutting off remote administration access, I also shut down all inbound message traffic. Now the only way a message could go out was through my console. Then I downloaded all of the messages that I had copied from Jin's data mat onto the server. When that was done, I downloaded an app that William and I wrote. The app was designed to send all of Shannon's and Viyaja's messages, along with an explanation of Shannon and Jamal's plan, out to every data mat. It was open kimono time.

Before pressing the SEND key, I said, "This is for you guys." The hairs on the back of my neck prickled. I felt like Rick, Lanka, and Senil were all in the data center with me.

The app worked. I looked at the console and watched as the emails began flooding the network.

By now, Viyaja was shitting his pants. I got up and walked over to the radio relay box. I grimaced as pain shot through my side. I looked down and saw that the blood stain was getting bigger. I also saw that I had left a trail of blood on the concrete floor. It would take the app about twenty minutes to complete sending the messages. I should be able to hold on until it was finished.

I sat down by the radio relay box, turned on the external speaker, and set the radio to scan mode. From here, I could monitor all voice communications on the net. There wasn't much chatter on the radio. Most of the calls were between the air traffic control tower and an incoming helojumper.

A high-pitched beep echoed around the data center. I looked over at the server and saw an alert indicator light up. Someone was trying to access the servers. I checked my watch. Another ten minutes and the app would finish.

Five minutes later, I heard the echo of footsteps coming up the stairs to the observation deck. I could tell there were two people. I prayed that it was some teenagers trying to squeeze in a quickie before dinner. Whoever they were, they had just reached the observation deck. I leaned closer to the hatch and listened. If they were lovers, then they were gay lovers, because the voices I heard were two men. I couldn't make out what they were saying, but it sounded like they were having an argument. The argument ended and I heard the metallic sound of someone climbing the ladder.

Those technicians had never once showed up on time when I was training them. Why did they have to develop a work ethic now?

I listened to the soft beeps as someone punched in the combination on the electronic keypad. A loud buzz let them know that the combination was invalid. He tried again. Same thing. After a short pause, there was pounding on the hatch followed by more arguing. This time I could make out some of it.

"The hatch is locked. I cannot get in," the guy on the ladder yelled.

"Well, you better call operations and ask for instructions," the other guy responded.

"To hell with you! I climbed the ladder. You call operations."

The other guy called operations. I listened to him on the radio relay box. Viyaja answered the call. He didn't sound happy. "You idiot. Break through the door and get in there."

"I am sorry, sir, but I cannot. It is a steel door and I do not have the equipment for that."

"Just stay there, you incompetent imbecile," Viyaja said. "I am coming over myself."

I smiled as I remembered the hours that Rick and I spent playing Texas Hold 'Em. It was my turn to bet. I was all in.

Viyaja's voice rang out from the external speaker again. This time he was on the MDF net. He ordered a helojumper to pick him and his personal guards up from the hotel roof. I checked my watch. It was going to be close.

I felt lightheaded, but I was able to write William a goodbye message.

I read it over.

Dear William,

If you're getting this message then I guess I won't be able to keep my end of the deal and join you. I'm sorry, but it'll be okay. We did it.

I know your mom and dad are out there somewhere and they're proud of you. I'm proud too and I'm not talking about what we did today.

I'm proud of how you stood up the bad hand that life dealt you. You're are a much braver man than I ever was.

When you go to the Mars colonly, you'll do great things. I wish I could be there with you, but I promise that I'll be by your side every step of the way.

I love you, William. Make me proud up there.

Aron

I didn't send it right away. I decided to wait until I heard Viyaja arrive. I didn't have to wait long.

I heard the sound of the approaching helojumper. Within a few seconds, the metal panels that sheathed the tower began to rattle like a hundred tiny thunder claps. I looked up and listened to the whoosh of the turbines as the helojumper hovered above the tower.

I wondered what they were doing. The pilot couldn't possibly be dumb enough to try landing on the roof. If he tried, he'd be in for a big fucking surprise. The roof was not very sturdy. It had almost caved in on Rick, Jin, and me when we went up there to install an antenna. A helojumper weighed a lot more than the three of us. It would bring the whole tower down.

The rush of wind came in through the vertical ventilation shafts and filled the room. I squinted my eyes as sand and debris flew through the air. Then I heard a loud thump on the roof followed by two more. A high pitched squeal echoed through the room. It was the sound of metal twisting. I looked up. A large metal panel that covered the ceiling fell into the room and crashed near the servers.

I covered my head with my arms and prepared for that giant blender to come crashing through. The sound of the helojumper blades was deafening. I looked through the dust cloud and saw a man wearing an MDF uniform laying motionless on top of a backup server. I quickly turned my attention back to the email server. It was fine. I sent my message to William and then crawled away from the servers just in case more of the roof caved in.

I looked up through the big hole in the ceiling. I could make out the underside of the helojumper. It hovered twenty feet above the roof. Through its transparent bottom, I could see at least two people inside. But then the helojumper pitched forward and it flew out of sight.

The roof hatch opened. They must have rappelled onto the roof. I hadn't considered that possibility.

A moment later, two men in MDF uniforms came down the ladder. I knew the first one in an instant. He had a bandage around his left hand and a giant, curved sword in his belt. It was Pun. He jumped off the ladder, turned, and pulled a pistol from his holster. He pointed it directly at me and motioned for me to put my hands in the air, but I held on to my side with both hands. The pain had reached a new leve. I doubled over.

I heard the second guy jump off the ladder. I looked up. He clumsily slid the rifle off his shoulder before rushing over to the guy sprawled out over the server. He checked for a pulse and then shook his head at Pun.

"Open the lower hatch," Pun said to the guy. He got up and went over to the hatch. He opened it using the manual override handle. Then he stood at attention next to the hatch as Viyaja climbed up into the data center. A technician that I vaguely remembered followed him into the room.

"You have caused quite a stir, Aron," Viyaja said wiping the dust off his shirt. "But you are too late. The ship's captain has already accepted the list from the Council." He walked over to Pun. "And this stunt will just be seen as the desperate act of a delusional man. A man who was killed by the MDF as they tried to apprehend him."

Viyaja's smile triggered something deep inside of me. Despite the pain, I rushed towards him.

Pun hit me on the side of the head with the butt of his pistol. I fell and darkness closed in. Somewhere in that darkness, I heard Viyaja say, "Do not kill him yet, you idiot. We need him."

The darkness receded and I lifted my hand to my forehead. When I pulled it away, I saw that it was covered in blood. I rolled over and pushed myself up to a sitting position. Viyaja was watching the technician trying to unlock the console.

I laughed.

"What is so funny, Mr. Atherton.?" Viyaja asked.

"Him," I said, motioning at the technician. "He's wasting his time."

"Why? He was trained by you."

I laughed again, but the pain in my head cut the laughter short. "Yeah, I know. But I never taught him how to fix what I did to that server."

Viyaja looked furious. Addressing the technician, Viyaja said, "Power down the servers."

The technician looked pale. "But sir...that could cause a cascade failure."

Waving his hand dismissively, Viyaja said, "I don't care about the technical details. Just turn them off!"

I could tell that the technician wanted to explain what a cascade failure was. They would have to rebuild the entire network from scratch. He looked back and forth between Viyaja's seething face and Pun's impassive stare. Then, with his hands shaking, he began to power down the servers.

I checked my watch. The messages should have all been sent out by now.

A minute later, the technician looked over at Viyaja and said, "It is done."

Viyaja called over to the guard and said, "Bring him here."

The guard grabbed me by my bicep and hauled me up. From the puddle of blood on ground, I knew that it wouldn't be long before I passed out.

The guard walked me over to Viyaja and held me there.

"I am going to ask you a question," Viyaja said. "If you answer it truthfully, I promise that my friend, Pun, will kill you quickly. But if you play games, then you will learn the meaning of real pain."

Addressing Pun, he said, "Unleash your Khukuri."

The Gurkha holstered his pistol and drew his sword. I stared at it and remembered how he had cut his own hand just to prove a point.

Viyaja stared at me. "So, Mr. Atherton, where is your friend's data mat?"

"What friend?"

"I told you. Do not play games with me. You know that I am talking about Jin."

"You're too late, asshole. By now the data mat is in the hands of the ship's captain."

I looked at Pun and spit in his face. "Come on, Pun. Stop fucking around and kill me already. My head and side are really starting to hurt."

"He will kill you when I tell him to kill you." Viyaja's face was flushed and sweaty. "You!" He pointed to the guard. "Run to the hotel and find the boy. When you find the boy, kill him and bring the data mat to me."

Eyes wide, the guard looked back and forth between Viyaja and Pun, but he didn't move.

"You fucking prick!" I yelled at Viyaja. "I'll kill you if anything happens to that boy." I took a step towards Viyaja, but Pun placed his sword in front of me like a crossing guard sign.

I glared at him and said, "I thought you said that you swore an oath to protect the people of the Maldives?"

He placed the point of his sword against my chest.

"If you honor that oath, then why in the hell are you taking orders from him? He doesn't care about the people. Look how easily he just ordered the death of a ten-year-old boy. He'd order the death of everyone in the Maldives if meant saving his own neck"

Pun's face was a mask of stone, but there was something I saw in his eyes. What was it? Then it hit me.

He didn't know!

"Why do you think he wants that data mat?" I pushed harder now. "I'll tell you why...to cover his tracks. He doesn't want anyone to find out how many people he's already killed."

"Shut up! The Gurkha has sworn an oath of loyalty to me."

I watched as Pun turned his head and looked directly at Viyaja for the first time. I saw beads of sweat multiply on Viyaja's forehead. He wiped them away with the back of his arm.

"You will kill him now. That is an order!" Viyaja screamed.

Pun lifted his sword above his head and set his gaze back on me.

"I can't believe that you are taking orders from Viyaja after what he's done to your people."

His eyes narrowed. "What do you mean?"

"Don't ask me…ask him. Ask him who massacred everyone on Hanikada."

Pun stared at Viyaja.

"He's lying!" Viyaja shouted. "Don't listen to him. He is trying to trick you."

Pun studied Viyaja's face.

Viyaja reached over and pulled the pistol out of the guard's holster. He took a step back and placed the barrel against my temple.

The room began to spin. I began to laugh again as I thought of how disappointed Viyaja would be when I died before he had a chance to kill me.

"Stop laughing!" Viyaja yelled in a high-pitched tone. Then, addressing Pun, he said, "I order you to kill him. Kill him now!"

I closed my eyes, ready for it all to be over. I waited, but nothing happened. With my eyes still closed, I lifted my chin and pushed my chest out.

"Just do it, Pun. For God's sake, do it. You know he doesn't have the balls to do his own dirty work."

I heard the swish of the sword and felt the wind as it passed in front of my face. I opened my eyes and looked down, expecting to see my intestines falling out on to the floor. I saw a puddle of blood, but it wasn't mine.

"I swore an oath to the people, not to you," Pun said before pulling his sword out of Viyaja. Then I watched as Viyaja collapsed to the ground. Pun looked over at the guard. The guard released me and sprinted for the hatch. He was followed close behind by the technician.

That tunnel of blackness was closing in again. But before I passed out I saw Pun smile.

CHAPTER 21

Familiar voices pushed their way into my dream and battled for attention. But I didn't want to wake up.

I was sitting in the backyard with Kelly. We were watching the girls run around. Kelly touched my arm and I looked into her eyes. She was smiling, but a single tear rolled down her cheek. I tried to wipe it away, but my arms wouldn't move. She said something, but I couldn't understand what she said because the other voices drowned her out.

"What?" I asked.

"Wake up, Aron." It wasn't Kelly voice.

Kelly, the girls, and the backyard began to fade way. I began to cry.

"Come on. Wake up."

My eyes felt like they were glued shut. After several attempts, I managed to open them, but I was assaulted by light and I shut them again.

"That's it, Aron. Open your eyes."

I tried again and this time I managed to keep them open long enough to see Helen. She was smiling.

She turned and said, "He's waking up, go get the doctor."

I turned my head to see who she was talking to. It wasn't easy moving my head. It felt like someone had tied a hundred-pound weight to it. I saw Mohamed just as he walked out of the room.

"Aron dear, look at me. Can you hear me?"

I looked back at Helen and croaked out, "Yeah. I hear you." Then I looked around the room and asked, "Where am I?"

The room looked like a hospital room or at least what I remembered a hospital room looking like. A monitor stood next to my bed and an IV bag hung suspended on a chrome pole. My eyes traced the clear tubing down from the bag to where it met a needle that disappeared into my arm.

"You're in the Male clinic, dear. You gave us all quite a scare."

I'd been in the clinic before, but I didn't recall seeing the monitoring equipment. It was clean and it actually seemed to work. They must have hidden it from us back when we were salvaging the electrical equipment to build the IICN.

"I don't understand," I said.

"So, our patient is awake is he?"

I looked toward the unfamiliar voice and saw a woman who had her hair pulled up tight into a ball, the old fashioned kind. But there wasn't anything else old fashioned about her. I tried to guess her age, but gave up. She had one of those ageless faces. She could be anywhere from thirty five to fifty five. But her eyes looked older. They were the eyes of a person who had seen her fair share of pain and suffering.

She wore a clean, white jumpsuit. I couldn't remember the last time I had seen anything that clean or that white. Having once worked in the satellite industry, I had seen a lot of people in jumpsuits like that. However I never saw anyone who could fill it out the way she did. She was too...too something. I couldn't put my finger on.

She walked over to the bed, looked at the monitor, and then pulled out a small pen light and held it in front of my eyes. "Try to follow the light with your eyes. Don't move your head."

Not moving my head wasn't going to be a problem.

"Good, good. Do you feel like you could sit up?"

I nodded. Mohamed came over and helped the woman elevate the head of the bed.

When they finished, I asked, "Who are you?"

"I'm Dr. Belkin. I'm the senior physician on New Hope."

"New Hope?"

"It's the Mars colony ship," Mohamed interjected. "They've brought a lot of medicine and other supplies." Mohamed looked as excited as a kid on Christmas morning.

A million questions swirled inside my brain, but there was only one that mattered.

"Where's William! Is he alright?"

"Yes, yes," Mohamed said. "The boy is fine. He is downstairs and very anxious to see you. He refused to leave the clinic, you know, and slept downstairs for the past two days."

I took a deep breath as a surge of relief washed over me. "Thank God."

"Did the messages make it out? The ones we sent?"

"Yes," Helen said. "Everyone got the messages. And let me tell you, people were pretty riled up. We almost had a full-scale revolution on our hands."

"That's enough questions for now," the doctor said. "There'll be enough time to talk later. Right now I want to finish checking you out."

She placed a hand on my forehead and I tried to knock it away, but the IV tube got in my way.

"Take it easy. Don't make me sedate you," the doctor said with a disarming smile. "How does your head feel?"

"Like a helojumper landed on it."

"It should. You had quite a concussion. You'll probably have a headache for the next few days, but you'll be as good as new before you know it."

I suddenly realized that the pain in my side was all but gone. I reached down to feel the stitches, but I only felt smooth skin.

"Oh, I see you noticed that we patched up your side. You ripped those stitches wide open and lost a lot of blood. The good news is that you didn't have any internal injuries."

"Where are the stitches?"

"I haven't stitched anyone together in a long time. I brought some Dermobond from the ship and fused your skin back together."

"How long have I been here?"

"Three days," she said. "I induced a coma so you'd rest. It was the only way to accelerate the healing process."

Three days. That means the ship will leave in less than a week.

"Well Mr. Atherton, I'm giving you a clean bill of health." She looked at Mohamed and Helen and said, "Make sure he gets up and starts walking around. The sooner the better."

"Yes, doctor," Helen said. "Thank you so much."

She walked out, but stopped and turned at the door. "I'll get you something for your headache and let the Captain know you're awake. He wanted to know the minute you were up."

Helen came over to the bed. She bent over, kissed me on the forehead, and then pinched my arm.

"Ouch!" I rubbed my arm. "What was that for?"

"That, my dear, was for taking off without letting us know about your plan." She pinched me again. "And that's for sending Mohamed and me that dreadful email. You scared us half to death."

"I'm sorry, really. But I knew you'd try to stop me."

"You're damned right!"

That was the first time I had ever heard Helen swear.

"You put William at risk and you almost got yourself killed," she said.

There was a knock on the open door. I turned and saw a man with a dark, Hispanic complexion standing there. His thick black hair was tinged with silver. Like the doctor, he wore a jump suit, but his was blue with a white stripe down each sleeve.

My heart rate skyrocketed when I saw William standing by his side. He ran over to me, hugged me, and buried his head in my chest, sobbing.

I wrapped my arm around him and said, "Hey, bud. It's okay. The doc said I'm going to be fine."

We held each other for a few minutes. His sobs began to subside. I looked up and saw Mohamed smiling and Helen wiping her eyes.

William let go and took a step back. He dried his eyes with the back of his hand. Then he said, "I knew you'd be okay, but that stupid message you sent me..."

"I know. I'm sorry about that, but things weren't looking too good and I wanted to make sure I had a chance to say goodbye...just in case."

"What's all this talk about goodbye?" the man in the blue jumpsuit asked.

I looked over. He approached the bed and held out his hand. I shook it.

"I'm Captain Ramos and you must be the guy who almost plunged the last civilized society on Earth into total chaos." A broad smile broke out across his serious face.

I wasn't sure what to say. "That wasn't my intention. I just wanted to stop them."

"Well, you stopped them alright. The Council got the hell off this island as soon as those messages started flooding the IICN. And speaking of the IICN, that was a pretty impressive engineering feat. Five of my best communications technicians couldn't get the network back up. If it wasn't for your friend, Jin, I wouldn't have been able to send out a message to let everyone know that a new list was in the works. I almost had a riot on my hands."

"Jin...he's okay?"

"If I was injured half as much as he was, I don't think I'd be able to walk, much less fix a network system. But he did it. He's a tough son of a bitch, that's for sure. That's why I asked him and his family to join us on the Mars colony. We're need more people like him."

The doctor returned and walked over by my bed. She used a syringe to inject something into the IV bag.

"There," she said. "That should help take the edge off of that headache of yours."

"What about Jin's hand?" I asked.

"Oh and don't worry about that," the doctor said. "I've already started to regenerate his fingers."

"Thank you…for Jin, I mean."

She nodded.

Looking back at the captain, I asked, "So you put together a new list?"

"Yes," he said. "My executive officer is finishing it up now. I hope you don't mind, but we started with the list that you had originally submitted to the Council. We found it on your data mat."

I smiled. "No, I don't mind at all."

"We're still tweaking the list, but I think that your suggestions line up pretty well with our requirements."

I began to feel more relaxed. I wondered if it was the medicine or hearing all of the good news. But the feeling was short lived.

"Wait! They'll be coming here. They'll attack us!"

"Easy, Mr. Atherton," the captain said. "Who are you talking about?"

"Them…the pirates," I said. "Shannon said they were going to attack Lohifushi, but when she finds out about the new list she'll attack here. I know she will. She's crazy!"

"I don't think we have anything to worry about," the captain said.

"Yes," Helen chimed in. "That nice man, Pun, took nearly the whole MDF over to Lohifushi. The priates where there and they were not expecting a visit from Pun."

"And Shannon?" I asked. "Was she there?"

The captain answered, "We don't think so. Nobody fitting her description was found, but some of the pirates managed to escape back to their mother ship. Luckily, with the information you sent out in those messages, it wasn't hard for my men to locate them."

"And?" I asked.

"And…well…my men discovered a new use for the shuttle's plasma ejection engine. It turns out that if you invert the polarization of the plasma coils it results in a pretty significant backfire. By significant, I mean that my men turned the mother ship into a new reef.

I wondered if Shannon was on board the ship when it was destroyed, but somehow I doubted it. She was a survivor. And the thought that she could still be out there somewhere sent a chill through me.

"Thanks," I said. "At least those of us staying behind won't have to worry about the pirates for a long time."

I looked at William, suddenly worried that he might not be on the list. As if the Captain had read my thoughts, he said, "And don't worry about William. He'll be going with us too."

A mix of emotions swirled inside of me. I was going to miss that kid, but I was so relieved that he would get off this dying rock and have a chance for a better life. I looked at the captain and the doctor. I could tell they were good people. William would be in good hands up there. Suddenly my eyes began to well up with tears and I said, "I'm really glad to hear that."

"He earned a seat," the captain said. "I was impressed with William from the moment he tried to give me your friend's data mat. He wouldn't take no for an answer." William smiled and the captain continued. "I had the opportunity to spend some time with him over the past two days, and he told me about how the two of you had figured out how to hack in to a Chinese quantum computer and program it to decrypt the messages. Initiative and innovation like that are the exact qualities we are looking for, so I feel pretty lucky to get him."

"You mean *us* ," William said.

I raised an eyebrow and the captain said, "Yes, of course. It turns out that William is also a pretty tough negotiator. He only agreed to go with us if you came along. He said that you were partners or roommates or something. Anyway, what do you say, Mr. Atherton? Will you join our team?"

As I waited for the lump in my throat to go away, I struggled with what to say. William leaned forward.

For twelve years, I'd waited impatiently for death to free me from this prison so that I could be together with my family again. I closed my eyes and pictured Kelly and the girls. I saw them as they had looked on the day that they said goodbye to me before my trip to India.

They smiled. Their smiles ignited a light within me, a light that burned away the shroud of guilt that had covered my heart for the last twelve years.

"Well?" William asked.

I opened my eyes and looked into his eager face. I wondered what he'd look like as a man. Kelly and the girls would understand if I went with him. William was part of our family now.

"Well," I finally said, "How far are you guys with the terraforming? Is there any place to fish up there yet?"

Everyone smiled.

"We have several thousand lakes and the beginning of two oceans, but we're about five years out from fishing," the captain said, "But I'll tell you what. I used to be a pretty fair angler myself once upon a time. So when we get back I'll push the biology team to thaw out some of those frozen fish eggs and see what it would take to stock a lake for us. How's that sound?"

Helen and Mohamed looked at me. I was going to miss them. It wasn't going to be easy for them, but they'd manage. They always did.

I looked up at the captain and smiled. "Hmm," I said. "No fish, huh?"

William started to look worried.

"Well, I suppose that William and I will find something else to keep us busy until then. Count me in."

ABOUT THE AUTHOR

G.S. Fields is the being heralded as one of the up-and-coming stars in dystopian fiction with his debut novel, Under Vanishing Skies. A masterfully crafted balance of action, drama, and science, he offers his readers a heart stopping tale of humanity at its worst and best in a world on the edge of destruction.

G.S. Fields served in the United States Air Force for over twenty three years before retiring to California. He rose through the enlisted ranks and was eventually commissioned an officer. He graduated from the University of Akron where he studied Computer Science and went on to earn a master's degree in Information Resource Management from the Air Force Institute of Technology. G.S. Fields lived in Europe for over eleven years and was stationed in numerous other places around the globe including the Middle East.

During his travels, he gathered together a rich arsenal of stories and characters that he expertly weaves together in new, fresh ways. It was on one such trip to the Maldives that the spark for Under Vanishing Skies was ignited in his head by a cold beer under a thatched umbrella on a pristine white stand beach.